LIAR

Copyright © Mitchell Tobias Publishing, 2022

Cover Design by Hang Le
Editing by Jenny Sims

This book is a work of fiction. Names, characters, places and incidents either are products of the author's imagination or are used fictitiously. Any resemblance to actual events or locales or persons, living or dead, is entirely coincidental.

All rights reserved. Except as permitted under the U.S. Copyright Act of 1976, no part of this publication may be reproduced, distributed or transmitted in any form or by any means, or stored in a database or retrieval system, without the prior permission of the publisher.

Visit Ketley Allison's official website at www.ketleyallison.com for the latest news, book details, and other information.

DEAR READER

My lovely reader, you're about to participate in the fetishes of Ember and Thorne, and while I loved every minute of writing it, I am not a professional in this dark playing field.

If you choose to explore this in real life, please do so responsibly and do not take anything I've written as a teachable moment!

But please, fantasize freely during your time with Thorne and Ember. I know Thorne would want you to.

CHAPTER 1

EMBER

Savannah Merricourt returns today.

Winthorpe Academy operates at a low hum this morning, whispers and theories floating through the cavernous hallways as students filter inside with the iced-over, frigid air tickling the backs of their necks.

I don't listen to the rumors—or accusations—as I shoulder through the meandering crowd, breaking up tight clusters of hushed mouths and flapping hands.

It's all rhetoric, anyway. Nothing that hasn't been picked apart, over and over, during winter break when conspiracies about her reappearance were flying through Raven's Bluff like their own restricted airspace.

Senator Merricourt paid a seven-figure ransom to get her back.

Savannah ran away to Boston but couldn't hack it.

She met a boyfriend online, but it turned out he was a 40-year-old pedophile who tied her up in his basement for twelve months.

She was in witness protection because she saw something she wasn't supposed to.

Savannah doesn't have her pinky finger anymore—it was cut off as proof of life.

Thorne Briar's known where she is this entire time and locked her up as his sex slave.

The gossip and rumors formed lives of their own, getting worse the longer Savannah refused to enter the public eye. No one's seen her since news of her resurfacing hit social media, and her family's kept her well protected, only allowing the Briars entry into their safe house.

I pass two girls huddled against the lockers, their lips moving rapidly as they ruminate on Savannah's return and what she'll look like. The same? A skeletal version of herself? Seven fingers instead of eight? I can't blame them or anyone else I walk by. Headmistress Dupris's mass email to everyone before the start of the new semester announcing Savannah Merricourt's re-enrollment and that all must treat her with courtesy and respect lit a fire the entire town was just *waiting* to surround.

Even the Societies stayed quiet, canceling all secret meetings and challenges until further notice. That *wasn't* through an email but murmured by the prince and princess of the Nobles and Virtues and down the chain of command on the last day of school before break.

I have no idea if I passed my last challenge or if I'm still a Virtue after Damion Briar's instructions to almost kill myself on the cliffs. In all honesty, I spent the entire winter break not caring. All I could think of is Thorne's brutal, scathing kiss, inking my lips with his brand before he ripped us apart and spoke his last words to me: *Savannah's back.*

I spent Christmas with his face rippling behind my vision, his ice-chip eyes spreading frost over my retinas as I tried to appreciate Malcolm's gift of a trip to Purdue University to explore their technology sector. I should've jumped at it. It's the first time he's offered me even an ounce of freedom, stepping foot out of the state of Massachusetts no less. Malcolm handed me an olive branch I couldn't fully grasp because of *him.*

Thorne.

Unlike the rest of the student body, I'm not thinking about Savannah. I'm plagued by the phantom touch of his hands. My thighs itch to be in his grip, spreading me open for his feast. My dreams are consumed by his weight, his body on top of mine, his breath tickling my ears and licking the corner of my jaw...

Then the fantasy morphs into how he was when I last saw him. Bowed over, bloody, and torn open.

Have Thorne's wounds healed? What do the scars

look like? Will he ever bare his back to Winthorpe Academy again?

Is he thinking of me?

We haven't exchanged a word since that night on the cliffs. I'm worried about him and what his father will do to him next. Savannah returning alive won't derail Damion's plans for long. He tried to get me out of the way once. But trying to kill me showed his weakness. I was convinced that I was on the right track in nailing the Briars to a wall. But Savannah being alive changes things. I'm terrified my theories were wrong.

Savannah might not be part of Damion Briar's drug trade. He'd never allow her to return if he's the one who made her go missing in the first place. Maybe she really *was* ransomed by an unrelated kidnapper. If so, that would mean I lost Aiko's friendship for nothing.

The conflict must be written over my entire face as I navigate through Winthorpe's halls, but nobody casts their curious gaze in my direction.

I'm not the target anymore, and I should be thankful.

Instead, I feel uneasy at the shift in tide.

A flurry of activity draws my head up, footsteps of increasing speed passing by me, skirts flapping and pants creasing as everybody scampers back to the entrance.

"She's here!"

"The car just pulled into the driveway."

"Omigod."

My heart rate kicks up at the words, and I allow

myself to be carried by the crowd, my thumbs digging into my bag's straps, my jaw tense.

The massive cathedral doors are propped open, the frigid air cascading into the stone foyer with biting accuracy. Still, nobody gives their lack of coats a second thought as they push outside and stop just short of the front steps as a sleek, black SUV with tinted windows comes to a stop at the bottom of the stairs.

The students fall into a hush as the passenger door opens. I remember to close my mouth and mentally coax my shoulders down from my ears.

A blazered shoulder emerges first, followed by a dark head of hair and a tall, sinuous body.

My sharp inhale freezes my teeth.

Thorne unfurls from the car, his profile exquisite and defined as he turns and holds out his hand. Delicate alabaster fingers appear out of the shadowed confines only to be swallowed by his chafed, firm grip.

Does her skin tingle against his calluses? Are her cold palms heated by his skin?

Pushing those thoughts out of my head, I focus on the rest of her as she slowly steps out of the car.

Her head's down, the blonde, beachy waves somehow catching the meager rays of sun leeching out from the dark, gray cloud cover.

Savannah's dressed in the uniform we all wear, colored in black, green, and gold, yet she stands out from us, from the brittle grass, stone carvings, and somber skies, bright and flushed and...

Beautiful.

Her hand doesn't leave Thorne's as she tilts her chin up, the green of her eyes flitting over the gathered crowd, then stopping on me.

Swallowing, I dig my thumbs harder into my straps. I don't break her stare, but my mind's in overdrive.

Does she know about me? What has Thorne told her? Are they *together*?

My heart hurts on that last question, but Thorne and I were never an item, so I shouldn't have feelings for him. Frankly, they're perfect for each other.

Light and dark. One can balance the other out. Unlike he and I, consuming each other in the shadows, neither one of us looking toward the light.

Bodies press into mine as I'm shoved sideways. I snap out of my rambling thoughts, glancing at the source of friction, and I'm not surprised to see Aurora jamming herself through the crowd and down the stairs.

Belle and Delaney follow her, both with shorter haircuts to match Aurora's textured pixie style. Aurora being Aurora eventually shook herself out of her shaved-head depression and turned Thorne's punishment into a fashion statement. Many of the freshman girls followed suit. A short bob or layered boy cut was the new winter statement, and any who did it received Aurora's praise and attention, which is a rare coup in a place like this.

My long, white-blonde strands falling past my elbows stuck out even more, Aurora's greedy gaze simply *wishing* she could telekinetically shear it off my head ... until Savannah.

Her hair length rivals mine. The volume and health of it far surpasses any quick comb-through I manage after a shower.

Savannah blinks and her attention shifts away from me, her expression impassive as she moves on.

I furrow my brows but don't question what she's thinking for long. Because my attention's moved on, too.

Thorne meets my eyes with brief efficiency. Where Savannah was neutral, he is frozen splendor.

He looks at me like he doesn't know me, like I'm any one of the other students filtering around the entrance, desperate for a glance of Savannah.

While holding my stare, he swoops his arm around Savannah's shoulders, bringing her close.

My throat works, thickened emotion making it hard to swallow. My eyes grow hot.

Our kiss flashes forward again as if I can feel the heat of his lips right now, his exhale consuming my inhale with suffocating accuracy.

I have no idea what's happening to my body, but it can't keep happening. Not in front of him. I swivel around, darting through the doors.

An *oof!* sounds out beside me, my shoulder smacking

against another's. I lift my head enough to apologize but skip to a stop when I register who it is.

Aiko stares up at me, her expression mirroring Thorne's.

"Sorry," I murmur. When she doesn't immediately bolt, I follow up with, "H-How are you?"

"Fine." Aiko shifts on her feet. "Good."

Her curtness rubs the wrong way against my skin. I don't want her to leave. I wish I could erase our last argument and return to how things were.

The sorrow at losing her tangles with desperation, so all I come out with is, "So is Savannah back living with you, or…?"

Aiko's gaze shutters. "You just can't help yourself, can you? Even though Savannah's here and your garbage theory of her drug running or faking her own kidnapping was disproven, you're still asking questions."

I lick my lips. "All I want to know is if she's settling in okay. If you're okay."

"Savvy's with her mom at a bed and breakfast in town." Aiko crosses her arms. "But you know that. Everyone in *town* is aware of it with all the press and news vans camped outside. Don't pretend to play dumb, Ember."

I try to speak through Aiko's verbal stabbing. "I know you don't believe me, but I'm glad you have your sister back."

Aiko snorts. "Are you also glad she and Thorne are an item again?"

I can't disguise the flash of pain her statement brings, and for a moment, Aiko can't hide the guilt at saying it. She adds, softer, "He's been instrumental in her recovery, apparently. Never leaving her side once the hospital allowed visitors."

"Good," I whisper, adding with more conviction, "Good for them."

Aiko searches my expression. "It's over, Ember. The mystery, the what-ifs, trying to move on without her ... that's all gone. Savvy's home, and I need you to respect that."

"I will."

Aiko doesn't believe me. "No more digging through the Societies or accusing Thorne's dad of"—A student pushes past us, his bag banging against his back as the rush to get to first period begins—"of drugs. We all want to start fresh, Savannah most of all."

"I understand. I'm not your enemy, Aiko."

Because what else am I supposed to say? Savannah's return doesn't mean Malcolm's stopped being an informant for the FBI. Her presence doesn't mean Damion Briar will discontinue his illegal business. The Societies won't disband because it turns out Savannah's still alive.

None of that matters to Aiko. All she sees is her stepsister, shaken but unharmed and willing to start again at Winthorpe. The fierce loyalty I admired in my friend was channeled into Savannah's safe return. I'd be stupid to think it'll only be Thorne who protects Winthorpe's lost princess.

Aiko pulls her lips in. "I'm really defensive of her. You've heard what happened, right? Where she was?"

I nod.

"I just—I can't believe she was held for ransom all this time, and Senator Merricourt *knew* it. Like, he's been paying them off every month in order to keep her alive. How crazy is that?"

"It's lucky they had a certain amount in mind and let her go when they got it all."

Aiko levels her stare against mine. She's unsure if I'm being sincere or a smart-ass. I can't quite keep the conflict from my tone. I'm suspicious of the circumstances surrounding Savannah's reappearance but have no one to voice it to.

I've lost everyone, including Aiko.

Aiko must decide that she's getting too conversational with me—our old friendship returning—because her expression closes off.

"Okay. Well..." Aiko turns to the door. "I want to walk Savvy to her first class, so I'll see you around."

"Yeah. Sure." I lift my hand in a wave, but Aiko's already dipped outside.

I watch her push through the gawkers, reach Thorne and Savannah, and loop her arm through Savannah's free one, forcing Aurora to step back. The three of them take the stairs together, Savannah's chin tipped high, her lips trembling.

She's beautiful, I think, stepping back into the shadows.

And she's retaken her place at Winthorpe.

Usurping mine.

CHAPTER 2
EMBER

Everyone is quiet as we take our seats in our first class after the holidays, world history. No one clusters together, catching up on what they missed. Instead, students take their assigned seats at the double desks and look forward at the classroom door.

The seat beside me is ominously empty. My fingers tangle against my thighs at the thought of who will occupy it.

Another vacant desk sits in the middle of the room, the circle of fidgeting bodies surrounding it making the gap all the more obvious.

Shadows flit on the other side of the frosted glass of the door. My peers stiffen at the sight.

As the knob turns, small murmurs lower into complete silence.

Zeke Aiden saunters through the door to a crescendo of groans.

"What, am I not what you cliterazzi want to ogle today?" Zeke arches a brow. "I'm gutted."

He moves through the aisle. My shoulders relax when he comes to a stop at the desk diagonal from mine.

But Zeke still manages to catch my eye and smile. "Are you also part of the mainstream desperate for a glimpse of Savannah?"

"No." I shift away from him, staring directly ahead.

"Too bad. I hear that's the only way to get Prickly Boy's attention these days." Zeke sits in my periphery, cradling his chin in his hands. "You look so much like her, too. It's no wonder he was so infatuated with you, then discarded you the instant his true love returned."

"Shut up."

"And she's *traumatized*. A classic case of missing white girl syndrome where she returns into the arms of a society desperate to find her. Or Thorne's arms, I should say. And his abdominals. Treasure trail. Not to mention his sizable—"

"I said shut *up*, Zeke."

"*Oooh*." Zeke's stare simply gleams when I jerk back from my desk. My nostrils flare, but I hold my lips tight, clenching and unclenching my fists.

"Ember darling, you're going to have to find more nerve than that if you're aiming to survive the rest of the year."

He's right, but damn if I'll let him know. Crossing my arms, I resume staring blindly at the whiteboard in front of us.

"I know it was you," I say.

Zeke studies my profile. "Me, what?"

"You told Damion how you and I broke into his home on the night of Thorne's Halloween party. And had me drugged for it."

It's subtle, but I catch Zeke's eye twitch. "I didn't know it'd go that far," he mutters, then swivels in his seat until he's facing the front like me.

Good. Finally, he shuts up.

The classroom door swings open again, and this time, the students get what their tuition paid for. A first row seat to Savannah's re-acclimation into student life.

Thorne strides in first. Air hisses through my teeth at the burn he casts over the entire class, daring someone to speak up.

His stare snags on mine.

Prickles of heat make the hair on my arms stand up. My knees lock together. My spine goes rigid.

The burn in his eyes turns into a full-fledged wildfire. White-hot and searing, but I force myself to blink and be the first to look away.

His attention doesn't stray from me. Not even when Savannah comes in behind him, fragile and quiet.

Zeke watches the exchange, humming with intrigue while he leans back and folds his arms over his chest.

Thorne's gaze darts to him. I sag in my chair, having escaped his scope, until he cuts back to me, his jaw so tense it sharpens the air with lethal warning.

My head lowers on instinct, but my mind scrambles for a foothold. Thorne had a thousand chances to contact me in the weeks following our last meetup on the cliff. He could've crossed the road between our houses any time or used one of the tunnels between our homes that slither through our walls like snakes. If he wanted my attention, he could've gotten it, yet he chose cold-blooded silence after melting my insides with a consuming, brutal take-down of a kiss.

I lift my eyes to his. Shaking. Determined.

I won't obey you. I'm not afraid of you.

His grow small as he studies my features, sensing the shift. His gaze dips to my lips, rests there, then captures my stare again.

I stop breathing.

Savannah comes to his side, touching his elbow. She's watchful, noticing the tension between Thorne and me faster than Zeke's unconcealed musings.

She steps forward, captivating the class as she moves through my aisle, her caramel eyes assessing me with every step.

"Hi," she says as she reaches my desk. Her voice is light and sweet, like spun sugar floating through the air. "I don't think we've officially met."

Nodding, I straighten in my seat. My throat's so tight that I don't trust my voice.

"You must be Ember," she says.

The entire class is swept up in her voice. A pencil could drop, and no one would look toward it.

"It's ... nice to meet you." My tone is scratched and as unsure. What else could I say? *How are you after being held hostage for a year? Am I in your seat?*

My eyes flare at the realization. I could totally be in her seat. I took her spot in this school, after all.

"Sav." Thorne's rough tone draws my head up. Savannah turns.

"Over here." He points at the empty seat in the middle.

Thorne's talking to her, but his penetrating stare remains on me. I can't read behind the white blizzard of his eyes. Does he not want me to talk to her? Am I supposed to pretend she hasn't shaken up the fragile foundation I'd built for myself at Winthorpe?

Probably, and he might be right. My trauma is insignificant compared to hers.

This time, I don't squirm under his scope. I meet his eyes, tilt my head, and wait for his next intimidation tactic.

The air is practically electric between us, sizzling with spite and flame. Neither of us decides to fucking blink.

Professor Ainsley steps into the classroom. His gaze

sweeps over the desks, then lands on Thorne and Savannah, the only other people standing.

"Ah, I see I don't have to make introductions." He drops his binder on the teacher's desk, revealing a plaid button-down shirt too tight at the neck and ill-fitting slacks. "Miss Merricourt, Mr. Briar, do take a seat."

Savannah quietly leaves my side, her lashes lowering as she says to me, "I look forward to getting to know you."

A promise or a warning? How much does she know about Thorne and me? Looking at him wouldn't give me any answers since his upper lip curled the instant Professor Ainsley wandered in and he broke our stare-off.

The only thing worse than Thorne confessing our entire relationship to Savannah would be if he—

—sat down at the open space at my desk.

My spine nearly fractures from how stiff I'm holding it. My muscles ache in protest.

Thorne's scent comes with him, chlorine, salt, and something distinctly him. A musk created solely for my nose, tantalizing and acting as a reminder of all those times his taste and smell consumed me.

Reminding myself to breathe, I huff out air through my traitorous nostrils.

"Now, you're all aware of our latest student and her long-awaited return," Ainsley begins, taking his place in front of the teacher's desk and leaning against it. "I would like to remind you she is not an exotic creature at the zoo. Savannah Merricourt has endured an unimaginable year, and I require you all to respect that. There will be no harassment in my classroom or inappropriate questions directed to her. Miss Merricourt, would you like to add anything?"

Every pair of eyes swings to Savannah as Professor Ainsley does the very thing he told us not to.

Her back is to me, that long cascade of warm blond hair covering her uniform from my vantage point. Despite the attention, those strands don't tremble. Her body doesn't shake. Savannah retains the same amount of mystery she had when she was plucked off the road by a passing pickup truck driver who thought she was a wounded deer.

She calmly lifts her arms and folds her hands on her desk. "No, sir. Thank you."

The barest hint of a sensation tingles across my outer thigh. I glance down in time to see Thorne's forefinger play with the hem of my skirt. Without thinking, I jolt, my knee banging on the underside of the desk and causing its legs to scrape across the parquet floor.

Professor Ainsley trains his eyes on me. "Miss Beckett? Do *you* have something to add?"

Thorne's hand darts back to his lap, his chin lowering to disguise his involvement.

I glance back and forth between him and the professor. Thorne, of course, gives me nothing.

"No." I clear my throat, then very obviously pull at the hem of my skirt, covering my thigh as much as I can. "Sir."

"I'm glad to hear it since your place at this school is now out of benevolence than right," Professor Ainsley says.

I jerk my head up, studying him more keenly. It's as if Damion Briar channeled himself through the professor and spoke what was so utterly apparent during my last Virtue challenge.

Zeke chuckles under his breath.

"That brings me to my next point." Ainsley claps his hands, redirecting the class's attention. "Outbursts in my classroom will not be tolerated. Miss Beckett, since you disrupted the class before I finished my rules, consider this a warning. Am I making myself clear?"

A chorus of *yes, sir* rings out. Ainsley responds with a smile, delighted with his power over a small portion of the world's one percent.

Fingers tickle my bare thigh again. I swipe at them, catching Thorne's middle finger in my palm.

"What the hell do you think you're doing?" I whisper fiercely, keeping my head down.

I bend his finger back. Thorne doesn't do well with questions, but he does respond to pain. Whether he enjoys it or takes it as a warning is anyone's guess. All I need is his attention.

He flexes his fingers around the one I hold hostage as if stretching into the sensation. A low thrum comes from his throat, my eyes darting toward it before I can tell myself to *focus*. Stop being distracted by the rush of blood in my ears and the sheer heat he's exuding, deliberately lighting me on fire with his touch.

Proving he still owns me. That I can still get wet for him.

My eyes shoot down, ashamed, but they scrape across his middle before returning to the task at hand—breaking his fucking finger. His pants are tented, clearly turned on by my "threat."

I release my hold with a hiss.

"Consider that a warning," he utters through the side of his mouth. "Don't fuck up my plans. Don't fuck with me. Stay away from Sav, and don't enter the catacombs again."

"Or what?" My voice is louder and more enraged than his cool tone of death. Ainsley glances over with a frown. I smile out an apology.

His hand clamps around my thigh, pushing into my skin and wrenching through the muscle. Thorne talks through my strangled groan as though he's asking what the weather outside's like. "Or else I'll fuck with you. You want to cause me pain? Do it harder next time."

I ask with my next small inhale, "You know what I'm going to do next?"

"Should I care?"

My hand spears into the air, catching Ainsley's attention. "Yes, Miss Beckett?"

"May I use the restroom?"

He swoops a tired hand to the door. "Go right ahead."

I leap from my seat, causing Thorne's hand to loosen. When he retreats, he takes the fire with him. I can breathe.

I no longer have the touch I've been dreaming about for weeks.

Damn him.

I power-walk to the door, lips pressed together and pretending this is the end of my time with him. There's an entire semester of having Thorne beside me, peeling back my layers and exposing all the softness he remembers stroking. Then shredding.

Unable to resist, I look back once. Just once.

Thorne's watching my departure, inscrutably still.

While Zeke stares at me with slitted eyes as if he heard the entire exchange

CHAPTER 3
EMBER

Savannah isn't in any more of my classes. I discover through the hallway grapevine that she's primarily taking eleventh grade classes due to missing out on the entire year, with Headmistress Dupris allowing her to resume one or two of the senior subjects she excelled at before her kidnapping.

Kidnap, abduction, and *taking* are used with surprising ease by the student body today, and it's around lunchtime that it finally makes sense as to why. These are the richest, most privileged children in the nation, even the globe. Kidnapping threats and ransom demands are probably factored into their parents' living wills and trust fund stipulations.

Forget secret societies and the underground drug trade run by the most powerful man in Raven's Bluff—the very real and obvious threat of being held hostage for money is regularly debated at the family dinner table.

Yet another reason I feel so detached from the world I've walked into.

Lockers slam and laughter rings out as the final bell rings. I huddle closer to my locker, students pouring into the hallway from every direction and brushing past me without a glance.

When I first came to Winthorpe, I wished I was invisible. Now that I am, I feel insignificant.

I blow out an exhale, shaking myself out of my self-loathing. There are more important things than popularity and friendship, like figuring out the Nobles' or Virtues' involvement in Damion's drug running and how much Thorne knows about it.

Calling Thorne a liar is one of the nicer names I can think up. But to accept that he tailored his lies specifically for me, that he might've sanctioned my near death by lacing my water with cocaine and fentanyl before a swim meet ... that makes it hard to swallow.

I felt something with Thorne, dark and addictive, and it still grows inside me like vines doused in oil, slick and cloying. Even now, it creeps into all my vulnerable spaces, between my ribs and into my heart, where it started to beat for him.

And he doesn't care if I'm dead.

Forget the touches he steals, the scrape of his nails on my skin. When it came down to it, he chose his family line. He stands with Savannah, holding up his end of the Briar heirship.

I'm so deep in thought that I don't notice the gaps of silence between other students' voices, becoming longer as the time between the end of classes and outside freedom ticks by. The cacophony of footsteps fades into single pair of echoing heels, and then nothing.

A prickle of unease spreads between my shoulders at the thought of being alone in a Winthorpe hallway. I hurry to spin the combination lock to my locker.

The locker door bangs when I pull it open too hard, the sound ricocheting up to the vaulted ceiling.

Well, if anyone was in hiding and waiting to pounce, I've given them my exact location.

Swinging my backpack to my side, I heft out textbooks with the intention of transferring them into my locker before heading out. Swim practice starts now, but I've been kicked off the team and have no reason to linger on Winthorpe grounds longer than I have to.

My stomach swoops with disappointment. I'm not a troublemaker, always seeking approval and thriving off pleasing others. That's reflected in my attitude, my activities, my GPA. To be cut from a team and accused of cheating the system... I'm about to cry and be sick at the same time.

I have to put it aside. *Damion's* drugs were in my system. His minions put them in my water—and one of those is his *son*. Both set me up to fail, and if I want to get out of Winthorpe, I need to rise above people pleasing and be the cause of fresh bruises instead.

Shutting the locker, I turn toward the middle of the hallway when a blurred figure moves in the corner of my eye.

A rough hand grabs my elbow. Instinct has me immediately recoiling, but he drags me into the corridor and slams my back against the brick wall before I have time to so much as screech.

I bring my furious gaze up. "What the—get off me!"

Hot, minted breath coats my cheeks. Eyes the color of whitened ash stare down at me.

"Thorne," I breathe out, stunned until I remember that I hate him. I jerk my arm out of his hold.

He grips me harder, pinning both my arms against the wall.

"Bastard," I spit, aiming for his groin with my knee.

Thorne easily blocks it. Smirking.

I struggle. Twist. Snarl.

He raises a hand to hook his thumb and forefinger under my jaw, pinning me by the neck. The move gives me the freedom to swing an arm, and in a spurt of anger, I mirror his actions, grabbing his throat, too.

Thorne grunts but stills in under my hand. "Seems we're at an impasse."

"What are you doing?" I grit out, my voice tight from the pressure on my trachea.

His eyes shine under the recessed lighting. "I'll ask the same of you. Are you going to squeeze tighter?"

My vision forms into a slit. I wish my glare shot fire. But I do exactly as he says, flattening my palm against his Adam's apple. My frustration over the past month singes down my arm, igniting my fingers as they dig through his stubble and cut into the softer parts of his neck. Thorne's passion, then his neglect. My parents' need for me, then their complete release. Aiko's friendship, then disregard.

Savannah's disappearance and return.

I am not nothing. But am I the problem?

Tears prick in the corners of my eyes, hot and burning.

Thorne's voice vibrates under my hand, a humming of approval. Growling, I hold on as tight as I can, picturing the bend of cartilage before I break his neck.

But he squeezes, too.

Thorne's fingers are under my ear. His thumb hooks under the corner of my jaw, rubbing against the bone. I can feel my face growing red, swelling under the deft squeeze-and-release he's deploying.

And the heat doesn't end at my neck.

It spreads past his fingers, tickling beneath my nipples and spiraling across my stomach. Nestling between my folds and pattering against the sensitive flesh there like the barest touch of butterfly wings.

My thighs clench, my brain communicating the need to fight against an attack, not submit to my arousal.

But this is what I've become. I am the dark.

"More," he murmurs.

Ceding to the call, I dig my fingers further into his tendons, the fine muscles straining. A coppery scent hits the air as my nails break through his skin.

Thorne molds his body against mine, our lips almost as close as our hands on each other's necks.

"You can't intimidate me, little pretty."

"Go back to your *girlfriend.*"

A crease forms between his brows. Thorne searches my eyes. Then his lips flatten with something close to calm acceptance. He bows his head, impervious to my palm pressing into his throat, and nuzzles the side of my neck he isn't squeezing the life out of and inhales.

I release my grip on his throat to push at his chest, my legs banging against his thighs like I'm doing the jig, but it's like fighting against a gnarled tree, stubborn and digging in its roots.

"I will once I get you out of my system." Thorne straightens on an exhale. He sneers before he frowns. "It's not working."

"You're—hurting—me." I speak between clenched teeth. Losing precious air is worth hissing at him. "I— preferred it when you ignored me."

"Ignored you?" Thorne angles his head, then drops his hand from my neck. He steps back. "I was saving you. From the fuckup that is my life."

I fall forward, gasping and slapping my palm against

the wall for support. While my breath recovers, the tingles between my thighs don't abate.

What's wrong with me?

"You haven't said a word to me in four weeks," I rasp, straightening. "Or seen me. And we live across the street from each other."

"All deliberate."

"No shit." After a droll look, I push off the wall, spinning out of the corridor.

He catches me at the crook of my elbow. "This isn't what I wanted."

"But it's the choice you made." I whip my head around, facing him. "You don't get to run through a forest and scale a cliff for me, in the dead of night, only to kiss me senseless then dump me like the trash at the side of your house." I rip out of his hold, and this time, there's no counterattack. "You said it yourself. You're finished with me. You chose Savannah. Now prove it and allow me to walk away."

Thorne's brows smooth, creating an eerie cast to his features, like a predator relaxing its muscles before it springs. "I would very much like to tell you to fuck off. You twist my brain around in its *skull*. You're so damn annoying." He bares his teeth. "I want to be rid of you. I'm determined to get your smell out of my nose, the taste of your cunt off my tongue, the look of you burned off my retinas. But there you stay, and I'm here to tell you to *leave*."

"Good." I fist my hands at my sides. "I agree with *all* of that."

"No. Quit Winthorpe. Leave Raven's Bluff. Go back to your parents."

I lower my brows. "You know I can't do that. Malcolm—"

"I'll deal with him. He won't come after the Becketts, I promise."

"Because your promises are so reliable."

"Ember, I swear to fucking..." Thorne casts his gaze to the ceiling, glowering.

I jolt, shocked at his use of my given name.

"Stop with this stubborn shit. Yes, Sav's back, and *yes*, she'll be re-inducted into the Virtues. Do you not understand what this means for you?"

I tilt my head to the side. "Let me guess, this is you 'saving' me."

"Yes! Jesus!" Thorne throws up his hands, the most emotion I've seen from him all day.

"Next time, maybe don't start by wrapping your hand around my neck."

"You loved it."

The furious whisper leaves his lips as hot as they formed in his throat. His eyes convey the same temperature. I squirm, not from uncomfortableness, but...

"You've missed the way I control your breath, much the same as I've missed your soft begs for more."

My cheeks warm. Thorne swims in my vision, his

porcelain features, his dark, raven-colored hair smearing in the same way my pupils must be when I look back and remember the haze of our sex, never going all the way, but torturing each other with breathless orgasms...

But then he almost killed me.

I blink, a mental shock of cold water dousing my brain. I say, with renewed vigor, "You and I both know I can't go anywhere now that your father was tipped off on what I was doing."

Thorne frowns. His fingers curl at his sides.

"I was drugged, Thorne, on your watch. With your family's illegal opiates that you're using the town of Raven's Bluff to make."

He shakes his head. "That was fucking Zeke Aiden. I have every intention of making him pay."

"After you do your father's bidding and stay by Savannah's side."

Thorne goes rigid, his stare never leaving my face. For a moment, guilt trickles in as I remember the lashes Thorne received on that fateful night, for reasons he hasn't expanded on. All I know is, Thorne was punished, the collar re-attached around his throat before the leash was hooked and gripped by Damion Briar. Thorne's been brought to heel, and the first course of action is to look good in the media, hold Savannah's hand, and gently bring her back to her rightful place as Thorne's girlfriend.

I'm not considering Savannah's feelings in this scenario. I can't—for if I do, I'll feel sorry for her, and that shouldn't be possible when she's so tightly wrapped around the Briars. Any involvement with the Briars, with the Societies, is sinister. I'm still not convinced Savannah's kidnapping was Society-free.

"She needs me," he says hoarsely, his gaze searing into my bones.

My stomach plummets at the simple statement. "I know."

"Leaving her to deal with the after-effects of her trauma would be like leaving you in that pool to drown."

I clench my jaw, at last looking away, unable to hold his too-intelligent stare any longer. "I've accepted that, Thorne. It's what I've been trying to tell you. I didn't contact you or try to see you all these weeks. I let you go to her. I'm willing to finish this semester without speaking to you again. If it weren't for you pulling me into one of Winthorpe's blind spots and accosting me, I would've *kept* doing it. So why—"

Thorne closes the space between us in one stride, cupping my face in both his hands, forcing my chin up. "Because I *can't*."

My lips thin despite the pain shooting through my jaw at his vise-like grip. "That ... sounds like a you problem. Not a me problem."

Wrapping my fingers around his wrists, I yank him down, to which he surprisingly complies. Probably because his gaze freezes me in the same way any of his strongholds do.

"There's a meeting tonight," Thorne says. "Don't go."

I pause before turning on my heel. "I'm one of them. One of you. I have to go." I level him with a look. "Or else your father might very well try to kill me for a second time."

Thorne's gaze shutters. His jawline grows taut. "Whatever's driving you to keep being a part of my life— of *this*—you need to put an end to it. Nothing is worth your life, Ember."

It's the second time he's used my name. I don't expect Thorne to comprehend what motivates me anymore, the same way he can't understand why he keeps doing as his father says.

I have my own family to protect.

"You live your Noble life, and I'll enjoy my Virtuous one," I murmur, then stride out into the hall.

Thorne doesn't follow. I hate that part of me wanted him to.

Distracted, I turn a blind corner toward the exit and don't see the wide expanse of uniform and the barrel chest that wears it until it's too late.

Black shrouds my vision. Cloth obscures my scream.

"Ready for some fun?" a scratched, eager voice whispers in my ear, then yanks me out of sight.

CHAPTER 4

THORNE

Ember is a succubus, consuming in every sense.

That theory's proven when I specifically wipe the sight of her from my view for an entire month, yet her scent remained in my nostrils, the vision of her in my mind's eye. Her peppery musk dancing along the back of my tongue, ruining my taste for anyone else.

I was whipped for her, lashed in front of the entire Nobility, and I should despise her for it. I get on my knees for no man or woman, yet my father bent me over for access to an amateur sex tape. A wide-angle view in night vision mode where our eyes glow like ferrets and our bodies came together in blurry, green twists, yet I protected it from my father anyway.

Protected her.

Chased Ember down on the night of the challenge that should've killed her—and let's be honest, she should've died a few times now, escaping death with the skill of a nimble hare until ultimately, jaws *will* sink into her haunches—and buckled in front of her. Me. Bleeding and weak, opening myself up to her, and for what?

I'm forever tied to the Briars, enemies of the Weatherbys. Savannah Merricourt is labeled as my intended, and I should accept it, as I do everything, because my father's too powerful and I've been locked in the Briar dungeon too many times.

Outwardly, I can do what he wants while actively forging my own pathway to independence, but that simply can't work when imprisoned for weeks on end.

And so, like I stated to Ember, *we're at an impasse.* All of us.

Will it leave room for a truce? Never.

"Turn into a vampire, that way you won't have to glare at your reflection all the time."

I turn away from the mirror and to Jaxon, glowering.

He finishes lacing up his shoes, then rises from the foot of my bed where he's been idling, waiting for me to announce that I'm ready and we can leave.

"How very obnoxious and uncreative of you to say." I step out of the en suite bathroom, then unhook my blazer from the valet stand, where Josh had it steam-cleaned and pressed. Jaxon's dressed similarly in a dark suit with a black silk tie—a requirement of the Nobles during a formal meeting.

"I'd just appreciate you wearing a new look now and

again." Jaxon smooths out the fabric between my shoulder blades as I find yet another mirror to glower at. "You've had a permanent scowl on your face for weeks now. I'd've thought you'd be as ecstatic as the rest of the town that Savannah's alive. More than ecstatic."

"I am." I fix my cuffs, then step back from the mirror. Jaxon darts out of the way just in time.

"Sure you are."

"Of *course* I am."

Jaxon follows me to the door, his resulting silence conveying exactly how convinced he is.

There's no need to fill the silence with puffed-up intentions and over-explanations. Jaxon and I spent more than a few nights musing under our breath whether the Nobles—and thus my father—were involved in her disappearance. Father's stone-walling of the police during her search certainly helped with that theory.

But in the end, that's all it was. A hunch.

When I went to visit Savannah at the hospital for the first time, I was well aware that my heart wasn't beating out of my chest at the prospect of seeing her. I was relieved she was alive, but I wasn't breaking down doors to get to her.

Go to her, son, Father had said. *You'll be the subject of unwanted talk if you don't.*

He means the Briars would be the subject of the Raven's Bluff gossip mill. It has nothing to do with my personal reputation and everything to do with his.

I move in front of Jaxon down the hall, our Ferragamo shoes echoing through the empty manor. Mine are slower than Jaxon's, and stiffer. The tightness in my back serves as a stark reminder of the consequences of saying no to Damion Briar.

Yet, I was willing to endure it for Ember.

We take the main set of stairs, and then the elevator into the underground garage, not bothering to turn on lights during our stroll. Jaxon's been a guest here so many times, he could walk an emergency exit route out of Briar Manor blind, and I've envisioned escape plans so often, the blueprint might as well be a tattoo on my brain matter.

My car gleams in the darkness, more alive than the shadows. Jaxon swings into the passenger side as I take the driver's seat, and once the automated garage door opens, I gun it into the dark.

Our drive to Winthorpe isn't peppered with casual conversation. Both Jaxon and I are lost in our own thoughts. We've never spoken about the last time we were in the catacombs and I kneeled at his father's feet while mine whipped a cable cord across my back.

We never talk about those things. If one of us shows up the next day carrying a fresh round of bruises or dried blood collected in the cracks of our lips, we merely nod in understanding, then spend that day entirely overprotective of each other.

Tonight isn't one of those moments, neither of us

burdened with our sires' rage for weeks now. I assume it's due to the damage control surrounding Savannah's reappearance.

Is she still a Society member? Does she have detailed information on her kidnappers and what she endured?

I guess we'll find out this evening.

As the car crests the final hill, Winthorpe's castle silhouette looms grand against the darkening horizon, like a scaled, spiked dragon curled up and turned to stone.

I use the back gates and staff parking lot as usual, Jaxon and I departing my car as quietly as we drove in. The same trapdoor hidden between stone and underbrush comes into view as we walk, this time without a line of freshmen behind us. Already, this is looking more pleasant.

Jaxon creaks one flap open and I descend without the use of my phone or a flashlight. He does the same.

It's eerily thick in the underground corridors, the air pungent with soil and stagnant water. If there were members before us, we wouldn't know. The dirt pathway is so downtrodden and flattened with time, it's impossible to discern the scuffle of footsteps by feel or by sight.

We round the corner into the octagon of the main catacomb, stone sculptures of the founders guarding each crypt on all eight sides, standing with their arms folded, the blankness of their eyes fixed at the middle of the room.

There, the Nobles are gathered, donned in all-black

suits. The viscounts, dukes, marquises, and barons are all dressed the same, the matter of hierarchy unimportant for tonight's events—except for the king, of course.

My father isn't here yet. The tightness in my chest relaxes at that realization alone. Jaxon gives me a quick pat on the shoulder before merging with the rest of the marquises. As the prince, I'm supposed to stand off to the side until summoned by the king. I have no problem with that. I'd much rather lurk around the edges, observing each and every twitch of my supposed brethren before the king enters.

Who will break out into a smile as soon as he enters? Which Noble stiffens at the sight of an unwanted leader? These are things I want to know after my treatment the last time we all met up at this location. My humiliation—*Ember's* downfall—were at the forefront of my father's motivations, and these assholes watched.

I can't fucking let that stand.

Light footsteps draw my gaze away from the small clusters of boys and men to the same entrance Jaxon and I used.

The queen, Headmistress Dupris, emerges first in a long, white silk gown with cut-outs that shouldn't be considered sexy on a school principal, yet somehow she makes it possible.

Aurora is next, her short, auburn hair smoothed back against her scalp. One corner of my lips tugs upward. Despite having her head shaved a little over a month ago, the girl knows her style. A white mini-dress caps off her 60's vibe.

She notices my attention too late, as I've already glossed over her appeal and have gone in search of who I *really* want to see.

Sadly, Belle follows next. Then Delaney. Then a few other Virtues, all in various white dresses, trotting in single file into the room like good little brides walking toward their fidgeting grooms.

Until there's a gap at the end of the line as if everyone's arrived and no more are coming.

Now, I know that not to be true.

The Nobles stand in a completed circle at the center of the octagon, folding in the Virtues until white and black alternate like the perfect numbers of a clock around the golden sundial in the center, engraved with the Societies' maxim. *We fly high in the dark.* Everyone faces outward.

My scan becomes more fervent as I bounce between the Societal circle and the entrance. It's not like Ember to send a deliberate message like this. By being a no-show, she's giving my father a big FUCK YOU, and that's not what my little pretty does. She's more subtle than that.

Ember's too perceptive and stubborn to just give up her seat like this and run home to mommy and daddy—even with my threats tucked into her stomach like sloshing bile. This town and this school have pissed her off too much for her to surrender so easily. And me. I'll never let her slip through my fingers and escape without my knowledge. Not without proper, punishing recourse.

My gaze narrows.

No, something else is at play, here.

Two large, eight foot torches at my nine o'clock blast with flame, drawing everyone's attention. A shadow flickers between the two columns, taking the form of a man as he draws closer.

My father.

He comes into the dancing light, all the other, smaller torches lighting up, one by one, around the room. The overhead light disappears, and we're left with flickering flames and undulating shadows as my father booms out, "Welcome, my Nobles, my Virtues."

He takes a breath, and I know what's coming. I stifle a yawn.

"In 1820, my ancestor, Thorne Briar Senior, consecrated our noble grounds and deemed it necessary that only the most capable, the most elite, the most *courageous*, could become what you are today. No more than fifty members per chapter, as is our Noble-given rule. His brother, my direct line, Theodore Briar, offered himself as the original leader to the Raven's Bluff chapter —our king—and became the creator of the challenges, an effort to lift our burdens and prove to one another our strength and capability above the common folk. It is a rite that does not exist in any other Noble or Virtue membership. Ours alone."

Father lowers his head, scanning his circle of members and unleashing a visible, serpentine smile, grinning with no teeth.

He continues, "We're all aware of our founder's mistress, Rose Briar."

The elders murmur stiffly to one another. The Virtues lift their chins, a few risking defiance in their glares.

"And how she came between two brothers, a secret affair that didn't come to light until hundreds of years later." Father lowers his voice. "We bear that shame."

A chorus of voices takes up where Father trailed off. *"Altum volair in tenebris."*

We fly high in the dark.

"That's right." Father lifts his chin and folds his arms. "We're able to overcome any shame, defy any inner demons, and transform into an unstoppable secret that can influence entire governments, control the largest corporations, and live like royalty without any civilian knowing the difference. It is a great privilege to be invited into our Society. To become one of us."

Father's voice echoes throughout the catacomb, every face, every expression, as stoic as the statues framing the members. I tuck my hands in my suit pockets, grateful I chose a shrouded position under an alcove so I can scowl freely. I sense where this is going. I'm not confident my expression can stay as blank as the stone figures.

"My queen, please take your position beside me."

Father lifts his hand, motioning toward Headmistress Dupris.

She complies. Breaching the circle, she lifts her skirt and strides up the few steps to reach Father.

Admittedly, she paints the better picture with Father than his wife, stoic and proud beside a man whose pride eclipses any woman he latches onto. Julie Weatherby simply wilts when he takes her arm, a haggard reflection of what she once was.

The unbidden comparison only serves to anger me—how could Malcolm let his wife be taken and treated in such a way? It's not beyond my comprehension, but it certainly prevents me from admiring or respecting him. When your girl is in danger, Societal rules should be damned. No control is worth her suffering unless it's by your hand and in *your* control.

He should've known that.

Idiot.

Speaking of which, is he in this room? As a tarnished member, Malcolm attends these meetings only when summoned. I haven't seen him mingling with our members since our ball when Ember's future was ripped out of her naïve hands.

But with my father's current speech, there's no doubt he'll want Malcolm to listen. He dips his chin at the head-mistress, allowing her the floor.

"It is with my greatest pleasure," she begins, "to re-introduce to you our former Virtuous princess, whom we thought lost, but has now returned to us. To say I am proud of her would be an understatement. This girl—no, *woman*—survived what no person should have to endure. She is our Virtuous sister, our Societal daughter, our endless treasure. Please join me in welcoming back Savannah Merricourt into our open arms."

Heads tilt up and staccato applause erupts throughout the room. I lift my hands in a soft clap, but I'm alert to the pauses between Dupris's words.

And my father's motives.

Ember's still not here. *Why isn't she here?* She wouldn't have picked this night, of all nights, to actually listen to me and stay away. The girl didn't blink at a night swim through November waters. There's no way she'd miss this.

Father and Dupris part, stepping to opposite sides and creating a gap that highlights the special entrance solely reserved to the king and queen of the Societies.

A slim silhouette appears in the middle of the stone archway, dressed in a long white gown and holding a bouquet of white roses.

She walks forward, and as her long, blond hair breaks through the shadows, my first thought is: *Ember.*

Her face comes next, pale, serene, flawless. Too composed to ever be confused with Ember.

Savannah's rosebud lips part in a small smile as she reaches Father and Dupris. Father kisses her cheek, which she demurely accepts. Dupris puts an arm around her shoulders and squeezes.

As Dupris fusses over Savannah, Father lifts his head and finds me, his eyes drilling like small daggers into the folds of my skin.

So much for my little slice of private viewing.

I was supposed to walk by Savannah's side as her prince. This is the first time I've so openly defied him and there's no doubt he'll up the ante later. This time, however, I'm prepared for it and would rather endure another whipping than perform as his puppet in front of some of the most powerful people in the world.

Savannah murmurs something to Dupris, then takes the small staircase down into the crowd of members, offering each person a rose as they welcome her and praise her safe return. I expect, after the distribution of flowers, she'll make a soft speech of her own before the members break off and gossip over cocktails and world domination.

It's the moment when Savannah gives a backward glance that I'm alerted to the *wrongness* that's been weighing on me all evening.

She stares between Father and Dupris, toward the stone archway she passed through, a single rose remaining in her grip.

It's half-wilted, the least desirable of the bouquet, bruised and losing petals.

Savannah holds it up, and, while in the center of the

circle of members, says, "This is for my temporary replacement. For there can only be one of us."

"That's right," Father affirms as Ember appears under the archway, as colorless as the catacombs, her eyes wide but her jaw tense. "As has been tradition for hundreds of years, there can only be twelve of you at any given time." Father's cold eyes find mine again. "And I'm afraid we're at the unlucky number thirteen."

I vault off the wall.

CHAPTER 5
EMBER

ONE HOUR EARLIER

I'm sitting in a family crypt, a windowless, granite box with a fire bowl in the center, illuminating the carved names on the wall.

Theodore Edward Briar

Sophie Morag Briar

Damion Anthony Briar

Thorne Asher Briar II

Damion and Thorne's are the only ones without dates chiseled under their titles. I shudder, thinking that Thorne's body is one day expected to rest in peace behind these cold, heavy walls, alongside his cold, mummified relatives.

I wonder if he knows his name is down here waiting for him, or if he even cares.

49

Either way, that sounds like a Thorne problem. I should probably be more cognizant of the living being I'm stuck in here with, because she looks like she's about to puke.

Savannah sits across from me, her sickly face illuminated between the glowing flames. We're each seated on a marble bench, though who would want to come in and take a load off in this creepy AF tomb is beyond me. Savannah's eyes shine like marbles as they dart around. She clutches her upper arms, humming to herself.

At any moment, she may fracture. The gall of these people—these *Societies*—truly outweighs any sense sometimes. Who was it that thought, *let's lock a girl who's been kidnapped and held for ransom in an underground crypt and see how she does. Oh, and add in a stranger who looks just like her and took over her life. She'll be fine.*

On second thought, I know exactly the kind of maniac who would do this.

"So did they lure you in here by leaving a trail of chocolate bars, too?" I ask.

The humming stops. Savannah glances in my direction. She stares at me with glassy eyes. Her throat clicks. A tear runs down her cheek.

My joke falls flat. Obviously, neither of us are stupid enough to follow a sugar-coated trap into a witch's gingerbread house, but here we are, anyway.

In an attempt to hold her attention, I add, "I was in the south hallway, heading out the doors to meet

Malcolm's driver Nash to take me home." I search for clues that Savannah recognizes either of those names. Her face stays blank. "Someone jumped me. Put a black pillowcase over my head, tied my arms behind my back, and dragged me here." Saying the words out loud puts it into my mind again. The unexpected force on my shoulders. The fabric against my lips. The hard, unyielding body behind me. I thought it was Thorne at first, deploying one of his fetishes again. My pussy even responded, throbbing in tune with my pulse, until I felt the scraping touch of my assailant.

Those weren't Thorne's hands. Too rough, eager, and harsh. My wrists were tied together so tightly I lost feeling in my fingers almost immediately.

"If you are truly Virtuous, you will submit and stop fighting."

I slumped in my captor's hands, but didn't bother to contain a curse. Another goddamned challenge was coming my way.

"My first bet was on Aurora," I continue, still searching for a reaction from Savannah. "She'd enjoy tying me up. But unless she had breast removal surgery along with her haircut, I doubt it was her."

Not even a glimmer of recognition when I back-talked Savannah's supposed best friend.

Sighing, I stand from the bench, smoothing out my rumpled, tartan skirt. Choosing my next approach cautiously, I say, "I'm sorry they're doing this to you. Do you know why you're here? Who they are? It's not where you were held before. I promise. You're with someone who cares. Me. You'll be okay."

Savannah gives one, slow, blink. Her voice comes out as a husky growl. "Don't pretend to understand what I'm going through."

I'm elated I got a response out of her but try not to show it in my expression. "This is some fucked-up shit, even for the Societies."

"They use our greatest fears against us, to test our stamina." Savannah recites it as if she's reading the sentence off a piece of paper. "It's no surprise they've latched onto my newest terror and are using it to test me."

I nod in agreement. "Like I said. Fucked-up shit."

"Yet here we are, anyway."

This time, I can't fight off a kindred smile. "My thoughts exactly."

I glance around the small room, peering into the spots the fire can't reach. "What do you think we're here for?"

Savannah's throat moves in another swallow. Her hands have stopped gripping her biceps and she lowers them carefully. Her breaths steady. My guess is, in the last place she was locked up there was nobody talking to her to keep her mind from spiraling. "There's supposed to be a ceremony tonight to re-induct me into the Virtues." Savannah's eyes catch mine, the whites of them liquid and alive in the firelight. "Aiko told me you were a Virtue, too."

The mention of my lost friend tweaks my heart, but I can't let it get to me. Not now. "It's recent. A few months old, really. I'm basically a baby."

"Not from what I've heard." Savannah folds her hands in her lap and tilts her head as she studies me. "Thorne doesn't say much about you, but I've learned through his silences that you've excelled at the challenges. Exceeded the king's expectations, even."

I don't want to think about Thorne, let alone talk about him. Not to mention Damion Briar. "I'm doing what I can to stay a member. They don't make it easy."

"Why?"

The question catches me off guard, though it really shouldn't. I've repeated my standard defense hundreds of times in my head if I'm ever faced with this kind of inquiry, and I use it now. "Because I want to be part of the best. You know as well as me that to be a Virtue means your future is set. Position, privilege, power. All of it is yours, so long as you continue to meet the challenges."

Savannah stares at me a few beats too long. Like she's peeling back layers of my skin, taking a peek at the secrets behind my tendons, then sewing me back together, frowning as she does it.

I forget that Savannah's dealt with Societal bullshit a lot longer than I have. She's kidnapped and held for ransom, and she *still* has to deal with their twisted rituals in underground graves.

"I'd ask you the same thing," I say to her.

"For the same reasons as you."

Savannah responds with a closed-mouth smile. I return it, both of us well aware of the fakeness of our words.

For a brief, vulnerable second, I'm about to tell her the truth—that I'm here to get the information needed to pass to Malcolm who can then give evidence to the FBI and bring the Briars down.

My mouth even parts to do it—until I force it shut.

I'm horrified at how easily swayed I am by a warm connection. Am I so lonely that I instantly trust the first person who's nice to me? Forget that this person is a traumatized human being, enduring God knows what for who knows how long. Just moments ago, she was on the brink of either a coma or hysteria. Only talk of being similarly bound and dragged into a locked room brought her out of it.

I *can't* trust her. I can't trust anyone.

"Do you have any idea why we're here?" I ask again. "Or ... why I'm with you?"

"My guess is, they're building up to something." But the questions prompt her to look around with me. "Hey, what's this?"

She lifts up a bundle that had been stacked in a corner and previously blocked by her body. As it comes into the light, I notice that it's white, expensive fabric. "Are those dresses?"

Savannah sets it down and takes the first piece of the top, shaking it out.

Silk falls from her fingers, shining and dancing along with the fire. She holds the shoulders in her hands, sleeveless and with a plunging V.

Setting it aside carefully, she unfolds the other dress. It's long as well, and covered in hand-stitched pearls.

I breathe out in wonder. "How much do you think these cost?"

"More than the price of our sanity."

We meet each other's eyes again. Smile.

Dammit, I like her.

"I suppose we have to wear them." I put my hands to my hips, studying both as Savannah lays them next to each other on the bench. "You choose first. I don't mind."

"The pearls."

"Wow. No hesitation there."

Savannah offers a sheepish, shadowy smile. "I'm not as tiny as you. I'd appreciate the extra detailing."

"Please." I wave her off, studying her from head to toe on instinct after a compliment that makes me squirm. "You have the body of a centerfold. I'd kill for your—"

Savannah shrinks under my scrutiny. Literally trembles and turns away. "Please don't stare at me."

"I—I'm so sorry." I retreat, throwing my hands up in horror. "I didn't mean ... I wasn't—"

But what could I say, really? She was taken. Held. Used. I don't know the details of what happened to her, but I shouldn't have to. "That was really insensitive of me." I clear my throat. "Something about being locked in a crypt. It throws me off."

"It's okay." Savannah turns back to me, smiling at my joke. "It's kind of nice to have someone who doesn't treat me like I'm a piece from the Chinese Dynasty, priceless and prone to fractures. It's only when I remember ... when my mind goes back to last year, that I..."

"You don't have to explain." I point at the gowns. "Shall we get dressed?"

Savannah nods, her long waves illuminated as soft, golden flames. "Would you mind turning around as we do it? I've been avoiding the girls' locker rooms and getting changed in the headmistress's office."

"Say no more." I spin around, taking the silk slip with me. It really is a square of fabric that will barely cover my nipples and show a lot of leg with that long slit on one side, but if Savannah's uncomfortable when it's just me she has to dress for, then it's up to me to be the sexual sacrifice.

"A Noble totally picked these out," I mutter as I peel off my knee socks and unclasp my skirt, then step into the dress. "There's no way any woman would make a fellow Virtue parade around a Society pageant like fucking Miss Raven's Bluff, Lingerie Edition..."

The crypt's door groans open.

Yelping, I cover my bare breasts as I turn.

In my swing, I catch Savannah, fully dressed in her

gown, cowering in the corner. The girl must've stripped in seconds. Nausea grows in my stomach at how she learned to be so quick.

A Noble, another senior, stares down at us at the entryway, one hand holding the stone door open. His name is Luke something-or-other and the size of his chest looks suspiciously familiar. "Hope you girls enjoyed your bonding session. Your presence is requested."

My hands come down. Suddenly, a free nipple doesn't seem so bad. *Why was it important to have us bond?*

Because I did. I totally like this beautiful, damaged girl and now I want to protect her.

Shit. That's not good for me.

Luke's dressed in a hand-tailored all-black suit. I think he's on the swim team, considering how tapered his torso is under the Armani fabric. His free arm swings from behind his back, holding a bouquet of exquisite white roses. "This is for you," he says to Savannah.

His pale eyes then land on me. "Pull your slutty straps up, Cum Bucket. You're coming, too."

Luke can't help it—his attention immediately goes to my breasts.

I stride up to him, openly displaying myself. His eyes grow dark as he lowers his chin, a feral murkiness obscuring his features. All except for his eyes, which dance against the flames behind me.

I purse my lips, gathering up a good suck of saliva.

Then I spit on his shoes. "That's for locking us in here and ignoring her screams, you fucktard."

He blinks. Readjusts his pants.

Fury overtakes his face before he gets it under control by breathing deep. "You're lucky Thorne's laid his claim on you," he seethes. "Otherwise I'd fuck you right here and now, whether or not you wanted it. Now cover yourself up, whore."

I roll my eyes, because of course I'm not leaving this room without a top on, even if it is two swatches of expensive silk that my nipples will *definitely* cut through once I leave the warmth of the fire.

"Cum Bucket?" Savannah asks quietly. She shuffles out of the shadows, folded in on herself. But her gaze is steady on mine, and I can practically read behind her eyes, like she's reliving Luke's revelation over and over again. *You're lucky Thorne's laid his claim on you...*

If she was unsure of me before, she's definitely on alert now.

"A gift from your bestie, Aurora," I explain. Sliding the last strap in place, I offer her my hand, reminding her I'm not the enemy in this underground of rivals. "Do you want to do this together?"

She focuses on my open hand for a few longing seconds before shaking her head. "It's better we stay separated. I don't..."

Want them using it against me later.

Savannah doesn't have to finish the sentence.

I swallow the instinct to help her and instead focus on doing the exact opposite of what the Society hopes for.

They wanted us to bond? Let's show them distance. Nodding at her in understanding, I'm the first to follow Luke into the torch-lit corridor.

"Thank you for standing up for me," she whispers at my back.

Happily, I watch Luke's shoes leave small wet splotches as he leads the way.

CHAPTER 6
EMBER

Shadows play across the old walls, aided by the mischief of fire sconces lighting our way through the passageway. I haven't been in this part of the school before, but I'm confident we're still at Winthorpe since my pillowcase captor—probably Luke—didn't drag me far before snipping off the zip-ties at my wrist and tossing me in the tomb with Savannah.

We don't have to walk far before an arc of light ahead illuminates our path better than the ancient sconces. Those tiny flames do little to stop the shivers trailing up and down my exposed skin. The crypt, as creepy as it was, offered little air and therefore a lot of heat. Out in the open, Savannah and I are both exposed and freaking freezing. I hear her teeth chattering behind me. I don't have to look back to assume she's hugging herself, her nose buried in the smell of roses, and that delicate spine of hers bowed over in some sort of protective fear.

Let the suspense be over soon.

I've found, during these months of challenges, it's better to know your enemy than face him blind. This time, I don't even have the clue of walking down the cliff-side to figure out what we're being asked to do next.

The tunnel glows with light as we make our way closer to an arched opening.

Abruptly, a forearm digs into my stomach.

"*Oof.*" I almost bite off my tongue at the unexpected force.

Luke's hard profile doesn't turn. His elbow digs into my ribs. "Stay here. Wait for your summoning."

"Yes, *master.*"

The sarcasm escapes him. One corner of his lips curves at my perceived submissiveness.

I move my jaw to collect more spit. He notices, jerking his arm away from my body.

He offers that same elbow to Savannah. "You're up first."

Savannah eyes his arm. "What do I have to do?"

"You don't remember?" he asks. "Come on, you weren't gone for a decade. You know the drill. Go out there, talk the talk, kiss the ring, enjoy being the center of attention as the long-lost princess of the Virtues."

My jaw unlocks. *She was the Virtue Princess?*

"F-fine." Savannah steps out of the safety of the shadows and turns toward the light.

Chanting reaches our ears and the low drone of Damion's voice. I've never been in the adjoining room, but it's easy to picture Damion standing in the center with a handpicked collection of members to hang on to his every word. And like Luke said, *kiss the ring*.

"Go on," Luke prods. Unlike with me, he doesn't yank Savannah around or push her forward. He merely waits.

At last, her attention strays from his proffered arm. She looks toward the archway. "I can do it myself."

"Good girl," he says.

I mime *gag me* behind his back.

Savannah catches it, her lips twitching with an amused smile. I reciprocate, then nod in encouragement. If Luke isn't forcing her, chances are she's only moving forward to be welcomed, not punished.

I save what could be planned for me in a separate compartment of my brain, reminding myself that it's nothing I can't overcome when there's nothing left to lose.

Savannah lifts her head. I watch as her features smooth, a confident mask settling in place.

She really is a vision, with the scoop neck, ivory dress covered in pearls and ending in a mermaid cut. Her hair and makeup somehow survived the transfer from wherever she was to the Briar crypt. Savannah puts one foot forward, then the next, as graceful as a swan, despite being barefoot. I picture her chanting in her head, *One more step. Just one step at a time,* before she disappears through the archway.

As soon as she's out of sight, applause erupts, Savannah's reception warm and encouraging.

Luke and I are left in the dark alone.

Shockingly, he ignores me, crossing his arms and staring into the open space Savannah once occupied.

I keep as silent as a mouse, unwilling to trigger his attention, even as a smart-ass. The closer it comes to my time, the more nervous I feel. There's no bouquet of roses for me, nor do I have hope that my appearance in front of the Societies will be followed by applause.

I'm a Weatherby legacy, but my biological father is a Noble disgrace. If the Societies knew to add "turncoat" to his list of sins, I'd not only be unwelcome, but likely killed.

After watching Savannah for the last few hours and contemplating what she endured simply for being the daughter of a senator, I'm realizing, now more than ever, how precarious my position in this privileged and deadly world really is.

Even the Societies couldn't save her.

Luke's hand slams into the middle of my back and shoves me forward. In my intense contemplation, didn't even realize he'd moved behind me.

"You're up," he says. "Cum Bucket."

"You know, you're really taking to the status of

'goon,'" I quip, lifting my skirts to stride forward. "Or is it 'lapdog'?"

Luke doesn't have time to snarl a response before I glide through the archway and into the light.

My entrance is probably how gladiators felt before stepping into the Roman arena to face a rigged battle.

I'm on a type of platform with Greek-inspired columns on each side. The room is circular—no, octagon shaped—with a stone statue on every side, with large fire bowls on stands interspersed throughout.

Members gather near the center, forming a circle. Strangely, the first thing my mind focuses on is that no one's wearing a cloak.

The Nobles are dressed in black, the Virtues in white. The small, lizard part of my brain rejoices in my survival —I'm wearing white, too. I must still be one of them.

They all hold a single rose. My gaze falls upon Savannah, standing in the center of the circle on top of a gold crest.

"Welcome, Ember Weatherby."

Damion's voice causes me to pause in my hesitant stroll to the front of the platform. I turn in his direction. He's dressed in an all-black suit as well, his silver hair and bright blue eyes in stark contrast. But his eyes aren't on me. I follow their direction back to Savannah, who holds up a wilting rose, the last in her hand, and says, ""This is for my temporary replacement. For there can only be one of us."

Excuse me, what?

I raise my brows as my mouth falls open. Gone is the vulnerable tremble to her voice. Her gaze is steady on mine. Unreadable.

"That's right," Damion says. "As has been tradition for hundreds of years, there can only be twelve Winthorpe members at any given time. I'm afraid we're at the unlucky number thirteen."

"She's earned her place here!"

The shout turns every head. Every one but mine. I know that tone. Could pick it out even if I were deaf, because I would still feel its vibrations as it traveled through my skin, embraced my bones, and claimed my blood.

Damion continues in an untroubled voice, "I see that my son, your prince, has finally decided to make himself known. Come up here, boy."

Thorne breaks the circle by shoving through two Nobles and storming up to the platform. He doesn't spare Savannah a glance. His stare bores through the air, drilling into the side of my face.

I don't turn toward him.

"Ember is a legacy," Thorne growls, stepping between Damion and me. His shadow almost swallows me whole. "Not only that, she's passed every challenge you've given her, including the impossible feat of beating my record to the top of Devil's Ridge."

So that's what that fucked-up relay race of my life was

called. I step to the side, Thorne's form so all-encompassing, it's hard to breathe under his protection.

"Indeed she did," Damion responds. Too mildly. My gaze darts to Thorne's back. Usually, any rebellion by his son is met with wrath and fury.

And any defense of me is met with torture.

"Thorne, don't," I say in a low voice. The members below stare up at us, enraptured. Savannah is no exception.

"I'll argue that Savannah Merricourt also earned her place here," Damion continues, "as she's proven by surviving the horrendous condition of being taken against her will and enduring whatever her captors wanted from her."

My eyes ping over to Savannah again. She hasn't moved from her spot in the center of the circle, but she's gone as white as her dress.

I'm forced to admit Damion has a point.

The responding slope of Thorne's shoulders tells me he sees it, too.

"So what shall we do with such a conundrum, hmm?" Damion pretends to contemplate the issue by sweeping his hand out to the members. "We've never had to banish a member due to an overcrowding issue. It is only when Savannah was considered dead that we added a new recruit. A legacy, yes, but one who was recently discovered through chance, when there happened to be a vacant seat on the Virtues."

By you, I want to snarl. *You set this up and you knew exactly what you were doing, whether Savannah was alive or not.*

Yet I keep silent, deciding to choose my battles against this monster. The last time I was too obvious, I almost drowned by his drug-happy hand.

"Banishment is only considered in the most dire of circumstances," Damion continues over the murmurs and mutterings of the members. Many unfamiliar faces pop out of the crowd, older and more world-weary, with the sharpness of quiet observation.

Damion's invited alumni, the Nobles and Virtues that are out in the real world. This meeting must be a big deal for him to premeditate their presence.

My stomach lurches at the repercussions of that. What are they here to witness?

"I'd say another challenge is in order, between the two girls."

The suggestion doesn't come from Damion. I search the crowd, finding the owner of the voice. A handsome man steps forward, his skin almost as dark as his suit. I blink, and I see the resemblance almost instantly—he's Jaxon's father. A viscount of the Nobles, if I remember it right.

Basically, an enforcer. Luke's dream job.

"What?" Thorne's head whips toward Mr. Murray. "That's impossible. Our challenges never involve pitting members against each other in a duel. We encourage solo skills, the ability to take risks and survive." Thorne scoffs, but I note the stiffness in his spine and the tightness of that sound. "We dominate and control outsiders, not each other."

"We've never had a situation like this before," Damion muses as if Thorne hasn't spoken. "Therefore, innovation is needed. I like where your head is at, Thaddeus."

"Once a member, we do *not* turn against each other," Thorne snarls. He throws a hand out in front of me.

I look down at it, my heart squeezing and releasing at the sight. First, he hates me. Then he protects me. Then he tastes me and despises me again.

I can't keep doing this.

His father blinks slowly, unfazed. "Correct me if I'm wrong, but I am the current king, not you, therefore I get to make the final decision. Along with the queen, of course." Damion defers to the silent shape beside him—a woman I hadn't noticed while dividing my attention among Thorne, Savannah, and Damion. Headmistress Dupris.

"The king is correct, I'm afraid," Dupris states. "It is in our code, our credence, that there can only be twelve members attending Winthorpe. Our Societies are to be cherished, not given out like Christmas gifts." She sighs, her fingers knotting together at her stomach. "Our founders never had reason to deviate from the rule they made with purpose. We must abide by it. If that means instigating an additional challenge between two members, I don't see the harm."

"If you allow this," Thorne says, "think of your *precious* Societies. Any time there's a conflict between members—"

"I'll do it."

Thorne stiffens. He freezes to the point that if it weren't for his flaring nostrils, I'd consider him one of the statues.

Slowly, painfully, he turns to me. "I'm sorry, are you speaking in tongues?"

"I'll do it," I repeat, straightening my shoulders. "I've won all the challenges given to me. This won't be any different."

Forget that it'll be against a broken bird of a girl. But I set my jaw and think of my family. Of Malcolm and what he's willing to risk. What Thorne can't escape. And how Damion's using this town as his personal drug lab and wielding power over the smartest, brightest students who could really make a difference in this world if directed properly.

For all these reasons, I hold my head up and pretend my bowels aren't turning into liquid.

"Ember, think about what you're agreeing to," Thorne warns under his breath. "My father is never impulsive. You could be asked to do the worst to Savannah. She could be asked to harm you. I can't allow it."

"I can protect myself." I move to walk around him.

"Maybe it's time you start believing in my ability to stay alive."

He whispers fiercely in my ear as I pass, "Don't make me watch you two kill each other. The only winner is *him*. Why do this to yourself?"

I murmur my response. "For the same reasons you submit to his brutal punishments. Because there's no other way to show him your strength."

Thorne rears back as if scalded. Really, he shouldn't be surprised I'm able to read him so well. He's not just a gorgeous specimen I want to climb and lick and suck. Thorne Briar is a person I'm getting to know.

And that, I think, is enough to make him recoil and allow me to keep walking forward.

Damion watches my approach as calmly as a snake waiting in the grass to strike. "I always wondered why my boy kept standing up for you." His lips lift in his version of a smile. "Now I'm beginning to see why. You're very unlike your father."

I'm exactly like him before you took away his will to live. I keep my thoughts to myself as I come to a stand next to him. I don't stop until Thorne's in my blind spot, because I know if I look at him, if I see the expression on his face as Damion metes out the challenge, I may falter.

"And you, my dear Savannah?" Damion doesn't acknowledge my close presence and stares down the platform. "You've been through such an ordeal. Do you wish to add to it in order to solidify your place with us?"

Savannah drifts forward in answer, the circle parting in a gentle, hushed way, the faces closest to her melting with pity. An angel in the midst of damned gods, and she owns every part of the role.

I can't hate her. I can't pity her, either. Her expression is so expertly still and serene, all I can do is admire her as she works to get her trauma under control.

She halts in front of me, holding out the last rose. I can't discern what she's feeling, which means no one else can, either. *Smart girl.*

"For you, my challenger," she says, her voice as musical and light as ever.

I grasp the stem, choking back a gasp of shock when my pinky scrapes against the top of her hand. A warm slickness transfers from her skin to mine.

There were thorns on the roses. She'd gripped them so tightly she'd cut her palm open.

Mirroring her expression, I bring the flower to my chest, and reply calmly, "May the best challenger win."

Savannah lowers her chin in acknowledgment.

"Very well," Damion says, then lifts his head to address the crowd. I still can't look at Thorne. "The two warring Virtues have agreed to a duel, of sorts. The girl who remains standing will prove herself the strongest, the most committed, and will persevere as an honored member. Thaddeus?" Damion turns his head to the left, at Jaxon's father. "Bring him out."

My forehead tightens. Glancing at Savannah doesn't help. She's just as confused as I am.

Mr. Murray springs forward and heads into the tunnel behind me, Savannah, and Damion. Headmistress Dupris watches his movements with grim acceptance.

As if pulled by an inner string of intuition, I finally look at Thorne.

His hardened jaw and intense gaze toward the same entrance Savannah and I used doesn't give me any reassurance. Thorne's lips thin as his eyes land on mine, leveled with acquiescence before he closes them slowly. *I warned you...*

Movement forces my attention to return to the archway.

Savannah's hand flutters to her mouth.

I gasp.

CHAPTER 7

THORNE

Jaxon's father disappears into Winthorpe's catacomb tunnels for mere seconds before returning with something in his arms. His biceps strain against his suit jacket as he lifts one-half of a chair, the other half raised by Luke, a jock who is basically a sentient steroid.

There's someone in it.

I can't tell who, since his head is covered with a black sack, but it's obvious he's as angry as a cat getting pissed on, thrashing his head in all directions, his neck straining as he fights against the binds tying his wrists to the arms of the chair and his ankles to the thick wooden legs. He's shirtless and barefoot, but thankfully, black slacks cover his lower half.

I keep my expression bland as Thaddeus and Luke lower the angry captive in the center of the circle. He's close enough now that I hear the strangled grunts behind the fabric covering his face—likely gagged as well as bound.

"Ah. He's awake." Father grins, beckoning the gathered members. The human circle moves closer to center. Everyone's too rapt with bloodlust, crowding as near as they can get, hoping for a front row seat.

I watch with wry amusement. Not just anyone can make it into the Societies. My father's predatory selectiveness in membership has always been on point.

My relaxed stance doesn't convey the rapid beats inside my chest, so loud they drum in my ears with incessant warning—*this is bad, Ember won't make it, Sav will collapse, fucking help them*—that it's nearly impossible to keep my expression carved in stone.

It's out of my hands. All I can do now is watch Ember willingly fall headfirst into the last ring of Hell.

I scan the members in a rapid-fire count. All are accounted for, so the bound man can't be any of them. I figured it'd be the most recent member to piss Father off, but honestly, the man wakes up angry. He probably rage-dreams long into the night.

Fuck, I don't know who it is. I don't specialize in man chest, so I can't tell by the shape of his fucking nipples.

He's cut. Fit. Tall. Medium-toned skin. Likely took two good syringes in the neck to knock him out long enough to be propped in that chair. I'm reluctant to admit ... the heaving torso is vaguely familiar.

My molars grind together. *Swim team?*

Leaning back against a column, I resign myself to waiting with the rest of these lost souls for the big reveal. Though my head won't stop screaming at me to do something.

"Now." Father clasps his hands together and moves next to the struggling prisoner. Father ignores him entirely. "Such a unique challenge requires a rare touch. Decades have passed since we were last in this position." Father centers his gaze on Ember. With the minutest movement, I straighten from my laid-back position, the clues falling into place in my head.

I know what Sav and Ember have to do.

The same thing Malcolm was required to prove in order to keep his place in the Societies.

He lost.

Malcolm refused to take it as far as my father was willing to, and for that, he gave up his independence and submitted to the worst punishment imaginable. A challenge so horrendous, even I don't have the balls to describe it to Ember.

My attention moves to her, searching for any recognition flowing across Ember's features. If she's putting the puzzle together the same way I am.

"What's going on?" Ember whispers, but I hear it as if it were a gong inside my head.

"My dears," Father said. "Come."

Reluctantly, Sav and Ember move forward into the

circle, stopping on the other side of the occupied chair. He grunts, fights, bucks the legs until they slam back onto the marble floor. Father doesn't pay him any mind. Sav is as white as the ground she stands on, and Ember can't stop staring at the trapped, flailing man between them.

Father signals to the right. "Thaddeus, the weapons."

Thaddeus breaks from his position in the circle, moving to the side and nearer to me. He doesn't acknowledge my presence as he disappears on the other side of the column for whatever he's looking for.

I find Jaxon standing on the opposite side of the circle, behind Father. The whites of his eyes are as bright as the flames encircling the room. In it, I see he's as on guard as I am—and had no way of knowing our fathers' plans.

Jaxon's eyes dart to the side. I follow their path to Thaddeus, who reappears with his hands full. He strides to my father, face grim. The new recruits quickly make room for him to pass.

Without further prompting, Thaddeus flattens out a leather satchel at the sacrificial lamb's feet. Metal shines. Wood sits a shade lighter against the leather.

Pliers. Knives. Paddles. Rolling pins. Screwdrivers.

A whimper draws my focus up. Sav shakes all over, her fingers pattering against her sides. Ember shakes her head, retreating a step and throwing her hands up. "No. I won't do this."

"Oh, but you have to." Father smiles. "Don't you agree, my queen?"

Headmistress Dupris breaks rank, coming to Father's side. While she doesn't appear pleased, she responds, "While it's unorthodox, this type of challenge is not unheard of. I'm afraid the king has ordered it."

"It is used in the most controversial of circumstances, and this is one such moment." Father dips his chin as if in serious contemplation. I wonder if I'm the only one who notices the maddened greed in his eyes. "Two Virtues. One must prove herself over the other." In a grand wave of his hand, ensuring he has each and every member's attention, he lifts the black hood in a flourish, revealing the boy underneath.

"Oh my god—Zeke!" Ember cries.

Sav mewls, covering her mouth with her hands and shaking her head emphatically.

Zeke's wide, terrified eyes take in the room. Sweat drips from his cropped hairline down his temples, dampening the silk tie wrenched between his lips. His grunts become an octave higher, his struggles against the bindings harder.

Fuck. I despise that asshole, but I don't wish this on him.

Father spreads out his arms. "The first Virtue to force him unconscious—or worse—wins." He takes Dupris's elbow and merges into the circle, his expression benign, but his eyes alive with intent. "Ladies, you may begin."

"I'm not doing this!" Ember's panicked stare goes from Zeke, to Father, to Sav. "*We're* not doing this!"

"Isn't he the one responsible for almost killing you?" Father counters mildly. "If it weren't for Zeke Aiden, I'd never know the lengths to which you'd go to besmirch your king's name. I wouldn't have needed to punish you to remind you of your insubordinance."

Ember looks at him, fisting her hands at her sides. Then she searches the circle in a blatant attempt to find me as if I could come in and save the day.

Not this time, little pretty.

I step farther into the shadows. She's on her own, though every fiber in me screams to take up weapons and do the dirty work for her.

Father chuckles. "Malcolm couldn't go through with it. But this time, I believe his daughter can."

Zeke screams beneath his bondage. His eyes latch onto Ember's, shining with tears, pleading.

"You can't make me." Ember shakes her head, crossing her arms. Her jaw works, chewing on a winning argument. "Zeke's famous. How will you explain any marks on him? Or worse? We'd be arrested for assault. It'd be all over the news, and your Societies would be uncovered—"

Zeke releases a muffled wail.

Ember's head snaps to Sav, holding a small scalpel in her shaking hand. It drips blood.

I find the wound in seconds, on Zeke's thigh, his slacks torn open with the efficacy of a surgeon.

"It seems our lost princess has the right idea." Father

folds his hands, his Noble pinky ring shining. "Start where it won't show."

"Savannah..." Ember says hoarsely. "Why?"

Sav doesn't react to Ember's shock. Her eyes bore into Zeke, the bones of her face seeming to protrude through her skin. Her knuckles grind white against the blade, and when she bears her teeth, they're just as pearlescent.

"You forget, Ember Weatherby, what our sweet Savannah has endured," Father continues. "For so long, she wasn't able to fight back. She was trapped, used, stored away until her kidnappers wanted to see her again. And see her they did."

Sav's breathing grows more erratic. Ever so subtly, the hem of her dress ripples. Her heels are lifting from the floor.

Ember opens her mouth to argue, or to soothe Sav, as she's always wont to do, but Father cuts in, "Those kidnappers are still at large. Unaccounted for. Free. This is a way for Savannah to channel her rage. Isn't it, sweet girl? Show us what was done to you. Make our members *see* the way you suffered and how strong you've become. You are a survivor. Your blood is royal. You are a phoenix rising from the ashes. *Show us.*"

A guttural cry leaves Sav's throat before she lurches forward, slashing the scalpel across Zeke's chest.

A red ribbon forms between his pecs, rivulets running through the lines of muscle on his chest.

"Savannah, stop!" Ember throws herself between Sav

and Zeke. "Please. If you and I both refuse, they can't make us do this."

Sav doesn't see her anymore. She's wild, vengeful, and free to take out her anger on the closest bystander. Including Ember.

"Too late," Father croons. "Savannah's begun the challenge. If you don't match her, you will become a pariah to the Societies, much like your father. An outsider who is no longer welcome. All privileges, including your tenure at Winthorpe, will be revoked. Is it worth it to you? To save this vain, self-worshipping boy's life?" Father angles his head. "What would he do in your position? Would he lower his arms rather than mutilate you? Or would he do what was needed in order to survive?"

"You're insane. A maniac!" Ember's voice is barely recognizable. It cracks and growls, hovering near the breaking point of sheer panic.

"And you're wasting time," Father says as Sav slashes her way closer to Zeke.

Ember screams when Sav's blade nicks her arm before she makes another go at Zeke. This time at his inner wrist, very close to the suicide vein.

Come on, little pretty, you know what to do.

She's quaking, my Ember, holding her bicep where Sav so easily swiped at her. Her white-blond hair hangs down her back in tangles, her slip of a dress revealing the pink of her nipples as she heaves.

Sav tosses the scalpel aside, grimacing with feral lips as she bends down and selects another tool.

She chooses the screwdriver.

Come on, *Ember!*

I step into the fire-lit room. As I suspected, the movement catches her eye. Ember sucks in a breath as she sees me, her perfect lips forming an *O* of longing.

I don't speak—can't—for any act of heroism will be seen as sabotage by my father. I can only stare, deeply and darkly, into her eyes, communicating through silence that she be as brutal as me, as quick-thinking, as *efficient.*

You know what to do. How to end this.

She pulls her lips in, moving her head to the side in a half-shake of denial, tears tracking down her face.

I lower my chin in an almost imperceptible nod. *Yes. Do it. You have to.*

The members forming the circle mumble impatiently, so close to seeing bloodshed only to have it reduced by Ember's refusal. Father notices. "Savannah, our princess, keep it up. Show the members that you've always belonged."

Sav lifts from the floor and in a savage arc that surprises even me, plunges the screwdriver into Zeke's thigh, possibly catching some scrotum along the way.

Zeke nearly breaks his neck tilting his head back, his eyes rolling to their whites. His voice box will carry scar tissue for years to come with the way he screamed.

Sadly, those screams die into whimpers. Soon, only

the squeaking sound of the chair legs against the floor can be heard in the resounding silence. Zeke, poor fucker, is still attempting to escape, even if he has to bring the chair with him.

"Fuck this," Ember murmurs. My ears prick with interest. "*Fuck this,*" she repeats.

She barrels over to the satchel, Sav stepping back enough to allow Ember to scan the various utensils. She's left the screwdriver in Zeke, her hands clenching and unclenching at her sides as she figures out how best to next attack.

Sav battles inner demons I can never come to understand, the fight obvious behind her eyes. She doesn't want this, but she does. She's trying to stop, but she can't.

Only Ember can end this, and I hope to fuck she succeeds.

Be quick, Ember, before bloodthirst takes Sav over for good.

Ember pulls out the wooden paddle, the type that fraternities use. The surrounding members groan with disappointment at the lack of creativity.

I smile.

She walks behind Zeke. Zeke tries to follow her path but loses her. He's shaking, pleading nonsensical words behind his gag. She lifts the paddle over her head. Closing her eyes, she moves her lips in a silent apology as she brings it down on the back of his head.

The *crack* sounds out through the space. Some members wince. Others applaud.

Zeke bows his head forward, groaning thickly. His eyes flutter, but he's still conscious.

Again. I stare at Ember, hooding my eyes.

Sav goes for the pliers, then lifts Zeke's fingers, cranking them back until they pop. Zeke's guttural cries don't reach her, but they freeze Ember, who watches Sav with horrified surprise.

"Savannah, don't—" Ember tries to say, but Sav's digging the pliers into one of his fingernails, peeling it back from his skin.

It's a minor move, but astute, since it causes the kind of pain that could make even the Hulk pass out. Unfortunately for Zeke, Sav grows bored, moving to his pinky and positioning the pliers so she can amputate.

I lift my attention back to Ember. *Hurry.*

"Fuck," she whispers again, her eyes as wide as I've ever seen them. She raises the paddle once more, bringing it down at his neck.

Then head.

Then neck again.

She swings and smacks, over and over, the sound becoming wetter, blood splattering onto her face, until Zeke goes limp.

EMBER

I *killed him.*

The paddle falls from my hand as I'm pushed aside by Jaxon, who scrambles to find a pulse.

My face feels warm—too hot, too tight. The dress's fabric sags against my breasts. I hold my hand to my mouth, tasting metal.

"I didn't ... I didn't mean ... is he dead?" I whisper through cold, numbed fingers.

"No." Jaxon removes his hand from Zeke's neck. "But he needs medical attention."

Obviously. Hysterical laughter bubbles up in my throat. I swallow it down so hard, it comes out as a garbled yelp. Jaxon turns back to me, arching a brow.

"Will he be all right?" I rasp out.

"I'm a doctor." A silver-haired man, his face handsomely lined, steps forward, separating himself from the circle that's become suffocatingly close. "Bring him into one of the empty mausoleums. I'll see to him there."

A couple of viscounts, Mr. Murray included, crowd around Zeke, elbowing me farther out of the way. Cold air drifts over my shoulders, spiking the hairs on my skin the more distance I gain from Zeke. As they start untying him from the chair, I look for Savannah over the tops of their heads.

She's shrouded by her father, protecting her with a thick arm around her shoulders and talking softly into her ear. Savannah shudders, her hands crossed over her chest as she struggles to breathe. Zeke's blood drips down her forearms.

Watching her jolts me out of my fugue. I look down at myself, at the splashes of blood against my dress, a vivid red cutting through the ivory.

A sound rushes into my ears. My own breaths escalate.

"Don't lose it. Not now." The voice travels into my ear, the low vibration of it managing to pull me away from the brink.

It's followed by a tight grip on my arm. I angle my head, though I know who it is. I always do.

Thorne holds me steady, his vise-like grip the only indication of emotion as he stares blandly toward his father.

Damion stands with three other dukes, all of them muttering to Damion and gesturing. Damion glances up, meeting my eyes. My insides shrivel underneath his cold, predatory focus. But the only physical reaction he'll get from me is the slight slackening of my jaw as I stare back.

Damion jerks his hand up, cutting the men off. He breaks from their group, striding toward me.

"Attention!" he booms. The room immediately quiets.

Damion does a slow spin, sweeping his gaze across all members, then Savannah, her dad, me, and Thorne.

"My peerage argues at the timing of Mr. Aiden's blackout," he says. "And whether it occurred during Savannah's ministrations. If that is the case, then Ember preyed upon an unconscious individual, thereby nullifying her attempts at maintaining her title as a Virtue."

"Bullshit."

Damion raises his brows at Thorne. "Did I say something to upset you, son?"

"You know as well as I do that Zeke was awake when Ember brought down her first blow."

The flatness of Thorne's tone causes a shudder to run down my spine. He tightens his hold in warning, but it's difficult to stay strong when they're arguing whether you beat someone while they were conscious or not.

I just needed it to stop. I couldn't watch Savannah succumb to her demons for another minute. The fragile, skittish girl I'd met in the crypt was gone. In her place was a ravaged woman who wanted to hurt as much as she'd been hurt.

I didn't recognize Savannah circling Zeke, salivating over the thought of maiming him.

I don't recognize myself.

Aurora adds, "I wouldn't be surprised if Ember cheated. That seems to be her MO."

Damion doesn't spare her a glance. "As you are no longer princess, your opinion doesn't matter anymore, Miss Emmerson."

I brace for Aurora's tantrum, or at the very least, a snide, jealous glare directed at Savannah, but nothing comes. Aurora's shoulders slope as she retreats into the comfort of her friends, Belle and Delaney, who each squeeze one of her hands in support.

My heart sinks at the sight. Aurora's a vile human being, yet even she has friends.

"I propose a tie," Thorne says.

I jerk my head up.

"Both Sav and Ember have displayed the attribute you tested, Fa—my king. Strength. Stamina. I know it's unconventional, but so is Sav's kidnapping, which was out of her control and solely due to her father's position in government. We replaced her with Ember, assuming that Sav wasn't coming back. That was our mistake. Not Ember's, not Sav's."

My jaw practically hangs open as I listen. It's the most I've ever heard Thorne say. And arguing against his dad, no less.

"The Noble prince has a point, my king." This comes

from Senator Merricourt, who hasn't released his daughter since the moment he was able to embrace her. "Why punish the girls for another's mistake?"

Damion's jaw clicks. His expression is controlled and resolute until I take a closer look. Fire ripples under the surface, boiling his skin and demanding to spread. He doesn't like being called out, especially in the presence of the entire Society, but he's put in a tight spot.

To demand my ejection now would seem personal, a goal Damion's worked hard to disguise. Thorne's argument leaves little leeway for Damion to pivot out of, not without revealing his deep hatred of the Weatherbys—a private vendetta not tolerated by members of the Societies. At least, not in front of each other.

Behind the scenes, he'll work his political black magic to destroy us.

But so will I.

Damion spears his son with a frown promising later punishment, but Thorne doesn't flinch.

"One might say you are favoring Ember over Savannah," Damion muses.

"I enjoy toying with Weatherbys just about as much as you do, Father."

Thorne's hand drops from my arm. Without its steadying force, I wobble, dizzy with leaking adrenaline—with what I've done.

Damion notices, narrowing his eyes at his son.

Thorne drifts over to Savannah's side, his movements

unhurried. Nothing Thorne ever does is relaxed, and I watch with bated breath, waiting for the moment he'll attempt to crush me.

I'm ready for it this time. I'm ready for you.

Zeke's blood splatter dries on my face, tightening the skin around my eyes. I hope my stare conveys my thoughts.

Another duke pipes in, "Are we sure about this? Ember Weatherby hasn't exactly displayed a sound mind in this recent month. If it weren't for her last name—recently and conveniently obtained, I might add—there is no way she'd be deemed a reliable member of the Societies."

"I also know to accord respect when it's due," Thorne continues as if the duke hadn't spoken. "And Ember, despite her mistakes and losing her spot on the swim team, has passed every challenge put to her." He levels his gaze at the duke, then slides its impact at his father. "Including this one."

Now *that* is not a statement I expected to flow from Thorne's talented, vicious mouth.

He's helping me. Why?

Damion makes no attempt to correct the duke, yet also doesn't argue with his son, or add that *he* was the one who "conveniently" attached the Weatherby name to mine. I didn't expect him to, but I keep my mouth shut, too, unwilling to show all my cards.

Dupris flows to a stop beside Damion, resting a

slender hand on his shoulder and tilting her fine-boned face to him. "Damion, the challenge is fulfilled. Let the viscounts clean up this mess, and perhaps we can move festivities above ground in celebration. It's not every year we welcome two strong, capable Virtues into our membership. They've more than proven themselves."

Never mind that one of Dupris's prized, precious, *famous* students is splayed out on the floor, tortured by more of her own. The headmistress seems more concerned with continuing the party.

To think, I'd thought she was one of the saner ones in here.

Damion parts his mouth, a slit of blackness against pale, colorless lips. "You may be right, Blanche. Perhaps I am taking the accords of our founders too seriously. As my son always mentions, we must grow with the times. I suppose this is a similar moment of consideration." Damion inhales, then says on a release of breath, "Very well. Members, please re-welcome our *two* Virtues, one our lost princess, the other a proven baroness."

My fingers stop digging into my palms. My exhales flow easier.

I've made it. I'm still one of them.

For now.

CHAPTER 9
EMBER

I've become used to the blatant staring at Winthorpe while I walk between classes. People avoid me because Thorne ordered it. People hate me because Aurora demanded it. Without Aiko at my side to distract me with coffee and chatter, I feel the aggressive studies even more.

But this morning, it's the warm smiles beneath all these eyeballs that have me slowing my strides.

"Morning, Ember!" a freshman chirps as she scurries by, textbooks clutched to her chest.

Another boy raises his chin in an aloof salute as he passes. Still others lift their fingers in a half-wave or curve their lips in a ... smile?

What the fuck?

I hurry to my locker, switching out my textbooks and

giving the hallway my back. Really, I should be glad for the shift in mood after spending so long dodging pointy elbows and pretending to be deaf to all the slurs. But I'm not that stupid. I'm suspicious.

The friendliness continues throughout my morning classes, including by the professors. A dude who loved covering the tip of his pencil in his spit and poking it into my neck leans forward on his desk and pats me on the shoulder when I answer a tough question, whispering, "Nice job, Beckett."

I whip my head around. "You still don't have permission to touch me."

He raises his hands in surrender. "You're right. I'm all for the #MeToo movement. I'll take it easy."

It's said without a hint of sarcasm. I narrow my vision into slits as I stare at him.

The bell rings, saving me from interrogating him further. Usually, I have to be wary of students crowded in the aisles of the classroom, deliberately standing in my way and forcing me to hop the desks to exit. Today, my pathway is clear, everyone ducking aside when I straighten with my bag on my shoulders.

"After you," Pencil-Spit says behind me.

I expect a wash of jeers and garbage to hit me as I head down the first aisle. Nothing comes. I haven't seen Thorne or Aurora yet to ask them what the hell is going on —since clearly they've sent a message down their royal line—so I'm forced to continue, pretending all this deference is normal.

"Did you see the *TMZ* post today?" someone on my left mutters.

"Holy shit, yes," her friend says, pulling out her phone to relive the moment.

I slow my steps, oddly drawn to the conversation.

"Look, they just updated it. He's in the hospital, resting comfortably. Thank god. They left season one on such a cliffy—I didn't actually want Dorian to *die*."

They're talking about *Golden Crest*. I didn't watch it, but my friend Kinsey from my old school in Boston was obsessed with it. Dorian is Zeke Aiden's character.

"A car accident." The first girl shakes her head in dramatic mourning. "Speeding around one of Raven's Bluff's insane curves. He's lucky he didn't drive off a cliff."

"What was he thinking?" The second girl raises her voice. "He grew up here. Even *Thorne* knows not to take those roads above forty-five. It's a death sentence."

"Broken ribs. Multiple contusions." The first girl scrolls through her friend's phone. "Concussion. Oh yikes, they had to amputate his pinky on his right hand."

The second girl gasps. "Oh my god, do you think he'll still be hot?"

"Of course," First Girl scoffs. "Just don't look at it too long."

Holy shit. My throat gets stuck on a hard swallow.

"Um, hey? You asked me not to touch you, so I'll just gently inform you that you need to move. You're kind of blocking the rest of us."

"Sorry," I mutter, sliding out from the front of the aisle. I send two more quick glances the girls' way, but they've moved on to theories of *Golden Crest*'s Season 2.

The rest of the class filters past me, including the two girls, and I fold in behind, head down and thumbs digging into my bag's straps. Zeke's fate repeats in my mind, the girls' revelations overlapping with the images of him screaming and sobbing while tied to a chair last night.

We did this. I did that.

My stomach curdles. I'd been forced to follow the Societies' challenge, but if this is what they do to a boy who helped the king uncover my duplicitous plans, what the hell are they going to do to Malcolm if they discover he's working for the FBI?

I can't think about it. My steps pick up in the crowded halls, heading with everyone else to the cafeteria. All I can do is move forward and protect Malcolm as much as I can until I gain enough information to take to him and bring Damion down.

Even if it means hurting others.

Badly.

Cringing, I push through the giant mahogany doors into the cafeteria, almost a building in itself with its large stations ranging from farm-to-table food, cook your own, allergen and gluten-free, kosher, and a cafe & sweets. Many other stations spear up from the crowd of students, all with trays and chatting freely with their friends as they pick out food.

With the dive my stomach's taken, I navigate to the soup station, settling on lentil and spinach soup with a warm tea to drink. Balancing them on my tray, I twist toward the historical area. It's a half-square of old trophies and photos with a few armchairs in the center, rarely occupied by students due to it practically vomiting sheer boredom.

"Ember!"

The voice draws me up short. Standing in the midst of scurrying students, I search for the source.

"Ember!" it says again. "Over here!"

A hand shoots up and flutters in a wave at one of the tables on the left. I follow the curve down to the shoulder, then the perfectly styled blonde head.

Savannah smiles at me, her hand still in the air, beckoning.

My fingers tighten on my tray. I can't seem to make my feet move immediately. I'm too busy studying her face, searching for the same guilt that must be clearly displayed on mine.

Her skin has a healthy sheen, her cheeks flushed with the exertion of being back and sitting among friends. Her hair is pinned back on both sides of her face with clips that catch the light and sparkle when she moves. Her uniform is impeccably tailored, the fabric bright with newness. I'd forgotten she was kidnapped while wearing her school uniform. I wonder if the previous one is soiled, if she was kept in it for long, or if it contains way too many memories for her to even acknowledge that she's wearing a brand new uniform two sizes smaller.

I remember Savannah stuck in the crypt with me, asking, soft and tremulous, *"Can you turn around? I've been avoiding the girls' lockers and dressing in the headmistress's office..."*

Savannah angles her head, her brown eyes warm and inviting. "Are you coming over?"

I snap out of it. "Sure."

It's easy to blend in with the other milling students until I reach her table. She pats the empty seat next to her, but my eyes slide over to the occupied seat on Savannah's other side. Aiko's there, her eyes downcast. Her forearms rest on each side of her tray like she's about to eat, but her flatware is clean.

I set down my lunch and sit.

Then come face-to-face with pale blue wrath.

I was so focused on Savannah, I hadn't noticed Thorne sitting across from her, his back to me as I headed to their table.

He sits with brooding stillness like he always does. The white fire of his eyes is fixed on my face. Our mutual dislike of each other is clear. We piss each other off. He orders me around, I ignore him, and while I try to forget how fucking good his tongue feels eating me out, he tries not to hate-fuck me right on this table.

I squirm under his intense scrutiny until I remember where I am and who I'm with.

Aurora and Jaxon sit on either side of Thorne, and a waft of too-sweet coconut perfume hits the side of my face as Belle takes the available chair next to mine and Delaney across from her.

Other guys I recognize from last night take the last spots available. Before I know it, I'm seated in the middle of the most popular kids in school.

It all falls into place—the kindness from my peers, the quiet deference to me in the halls.

"Ember? You okay?"

Savannah's gentle expression drifts into my focus, forcing me to sit straight and relax my tense lips.

I reply, "Yep, fine, considering what happened last night."

Savannah doesn't give me the reaction I'm hoping for. Guilt, regret, fear even. All I get is serene blankness when her glossed lips curve into a placating smile.

When I don't respond in kind, she adds softly, "Aiko has something to say to you. Right, Aiko?"

I'm all too aware of Thorne's attention as I lean forward so Savannah no longer blocks my view of Aiko.

It's easy to refuse to talk to him. What I didn't consider was how hard it would be not to look at him.

Even in my periphery, he's all hard edges and irresistible angles. No one looks like Thorne Briar, so vampire pale and ethereally handsome. *He's* the wicked god creating havoc in a prep school—not Zeke's character on *Golden Crest.*

For one suffocating second, I meet his eye, holding his focus until it becomes too intense and I have to look away. Heat pools at my core at the same time cold thoughts battle against it in my head. It doesn't take long for them to lose. I can *actually* picture spreading my legs on the cafeteria table in front of everyone while he buries himself inside me.

I hurt someone last night. Thorne's probably done the same thing many times. It's that darkness, that animalistic rawness in him that calls to me in the middle of a school day.

"Um..." Aiko's quiet voice redirects my attention. "I'm sorry."

I pull my brows in. "What? Why?"

"For how I treated you." Aiko lifts her gaze from the table, vaguely centering me in her focus. "I shouldn't have yelled at you or insulted you the way I did. All you were doing was trying to find Savannah when everyone else gave up."

Savannah rests a hand on Aiko's shoulder and squeezes, nodding her head in approval. She regards Aiko with the same warmth she directed at me, but even from this angle, I notice her gaze is oddly empty. Drained and endless. My brows pull in harder.

Aiko abruptly stands, Savannah's hand dragging down Aiko's arm until it drops. "Anyway, I have to get going."

"You don't have to apologize." I glance back and forth between Savannah and Aiko as Aiko picks up her tray, holding it so hard against her stomach that the edge digs into the soft muscles. "You were worried about your sister. She's lucky to have someone who never accepted that she was a lost cause. Right, Savannah?"

My voice picks up at the end, my brain scrambling to solve the weird dynamic between the two of them. Aiko should be overjoyed that Savannah returned relatively unharmed. She has no idea what Savannah and I got up to last night—or who we beat up. I can understand why she'd continue to be wary around me, but why is she so tense around Savannah?

"That's right," Savannah answers, her attention gliding over to me. I swear, it's like conversing with a silicone doll right now. Her two faces from the night before are gone—the girl who trembled while putting on a dress and the one who grew claws, the tamed and the vicious. It's like those two dualities took all the energy that remained in her after being held captive for over a year.

"Aiko, you know I love you," Savannah continues softly as Aiko shows us her back. "Never forget that."

Aiko turns in profile. "I love you, too," she murmurs, then leaves the table.

Throughout the strangely banal three-way conversation we were having, the rest of the table chatted about school stuff while keeping an obvious ear on us. Aurora is the least subtle, saying loudly as soon as Aiko departs, "Aren't you lucky, Cum Bucket? All is forgiven, and you're back in Aiko's good graces. You got your only friend back."

"Aurora," Thorne warns. He doesn't glance in her direction. Zero muscles in his face contributed to that warning, but Aurora shrinks as if he roared it. Thorne's attention remains on me, and being the target of a flattened expression with burning, hate-filled murder eyes somehow tightens my nipples. They tingle with sensuous fear like they can't wait to be under his command.

Or punishment.

I resist rubbing them with my palms or pinching them to remind them what real pain feels like. Thorne is not mine. I am not his.

A warm hand on mine jolts me back to the present.

"Nonsense," Savannah says, her thumb rubbing the top of my wrist. I look down, filled with a creepy sort of awe. "Ember has me and everyone else at this table. She proved that last night, the same way I proved I still belong." For a moment, Savannah's eyes flash, and her stare mirrors Thorne's. Hateful and murderous. It hits me without the erotic afterthought, however, and instead wraps around my bones like slimy green seaweed.

"I am the uncontested princess," Savannah continues, "and I decree, along with our prince"—another warm, empty glance at Thorne—"that Ember will not be your plaything anymore. You're finished, Aurora, both in status and in your twisted games." Savannah's hold tightens on my hand. I haven't yet communicated to my arm to *pull the fuck away*, despite Savannah's promise of protection.

Aurora's mouth drops open. "But—"

"You haven't hurt the way she hurts," Savannah cuts in, softer now. "Your challenges mean nothing compared to hers. Until you draw blood..." Savannah shrugs as if almost killing a person is the latest viral trend that Aurora has no hope of copying. "You have no standing with me."

Aurora's hands clench around the table, everyone else looking on with widened stares and empty forks hanging in the air, lunch long forgotten. Only Thorne sits back, idly twirling a steak knife, the sharp blade coming close to the tender skin between his fingers before expertly circling away while he catalogs the conversation.

What is he thinking? Is this normal behavior at the cool kids' table? I try to catch his attention, but to no avail. He's too busy staring at her, Savannah. *No*, I remind myself, *his girlfriend.*

It finally becomes easy to pull my hand from under hers.

"I'm your best friend," Aurora says, her tone high with hurt. "And the interim princess. I promise I wasn't trying to steal your spot. All I wanted was for you to come back.

In fact"—Aurora's eyes knife into mine—"when it was announced your place at Winthorpe was going to be taken by an outsider fake, I fought loud and hard. Shouldn't it be me you're defending against *her*?"

I've never seen Aurora so supplicant and unsure. To be honest, I kind of enjoy it, especially when framed by a haircut she never asked for.

Thorne must read my amusement. His upper lip twitches, as if fighting off approval of my insatiably cruel side. *A side he feeds off.*

Shifting in my seat, I look away from him.

The bell rings, signaling the end of lunch. Delaney's the first to pop up while Belle cajoles Aurora to come along. It takes a few seconds, but eventually, Aurora gives up her silent pleading against Savannah's unaffected calm and rises.

"I defend those who deserve it," Savannah says while smiling. "We can still hang out, Aurora. I'm around for that now."

Aurora responds with an unsure twitch to her lips, then a scathing glance at me, before following her friends out of the cafeteria.

Thorne's the last to stand, and with a rigid, automatic movement, holds out a hand across the table for Savannah to grab as she rises. He won't look my way.

"I'll walk you to class," he says to her, his gruff voice a dark rumble against my rib cage.

Savannah doesn't take his hand. I'm sorry to say I'm

relieved I don't have to see it. "I'd like to hang back for a bit. Talk to Ember."

Thorne flicks a disinterested glance my way. "Suit yourself. I'll see you at the end of the day."

His cold departure doesn't affect me the way it should. Maybe because it's happened so many times I've grown used to it, since he more than makes up for his shitty attitude with an expert tongue.

Damnit, stop this. I scrunch my eyes shut, hating how much my body responds to him.

"I meant what I said." Savannah's voice cuts into my thoughts. I open my eyes. "You're one of us now. Don't worry about Aurora."

"I never have." I chew on those dishonest words, unable to confess to Savannah how close Aurora came to assaulting me. Savannah probably endured worse. "But thank you for standing up for me." Those next words feel just as untrue. I click my tongue, wondering why. Savannah's been nothing but nice since I met her. Besides, shouldn't there be a bond between us, now that we've mutually destroyed a guy?

I search her eyes in an attempt to find a thread to connect us. I see nothing.

"I'll always be on your side," Savannah says. "Just like you'll be on mine."

"Yeah. Sure." I swallow while keeping a wary eye on her. I've seen Savannah snap. I'm not about to cause it in the middle of the cafeteria.

"Do you wonder how Zeke is doing?" I ask her. Gently. "Because I do. I don't know why I did that. I've never been so violent before. He's an asshole, for sure, but I regret it. I regret hitting him while he was down."

"It's the fervor. When the Societies surround you, chanting with centuries-old wisdom, it's like they're funneling their strength into you and suddenly, you have the power of twenty-four elites. It's no wonder we needed to unleash." Savannah's expression doesn't shift despite her passionate words. "I only wish I had that power when I was alone."

"Agreed," I say in a hushed tone. "But don't you think it's … poisonous? Like, if we take too much, it'll kill us?"

She shakes her head. "It only makes us stronger. If it weren't for the Societies' teachings, I wouldn't have been able to withstand what I went through."

I shut my mouth, my argument silenced by the meaning of her words. When put in that kind of context, I can see why Savannah would want to possess that savagery and fearlessness, the ability to fell a man when so often, she was made the victim.

"It's why I was the first to choose our sacrifice," she adds lightly.

My stare shoots back to hers.

"The king and queen both overrode my suggestion, though." Savannah shrugs.

I speak through the ball of dread building in my throat. "What are you talking about?"

"The king and queen wanted to respect what I went through and gave me the option of choosing who we would torture. But they didn't think it was wise to pick someone with so little knowledge of the Societies. She'd see too much if we didn't kill her. With Zeke, they had a much better chance of manipulating him into silence, because of *course* we wouldn't kill him." Savannah laughs under her breath, like she'd just stated the obvious.

I can actually feel my face draining of blood. "You knew? The whole time when we were stuck in the crypt together, you know what we'd have to do?"

"Well, yes." Savannah stares at me like I was failing her personal math quiz that she worked really hard on. "I've been a member since I was twelve. I'm well aware of how far the Societies go. Do you honestly think I'd be this sane after my abduction if I hadn't?"

I pull my lips in, because I sure as hell can't answer that. "Who did you choose, then? Who did Damion and Dupris override?"

Savannah flinches at my use of their names, but the cafeteria has emptied out. It's just she and I sitting side-by-side at a long table, yet I feel like there's a chasm between us.

"I thought it'd be obvious," she says, cocking her head at me. A owl assessing the mouse below.

"It isn't." There are too many people to choose from, frankly, but I don't tell her that.

"Aiko." Savannah rises at the same time my mouth

falls open and the rest of the blood leaves my face. "I nominated her as the sacrifice. She needs the strength we possess, don't you agree?" Savannah picks up her tray before turning to leave. "I was offering her a kindness, considering she now has two of the most powerful Winthorpe Virtues as her best friends."

CHAPTER 10
EMBER

Later that evening, dinner with Malcolm does not go as planned.

He and I are in a convenient sort of cease-fire and I was hoping to use that when I sat down with him in the formal dining room. I could comfortably go over Savannah's benign revelation that she wanted to maim Aiko. Malcolm's aware of my involvement in the Societies and is fully accepting of how violent it can get, yet it's still rather difficult for me to explain that I laid into a fellow student with such unfiltered rage that I dented his skull. All while Thorne and Damion, the two people Malcolm despises most, looked on.

Yeah, this truce should've come in real handy with both of us enjoying safe topics of discussion with the possible light treading into the status of the FBI investigation into the Briars, but nothing more than that. Not if we wanted to keep dinner at a low decibel.

The first sign that my plans were about to go awry was when the dinner plates were set before us. Marta fixed Cornish hens, their little corpses roasted and browned just for our tastebuds.

I stare down at mine, swallowing a lump of bile while picturing Zeke's bloody head sprouting out of where the hen's neck used to be.

Malcolm hacks into his chicken with aplomb, his sharp knife splitting the breast open. Of course he has to pick this time to actually eat his dinner instead of allowing it to cool untouched on his plate before he storms out.

He sticks a forkful of juicy meat into his mouth, a flap of crispy skin hanging out before he sucks it in, leaving his lower lip shining with grease.

My body jerks with a barely contained gag. I reach desperately for my glass of ice water and chug.

Malcolm frowns. "Something wrong with your dinner?"

An ice chip breaks hard against my molars. "It's—uh, I think my hen's undercooked."

Malcolm's lips pull down even lower. "Really? That's rather unlike Marta." He snaps his fingers for Dash, who manifests from the walls and swoops up my plate.

"Oh, you don't have to—I'll just take a salad. Tomatoes and cucumbers only. No meat." I swallow thickly again.

"Is this the part where I ask my unpredictable teenager if she's turning into a vegetarian?"

"Vegan, actually," I mumble into my place setting. "Definitely vegan."

Malcolm makes a thoughtful sound in his throat. "Very well. I'll give Marta grocery instructions for tomorrow."

I shift uneasily in my seat, finishing my water. Dash somehow reappears in record time, refreshing my glass with a pitcher.

"I was about to ask if your quietness was due to the news this morning," Malcolm says.

I lower my drink. "News?"

"Of a fellow student's car accident." Malcolm dabs the corners of his lips with a napkin, somehow failing to notice my spine fusing with the back of my chair. "Zeke Aiden. Isn't he a celebrity's kid?"

My hand slides from the icy-wetness of my glass as I study Malcolm closer. He knows very well who Zeke Aiden is. Why is he playing dumb?

"Zeke's the celebrity, not his parents," I correct with deliberate calm.

"Terrible tragedy." Malcolm takes another bite. When he sticks the fork back in his mouth, his eyes never leave mine.

I don't have silverware to fidget with, so I force my hands to my lap instead. "It is."

"Do you think the Societies had something to do with it?"

Direct fire. Shit. I level my shoulders. "He's not a member. Not that I know of."

"Indeed." Malcolm pauses to chew. "But that's never stopped their punishments before. What do you suppose he did, and who did it to him?"

"I ... wouldn't know."

As of now, Malcolm believes me to be low on the hierarchy list in the Societies. I hope to keep it that way, at least until I understand myself and my position a bit more. I *want* to help him. I'm happy to bury the Briars and stop Damion's illegal run of this town. My morale is practically made for this shit. Perfection and praise for doing the right thing is in my veins. So why am I stalling?

Because you're the one who helped put Zeke in the hospital. And you liked it.

My back aches with how tightly I'm holding it. Maybe, just maybe, it's not because I enjoyed the power and I just I don't want the hopeful light to die in Malcolm's eyes when it comes to me. He has so little left to cling to.

I lower my eyes in shame. If only it were just that.

"Ember."

Malcolm's soft command reluctantly draws my gaze up.

"I don't want to have to ask you this. Believe me when I say that I thought of all other options."

My brows tighten, but I wait for him to say more.

"The agent I'm in contact with, they're about to close the investigation."

"What? Why?" I can't stop the panic from infusing my voice any more than I can halt the thought that if there's no investigation, there's no further reason for me to continue acting the part of a Virtue.

"There's not enough evidence." Malcolm sighs, carefully laying his knife and fork on either side of his plate and sitting back. "It's been a few years now with no further developments, and his boss—or his boss's boss, I should say—is making noises to divert the funds to a more pressing investigation." Malcolm shakes his head solemnly. "We're Raven's Bluff. A small town with nothing special to offer, other than a drug ring, among thousands of other drug rings across America. A losing battle."

"Malcolm." I lean forward. I've never heard him talk like this. So defeated. So empty. *So Savannah-like.* "That's not true. The Societies aren't just in Raven's Bluff or even Massachusetts. They're *everywhere* and have the most powerful people in play. The Nobles and Virtues control governments, siphon corporate funds and own a shitload of cryptocurrency. Give them time and they'll have more control than Congress and the President combined."

"Honey." Malcolm's expression sags, staring at me

like I'm a new puppy who just peed on his Persian rug. "They already are."

"Okay, so, that's why the FBI needs to stay involved. If the Societies are busted open—if gossip rags even get a hold of them, their secret is over. They're exposed and vulnerable. Damion could be forced to stop his operations. If we have a chance to do that—"

"Exactly."

That brings me up short. "You're not giving up?"

"The opposite. I'm doing so much worse. I'm asking you to bring me proof of their violent existence."

Dash chooses this moment to project himself into the room with a large bowl of salad. He sets it in front of me, and Malcolm and I wait in pensive silence as Dash places saucers of various salad dressings around the bowl.

"We were unsure of your vinaigrette preference," he explains. "Marta's provided you with a plethora."

"Uh-huh. Thank you." I choose blindly and dump some on my salad to speed him up. I wrinkle my nose, realizing I'd poured stinky blue cheese all over it.

"Not a problem." Dash bows, then becomes one with the walls again.

"I don't know if I can do that," I say to Malcolm, picking right up where we left off.

He nods. "I realize I'm putting you in an impossible situation, but look what happened to your peer. Zeke. I'm positive Damion had something to do with it. His manipulation of power, of pitting students, *teenagers*, against each other, has to stop. If you can record the next challenge or punishment, if you can obtain one of the manuals or records kept in the tombs…"

I'm already shaking my head. "Their security is insane. I haven't been granted access into any kind of records room, and if they saw me with my phone raised, I'll be the next one in the hospital."

"You already were."

His quiet statement strangles any further argument from escaping my throat.

"I cannot allow it to keep happening. If I could get in there myself, risk my own body, I would do it. No other person should suffer as I did. But I'm cut off. The further they induct you, the more they push me away. They have their new Weatherby. I need you, Ember. I'm sorry, I despise saying this, but the Societies' future victims need you, too."

I scrunch my eyes shut, battling with my will-power. If I do this, I risk exposing myself and Malcolm to huge danger. If I don't, Damion wins. It should be an easy decision, but Thorne's infuriating face keeps wobbling into my mind's eye as a stark reminder that my loyalty is in question.

"I'm not entirely convinced they had nothing to do with the Merricourt girl's disappearance, either," he adds.

I'm curious enough that the guilt leaks out of my

expression and I open my eyes. "You think the Societies were behind her abduction?"

Last night would be an excellent argument against that assumption, but I still can't bring myself to admit my involvement to Malcolm.

"Agent Colt doesn't tell me much about the investigation into her kidnapping, but I get the sense it has stalled, as well. No trace of the kidnapper—or kidnappers. Savannah Merricourt can't be sure. She doesn't remember where she was held or how far away it was. Her memory is a blank slate. Other than severe amnesia, I can only think of one other way to silence her."

Malcolm waits for me to fill in the blank.

"The Societies intimidated her into submission," I whisper, but shake myself out of it. "No, there are a ton of other causes of her memory loss. And she hasn't lost everything."

"No?" Malcolm perks up.

"I mean—last night, at the meeting"—because Malcolm *does* know the Societies met—"she was there. We had to change out of our uniforms and into formal dress together, and she was terrified."

Malcolm nods, humming in thought. "Which only adds to my theory. Torture."

"Senator Merricourt finally paid the ransom. That's why she was let go. The Societies don't need extra money, especially from a member."

"All smoke and mirrors. Why suspect the very enterprise that was wounded in the exchange? A clever ruse, but I would never expect anything less of Damion."

"I—" I hold back my point. If I keep arguing *for* the Societies, Malcolm will no doubt become suspicious.

"If you find any evidence of Noble or Virtue involvement in Savannah's abduction, you must bring it to me. Agent Colt and his team are primed for a raid of the Briar residence. I know for certain Damion holds evidence of the Societies in that manor. He's held ceremonies there, challenges, and there are enough passageways to hide a damned body if he so chooses. He could've locked Savannah in there for as long as he needed to. I *need* to get the FBI in there. You're the key, Ember. Please."

Malcolm's eyes are fervent, latching on mine like I'm his last source of water in the vast desert of his suffering. Warning bells clang in my head the more passionate he becomes. Obsessed. Almost unhinged with his desire to topple Damion from his throne.

I can't bring myself to deny him. I know firsthand how devastating the Briars can be.

"Okay," I say, lifting my head higher. "I'll do everything I can to help you. I promise."

Malcolm reaches across the table and grabs my hand. His hold is tight, warm, and dry. It's also one of the rare moments we touch, and I'm reminded of how strong he's managed to stay regardless of Damion's attempts to cut him off at the knees.

If he can survive his losses, I can bear mine.

"Thank you, Ember. From the bottom of my heart."

I hope my smile transmits my thoughts when I squeeze back. "I want to bring them down just as much as you do."

But even as I promise it, the bottom of *my* heart stays dark and sharpened to a point.

CHAPTER II

THORNE

Of all Malcolm's transgressions, I didn't think I'd become most pissed at him for glue.

Traipsing around the underbrush of Weatherby Manor changed all that. My hand scrapes against the gray brick, testing for the hidden entrance that I know is around here somewhere. The restriction of my access to Ember's room rubs like a festering wound the longer I can't locate it. I'd spent most of the early hours before school poring over the blueprints stashed in my father's office instead of swim practice. I told myself it was more due to a reluctance to show my fresh scars on my back and think up a viable explanation, but I knew the truth behind my actions.

Ember. Always Ember.

I was damn well going to make sure the skipped training was worth it.

At last, one brick gives ever so slightly against my testing weight. I put my shoulder into the next push, pacing into the wild rose bushes to give me enough distance to run my side against the wall, heaving the makeshift door open a crack. It's so heavy, I need a few running starts before a large enough space opens for me to slip through, then ram my back against it to shut it partway behind me.

I'm not worried about making noise. All occupants in the manor should be asleep on the second or third floors by now, including my little pretty. I'm also taking pains to keep my pissed-off grunts at a minimum, hating that I'm reduced to breaking in from the outside like a prowler. I much preferred the anticipatory stroll from my hallway to hers, with a row of wall sconces lighting the way.

The next sound I hear is the flick of my lighter against my side before I raise it to eye level, taking in my surroundings. The blueprints didn't show much in terms of decoration, only the barest layout of a thin corridor weaving through the manor's walls. I slink carefully along, heading west. I don't use my phone's flashlight because,if this passageway is anything like Briar Manor's, such a bright light would risk showing through consciously placed paintings along the way, the canvas made thin to better to peep into the home. There's a chance Malcolm remains nocturnal, despite the calming presence of his recently discovered daughter under his roof. I don't want to tip him off before I've finished what I came here for.

The toe of my shoe knocks against something hard. Cursing under my breath, I wave the lighter lower, its tiny flickering flame illuminating a set of stairs, or, more like giant children's blocks stacked as high as they can get.

I follow the flight, muttering under my breath when I stare at the ceiling. It doesn't follow the height of the stairs. I'll have to crouch.

Thanking my good sense for rigorous routine of stretching in the mornings regardless of making training, I crawl up the old staircase on all fours, using the heel of my hand while maintaining my hold on the lighter.

At the top, I stand, walk a few feet, duck, and crawl for ten more minutes, navigating the route I'd measured in the manor's plans until I make it to the section of wall I need.

It requires the same push as before, but this time I'm much quieter. I press against the stone, heaving and gritting my teeth until at last, it gives. A long time has passed —centuries, probably—since this access point was last used. Likely when Weatherby Manor was owned by my great-great-great uncle, Thorne Briar I, when he and my 3x great grandfather squirreled around between their manors, concocting whatever nefarious schemes as the founders of the Societies.

I step into a darkened room, cast in enough moonlight from the large bay window that I flick my lighter off and stuff it back in my jeans. The section of bookshelf I'd come through clicks back into place with a press of my palm, much easier to maneuver from this side of the hinges. I've made it into the library, much smaller than my family's, but well-read with first editions and ... a concerning amount of crime novels.

I don't linger on the spines too long, what with Ember being so close I can smell her. I'm not a beast with heightened senses, but the scent of her pussy lips lingers in my nose, a triggered memory that becomes stronger the closer I come to her bedroom door.

My cock tents in my pants, straining against the denim. It's so uncomfortably pleasing that I have to reach in and adjust until it's flat against my stomach, the tip already wet with precum. In a flash, my fingers become hers and I groan. What *is* it with this girl? I can't get Ember out of my head. The image of her swinging at Zeke loops in my mind. The spray of blood across her cheekbones and forehead, the feverish light in her normally black eyes, the tips of her long, ash blonde hair wet with it...

Except in my mind, Ember's not wearing an ivory dress. She's naked, her breasts splashed with blood, her nipples erect, and she saunters toward me, handing me the paddle and pleading with her swollen lips to smack it against all her soft parts before taking her from behind...

I growl. Maybe I *am* a beast. The Beast of Weatherby Manor has a nice ring to it.

But no, I have to remind myself I'm here for the opposite of taking Ember's virginity. This time, I need her out of my head for good. If last night showed me anything, it's that Ember's in too deep and falling into my father's clutches far too easily.

Her door forms out of the darkness. I place both palms against the paneled wood as if I could feel the heat of her through the thick, varnished pine.

Is she sleeping? I hope so. I'd love to wake her up before I push her away.

The brass knob gives in my grip. My cock twitches at such easy entry, and I have to coax it down, reciting over and over that I'm not here for her tight, wet pussy, though I'm groaning with want.

Over a month with only my hand for company has done its damage. I wouldn't dare touch Savannah after what she's gone through. More than that, I don't want to. She's not who commands my dreams and warps my fantasies. It's not Sav who twists my balls and turns them blue.

It's ... *her*.

The door swings open on oiled hinges, nothing but a quiet *swish* against the threadbare carpeting.

Surprisingly, her bedside light is on. At three in the morning, I was confident she'd be asleep. Narrowing my vision, I pause in the doorway, sweeping the bedroom, noting the undisturbed bed and—

"What the *fuck* are you doing here?"

The screech comes from my left. Ember pushes the door shut behind me, revealing herself in one of her worn-down cartoon T-shirts and nothing else.

Well, not exactly nothing else. She's brandishing a pickle ball paddle.

The vision of her naked in someone else's blood, begging for a spanking, comes at me in such a rush that the most animalistic parts of me roar for dominance.

Outwardly, I arch a brow. "Care to challenge me to a pickle match?"

"Fuck you," she seethes, her hair a tangled halo around her wide eyes. "This is all I had on such short notice. I didn't expect an intruder to saunter through my door after midnight."

"Maybe put a knife under your pillow next time."

"You'd like that."

"I truly would." I step deeper into her room. Ember circles me, tracking my movements.

Still holding the paddle in the air, she asks, "What do you want?"

I turn back to her, ignoring the question. "How did you hear me coming?"

She jolts, taken aback by the question. "I'm used to the sounds of this house at night. When one's less familiar, like the groan of a moving wall, my hearing tends to perk up."

"Hmm." I mull this over. "I woke you? I'm usually stealth in human form."

She scoffs. "Don't flatter yourself. I was already awake. Can't sleep." Her eyes shift away.

Watching the memory of last night flicker across her face causes a certain possessive buzz in my body, growing louder the more I realize just how much she's thinking about Zeke.

I give a dismissive grunt. "It's nothing the rest of us haven't endured before. That crusty mole of a guy will be just fine."

"Zeke's not part of the Societies or their training. In fact, he denied his invitation. Zeke didn't consent to any of this. Do you know how I know that?" Her throat bobs as her eyes develop a sheen. "That terrified look that flashed across his face..."

"You're defending him."

I don't ask it. It's said as more of a warning. *Don't test me.*

"I also know what I did." Her voice grows husky, like velvet caressing my dick. I clench my jaw to remain in control. Why the fuck did I think it was a good idea to come here?

"I'm the one who dealt the worst blow," she says.

I find myself rushing to defend her. "You weren't the one with a blade. Pliers. Willing to mutilate him." I continue, softer, "I know you, Ember. You hit him hard so you could knock him out quick. So you could end it."

Her forehead wrinkles with conflict. "Speaking of,

when were you going to tell me Savannah's lost her mind?"

I tip my head back, studying Ember. She's dismissed my excuses for her actions and gone straight to the source. It's a hard reminder that I have to measure my words with her. Always. She cannot make me weak.

"Sav's traumatized by her experiences, as you can imagine."

"So you give her weapons?"

"No, we weaponize her."

Ember draws up short. "Oh my god, you're serious."

"What part of the Societies has you hesitating at admitting their ruthlessness, little pretty? Yes, Sav has trauma counselors, funded by the Societies to 'help' her, but underground, it's a different sort of assistance. My father thinks she'll come in handy when he needs information extracted from certain individuals. She's both an excellent lure and a willing torture device. Tell me you couldn't see it last night."

"No." Ember shakes her head. The paddle drops onto the bedsheets. "*No*. What we did was forced, and worse, she's vulnerable. I saw the sweet side of her yesterday as much as I witnessed her savagery. Savannah needs actual *help*. She's still in there. Your girlfriend can be saved, Thorne. Why aren't you fighting to stop this?"

"For the same reasons you're not willing to *leave*."

My voice whips through the air. With the way she lurches, it feels like I've cut through her.

"My father manipulates you into the darkest version of yourself, or haven't you noticed?" I point at my chest as if I can directly show her the evil nestling within, cultivated and pruned like a rare, poisonous plant. "He's awakening it within you. You feel guilty now, but at that moment, you were his creation and out for blood. It'll only get worse the longer you stay with them. Why didn't you escape when you had the chance?" I sharpen my gaze on her, hoping my intensity slashes into her soul. "Sav's back and happy to resume her position. You could've stepped down. *You* could've stopped her from proving to everyone what a valuable asset she's become. There was no longer a place for you until you carved one for yourself by winning yesterday's challenge."

Ember doesn't waver. "Is that why you broke into my home? To tell me how much I've screwed up my chances to be free?" She laughs, low and bruised. "My future was fucked the moment I met *you*, Thorne Briar. Anything I do now is merely a bonus trip to Hell."

She's telling the truth, and it hits hard. Her defeatist attitude twists my heart in a way it was never meant to register.

"I've come here to warn you." My tone comes out rougher than intended. "I've finally figured out what my father wants with you, and that's to make you one of his weapons or break you while he does it. Either one will suit him."

"Like he did with Malcolm?" She whispers it. "Or is it Savannah? Who are you comparing me to?"

I cross my arms, the muscles there thrumming with the need to tie her to the bedposts and force her to submit. The craving heats the backs of my eyes. It's the only feature I can't warp into stone.

"I can take care of myself," she says. "I certainly don't need you to slink around Weatherby manor's sewer lines and pop up when it's convenient for *you.*"

I stare at her. "*Me?* You think my constant saving of your ass is about me?"

"Oh, that's rich. I don't recall you swimming beside me during Damion's rock-climbing challenge, or yesterday when a pile of torture devices was thrown at my feet. *After* I was told to dress like a virgin and hurt someone until they passed out."

Ah. It starts making sense. "You liked it."

She balks. "Excuse me?"

"You liked smacking Zeke around, you enjoyed the risk of death while swimming in the pitch black, and you like it when I tongue that pussy of yours with my hands around your throat."

I step closer. She skitters away, retreating until her back slams against the wall.

"You feed off adrenaline. It's what motivates you. Fuck, it's what keeps you with the Virtues instead of doing the smarter thing and walking away."

I smack my palms on either side of her head, caging

her in. Ember flinches but doesn't shrivel under my stare. I bend until my nose almost touches hers. "And yes, you finished my father's impossible challenges all by yourself because you couldn't be bothered to heed my constant warnings to get the *fuck* out of this place."

Ember bares her teeth, her nose bumping against mine until I snap my head back. "Would that be before or after you set your own challenges for me? Or had me naked under you, recording me sucking your dick to use for your future perverted use? Quit making yourself out to be a hero, Thorne. You're clearly the villain in my story."

I get right in her face, rasping, "I never knighted myself as anyone's savior. I want you gone so you can quit distracting me with your sweet cunt, and I can get on with my life."

Ember's hand whips up. My head snaps to the side as sharp, hot pain rides along my cheek. Without moving my face back to center, I smile without teeth. "Did I say something to piss you off, little pretty?"

"Get out." Ember holds her expression so stiff, it vibrates underneath her skin. "Get the *fuck* out of this house."

"Or what? You'll slap me again?" I face her. "Don't you remember? I love this shit."

A vengeful mewl escapes her throat as she pushes against my sternum, her knees coming up to help her. I dodge each blow, pivoting when she thinks to go for my crotch.

"Slap me again, Ember. I dare you."

Ember does just that, using her less dominant hand since her right tangles in my shirt, pulling me in for a good smack.

I let her, keeping my grin in place. The heel of her palm hits my top lip, a coppery tang soon following. She split it open on my canine tooth.

The smile falls from my lips. I grab both her wrists, trapping her. "Developed a taste for blood, have you?"

I push into her body, flattening her between the wall and my hard, aching cock. Her eyes turn into tinder, the sparks of a burgeoning wildfire, carelessly lit by my inability to let her go. I didn't come to her for this. I wanted to give her one last warning before shit hits the fan and I can't protect her anymore.

Except here I am, close to tearing Ember's clothes off and lifting one of her legs so I can thrust into that tight, wet center.

The thought of it makes me groan near her mouth. "So long as it's my blood you crave, have at it, little pretty."

"What is wrong with you?" she cries.

"I don't like the thought of you wanting to draw *his* blood," I find myself saying. Surprise fizzes into my mind, but I can't stop. Anger boils to the surface. "The only one you should touch, the one person you're desperate to unleash your violence on, will always be me."

Ember wriggles against my body, electricity snapping

between us. I see it in her eyes, the wildfire gaining ground.

"I may have done unforgivable things, including hurting Zeke, but I'll never stoop to your level," she spits, her warm saliva sprinkling across my mouth and mixing with my blood. "I don't want anyone's blood on my hands, especially yours."

Her thigh rubs against my dick and her brows crash down. "Get yourself off with your own blood as lube and give me peace."

Angling my head, I croon, "Would you like to watch?"

"Fuck off, Thorne."

"Admit it. You liked it."

"Liked *what*?"

"Hitting. Hurting. Dominating." I press closer. The heat of her body sinks into mine. Ember's nostrils flare like she scents my desire. "You would've kept going given the chance. I'm coming to know you, little pretty, and you're just as fucked up as I am."

To prove my point, I release one wrist and close my hand over her throat, squeezing.

Ember grits her teeth, but her struggles weaken. Her eyelids grow heavy with want.

"In different ways, of course," I continue, massaging her throat, harder, then softer. "You've lost your family and wandered into the dark history of the Weatherbys. Whereas I want nothing more than to leave my heritage and live the rest of my life untethered from everyone." I slink my thumb down the center of her throat, nestling into the dip of her collarbone and pressing hard. Her muscles ripple under my grip, her instinct clawing to breathe. "You have no idea what runs in your veins, and I'm all too aware of the venom traveling through mine. We're opposites, you and I, yet..." I lean closer, breathing in her quick exhales, tasting the sweetness on her breath, "...we can't resist exploring."

Ember's breathing shortens. Her eyes stay on mine. Her lips part, and I tip my head back, expecting the denial to shoot from her delicious mouth. As if she can't feel the thrumming between our bodies and how our pounding heartbeats are matching speed.

Instead, she does the opposite. She whispers, "Squeeze harder."

My eyes widen.

EMBER

Thorne doesn't need to be told twice.

He digs in, the heel of his palm crushing my larynx. Black stars explode behind my eyes. A feeling of lightness releases the guilty weight on my chest, my heart pounding with the adrenaline to live, to fight. If I could moan, I would. Ever since the first time Thorne cut off my breath, I've been chasing this high. The toeing of the line between life and death while my center grows hot, swollen, and wet, it's like a new world is forming inside me with Thorne as its god.

He's an addiction, one that stumbled into my bedroom in the black of night, threatening and tempting and *daring*.

Thorne's hard-on rubs against my belly, my thin, old, angry unicorn T-shirt doing nothing to cushion the friction. Heat flows between my thighs. I feel faint. Dizzy. That I might...

A gush of air opens my throat, the oxygen rushing into my lungs.

Thorne steps back, his hand dropped at his side. He tilts his head, assessing.

"You don't mean that," he says.

It's difficult for me to swallow, the tendons in my neck already reacting to Thorne's grip and swelling. Worse, the muscles strain.

Like they want more.

I croak, "You don't get to tell me what I want."

Thorne paces forward, his eyes dark craters aiming for mine. "If you keep asking for this, that's exactly what you're allowing. I don't do tame or soft lovemaking. I *fuck*. And I do it while in control. I order you to suck my cock; you do it. I spread your legs; you ask me how wide I want them." Thorne's close enough to yank me by my hair, his stare dropping down to my exposed throat. "I demand you hold your breath; you willingly stop breathing. Does that sound like something you want?"

He pulls so hard that my scalp burns. But that burn travels, wrapping around my neck before spearing between my legs. I've never been dominated like this. I was curious, sure, on how it would be to have someone so cocky and confident take my body for his pleasure. I just never considered I'd be in a situation where it was an actual possibility.

My heart slams against my ribs while nerves fire out from it. I've only now regained breath, and I'm about to ask him to stifle it again.

I know I am.

Thorne's seen me at my worst. He witnessed the dark fetish that cracked through my resolve when I first lifted the paddle to swing toward Zeke's head. He's tasted my desire, both for the Societies' secrets and for him. Thorne is fully aware of the black ink traveling through my veins and polluting my blood. And he's calling to it.

I respond with a shaking whisper, "It sounds like something I'm desperate for."

Thorne's pupils eclipse any light remaining in his eyes. I've asked the god to keep creating his dark kingdom inside my chest. There's no turning back.

He understands the darkness. Which means when I'm with him, I'm not alone.

Thorne shadows me, still as a statue, while I tremble with my back to the wall. For a moment, everything is quiet. The howling manor has grown sentient as if waiting for his next move as much as I am.

My heart flutters along with the pulsing at my core.

I can't wait for Thorne to go through all the wrongs of this in his head.

Won't.

I leap for him, crushing my mouth against his while my arms wrap around his neck and my thighs thread over his hips. He absorbs the impact like he was waiting for it, his fingers spearing into the fatty tissue of my ass and his mouth opening up, then clamping down.

Metallic salt explodes in my mouth along with a flash of pain, my bottom lip bursting open under his teeth. Instead of reeling back and shrieking—like he wants me to, like this is his last warning before his demon breaks loose—I push into the kiss, my tongue swooping in and swirling into his mouth, lapping up the blood before he swallows the rest down.

Thorne swivels us on a bone-chilling growl, the length of his dick digging into my underwear, close to my folds where I'm practically soaking him with need.

He rips his mouth from mine and tosses me onto the bed. I land without grace—gangly, surprised limbs every-where. Thorne looms over me with blood at the corners of his lips.

Thorne's voice is low, carnal. "Don't ever lay claim to my mouth again."

The feel of his stubble still burns against my quickly swelling lips. I tongue the fresh cut, reveling in the brief re-awakening of pain. We've only kissed once before, when Thorne was at his weakest, both of us trembling, cold, and vulnerable on top of a cliff. Kissing to him is the equivalent of wearing your heart on your sleeve. Unac-ceptable. "No kissing. Got it."

"Wrong response. Say, 'yes, sir.'" He thinks for a moment. "Or 'yes, my prince' would also be acceptable. Your choice."

The urge to rebel is instant. My mind immediately swings to all the various punishments he has in store for me if I refuse. That is, until I remember how green I am, and it's not just dominance that's new to this body.

Swallowing back the retort, I utter, "Yes, sir," instead.

"Good girl," he purrs while unbuttoning his shirt. Thorne untucks the bottom, his 8-pack rippling between the black fabric. He sheds it like a cape, the lines of muscle on his arms, his pecs, and his pelvis crisscrossed with moonlight and my bedside lamp.

His eyes stay anchored on mine as he unbuckles his leather belt and pulls it through the loops.

I watch all this with terrified anticipation, outwardly cool but inwardly freaking the fuck out. My pussy gushes with want at the same time my fight or flight kicks in. I wriggle on the bed to release some of the ache, but all it does is cause more.

Thorne's attention snaps to my middle, his Adam's apple bobbing as he restrains himself from doing ... whatever's in his mind as he looks me over.

I gulp.

"Sit up."

Pushing onto my elbows, I do as he says.

Thorne cocks his head. "What do you say, little pretty?"

"Y-yes, sir." My body's so amped that I can barely relax my vocal cords enough to speak.

He crooks a finger, unsatisfied with where I've

decided to perch. I scoot forward, breathing through my mouth. My nose just simply isn't sending enough oxygen to my heart as it tries to break my chest open and flee.

Thorne snaps his belt tight with both hands before looping it behind my head. I stiffen as he wraps it around my neck, pulling it through the buckle until it tightens against my throat. A small whimper escapes me as he goes through his ministrations, and his eyes swoop up to mine.

"I warned you."

"I know," I croak against the belt collar. "Keep going."

He smiles, but combined with the iniquity in his stare, it's like being grinned at by Lucifer himself. "I wasn't about to stop." He nips at my nose, his teeth making an audible *snap*. "I can smell your sex now. There's no fucking way I'm leaving until I've had you."

Oh, fuck.

CHAPTER 13
EMBER

"Lie back, little pretty, head against the pillows. Then slide your panties off and spread your legs. Wide open."

"Yes, sir."

I straighten my legs and lie back as he demands. Hooking my underwear, I lift my butt and weave it the rest of the way to my ankles and off, tossing them to the side.

It's slightly humiliating and very gynecological to bend my knees and spread for him with my shirt riding up my stomach.

Until his eyes eat me up. There's no way any doctor would look at me with that type of hunger.

Thorne's so hard that the tip of his penis has escaped his pants. The tip glistens. My mouth waters in response, but I stay still, as instructed. I'm vibrating with desire, but if he senses it, he has the restraint of a Komodo dragon, who can survive months without prey.

An apt comparison, if I do say so myself. Venomous bite. Nocturnal. Prefers rough sex...

Thorne gets to his knees at the foot of the bed. I lift my head to follow his descent, but he grabs me by the ankles and pulls me until my pussy is in line with his mouth.

I claw the bedsheets on instinct, the rough yank sending my pulse ricocheting in my neck and reminding me what he's wrapped around my throat.

"Fuck. You're glistening," he rasps as he unabashedly takes me in.

Thorne pushes his nose into my pussy, inhaling deep as I gasp in shock. His resulting groan sends unbearable shivers into my body. My head falls back as I moan.

"Delectable," he says as he sits back, his tongue scraping along his top lip.

Thorne blinks and looks up at me as if remembering who's attached to his latest craving. He spots the belt around my neck and smiles. "This is very important, little pretty. Every time my tongue circles your clit, I want you to pull that belt tighter around your sweet neck. Eventually, it will get so tight you can't breathe. I want you to keep it there until I tell you to release it. Do you understand your instructions?"

I hesitate.

"That's right. It means you have to trust me, but not all the way. You're in control of that belt loop. I won't lay my hands on it. I'll be too busy with your pussy." He traces a finger down my inner thigh, and my breaths turn shaky.

My throat works, but who am I kidding. Thorne is inches away from eating me out, something he's done a few times before, and granted me the best orgasms of my short life. Each time I'm with him, the pleasure ratchets up. Why would I deny him now?

"Okay—yes, sir."

The corners of his lips lift just enough so I can see them over my apex. "Lay your head back. You'll be staring at the ceiling for the duration. Do *not* look down at me. I want you to exclusively ride the feeling, not the visual. Failure to do as I say, and..." A sharp pinch on my ass makes me yelp. "...your punishment will be swift."

I jerk my chin in a nod, wincing. That's sure to leave a mark, which is exactly his intention.

His deep voice hits my skin with heated breath. "Pull."

My mouth opens to ask for more clarification as I blink up at the ceiling, but his mouth is on me before I can so much as breathe one syllable. Thorne's agile tongue circles me, and I squirm, a groan escaping my throat as my thighs turn into liquid in his hands.

However, my brain's able to compartmentalize and remembers to pull at the belt, tightening the strap against my neck. Just a little bit, because I'm not sure I want to—

He laps at my clit again. My hips lift off the bed, the

sensations excruciatingly pleasurable, but he pushes them back down, his large hands spanning my hips.

I pull slightly more, the strap making itself obvious on my skin now, digging in and pressing against my trachea, but I can still breathe.

Thorne explores lower, slipping in and out of my folds, swallowing every drop of desire that's accumulated there since he stormed into my room.

It's when his wet warmth gets too low that I squirm, my heels digging into the mattress to escape. It's magical, this sensation, but I don't want him at my back door. Do I? I'm a virgin in both places, and I'd rather not—

The tip of Thorne's tongue pushes into my anus, sending pleasure signals to a place that's been dark since the moment of birth, and I squeal, my hands knotting the sheets. Thorne tongues me all the way from my butt to my clit, the long sweep like molten ecstasy pouring into my soul and fucking destroying it.

I remember to pull the strap tighter. Tighter still.

My back arches, an automatic response to my shortened breaths. Adrenaline seeps through the zings of pleasure as Thorne sucks and nips and laps. My heart resumes its loud pounding, a warning drum in my ears and throbbing against my core.

It can't compete against Thorne.

He adds his fingers, pushing one into my ass while his other hand pushes three fingers into my pussy and spreads them, giving him better access to—everything.

Writhing, I'm unable to stay still, overstimulated and aching as all these polar opposite feelings rush into my center and battle for dominance. My head is so cranked back that my eyes are welded to the ceiling as the pressure builds and builds...

Thorne demands I go tighter still by pressing the pad of his tongue on my clit while curling his fingers inside me, hitting a deep G-spot I didn't know existed, especially combined with the one in my anus.

This time, pulling at the belt isn't from conscious thought. I'm so in the throes of a building orgasm that my hand jerks on the strap, pulling as tight as I can as I buck against the bed, and ecstasy shoots through me so furiously that I can see into outer space.

Dizziness and weightlessness war with the shooting stars of an orgasm. I pull and pull at the belt, strange noises coming from my mouth as I fight for both pleasure and life. Thorne doesn't stop until he's consumed every last drop of my orgasm, and I fall limp against the bed.

I can't see properly anymore as more shadows than light play off my retinas. I register the dip of the mattress as Thorne crawls on top of me, his arms falling on either side of my head before his imposing form lifts up, and he pulls my hand from the belt, then loosens it himself before pulling it off my neck.

"Very good girl," he says while pushing my legs back apart with his thighs.

It's harder to regain breath this time. I'm not sure how

close I was playing at the precipice of death, but my heart struggles to find its natural beat, and it hurts to take in full breaths.

"Easy, little pretty."

Thorne's warm, dry hand rests against my cheek as he pulls my face toward him. "Now lick your pussy juice off my face."

My eyelids flutter, and my lips part as I try to speak, but I'm much too hoarse and supple to do anything but obey his commands. At least until I get my limbs back.

He bends his face close to mine, waiting patiently with a hooded, desirous stare. I dart my tongue out in experimentation, hitting the edge of his bottom lip. Saltiness coats the tip of my tongue, which slips back into my mouth in surprise.

"I won't even demand a 'yes, sir,' this time. Take it off my face, little pretty. Or else I'll be forced to fuck you until I pull out and spill all over your face."

That wakes me up.

Lifting my legs, I can feel the soft fuzz and bareness of his skin. Thorne's slipped out of his pants and has centered himself at my entrance, his dick pressing into my heat, then pulling back. His tight breaths dust the lower half of my face, maintaining control, but I don't know for how much longer.

That's when it hits me. Thorne's as desperate for me as I am for him.

My eyes flutter all the way open, meeting the yin and yang of his. "Say please," I whisper.

His stare narrows in warning. "Don't test me."

My pulse skitters in warning, but I persevere. "Say, 'please, Ember.'"

Thorne growls, his eyes somehow reflecting brighter than the light in this room. "The only person begging in this room will be you." He pushes, deeper this time— almost too deep. And he's not wearing protection. Thorne's head angles as he watches my thoughts flit across my expression like he knows exactly the dangers he's playing with.

"You're soaked enough that one thrust is all it will take," he says with a grin.

Damn him.

I lift with sore neck muscles, sliding my tongue across his closed, smart-ass mouth and collecting my juices along the way. Despite my frustration with him, something is deliciously hot about mixing my taste with the tang of his skin, the potent cocktail zinging against my tastebuds as my mouth waters for more. I scrape the pad of my tongue across the stubble on his cheeks, going slow and maintaining eye contact as he stays unbearably still, submitting to my licks and sucks like a marble carving would.

Except ... a statue doesn't tremble under its stone. Muscles don't strain as they maintain their position on either side of me, the tendons of his arms bursting out of skin as he knuckles the bed.

His cock rests against the soft hair at my apex, but his hips sway in a gentle pump, his precum turning into lube as he instinctively strokes against my belly while I tongue him toward ecstasy.

When I lift my hands to scrape my fingers down his back, he jerks his head away. "Enough."

Contrition sings along my veins. He's sensitive back there because of *me*. While he won't let me see them, I know what marks his flawless form now.

An apology would only piss him off. Instead, I say, "Yes, sir."

I say it with such sass that his brows come down. Then a sharp-edged smile takes its place. "What was I thinking, taking you for the first time in a missionary position? You deserve to be on your stomach where you can collect my cum on the small of your back."

Anger flashes through me, and I rear up on my elbows. The *Cum Bucket* nickname isn't something I want to hear right now.

Thorne chuckles. "Relax, Ember. I'm about to be your undoing. You'll be so spent when I'm through that you won't care where my cum lands."

The cockiness should be a turn-off.

It really isn't.

Thorne rises on his knees, his cock jutting out like a sword. I stare—aghast every time I see it, it's so *big*—and he takes that opportunity to flip me over, nestling a pillow under my hips and spreading my ass cheeks before I can so much as say, "Huh?"

"I'm not a goddamned blow-up doll." My voice is muffled from my face being mashed into a pillow. Scraping my hair out of my face, I lift and crane my neck to stare him down as much as I can from this angle.

"Wrong. Tonight, you're my little plaything."

"That's incredibly—" *rude* is lost on my lips, a gasp taking its place as Thorne fingers my asshole again.

"What do you think I should take first? Your ass or your pussy?"

"I—" Oh crap, I didn't sign up for this. "That's—this isn't—"

His thumb swoops across my pussy lips, dragging the moisture up and around my anus.

"I don't think we'll be needing lube for this." Amusement vibrates in his throat.

Two fingers slip in, the feeling so foreign and strange that I both writhe and submit to what he's doing. My hands ache from clenching into fists for so long and my pillow quickly turns wet from my salivating mouth. *What the fuck is wrong with me? I'm acting like an animal in heat...*

"Inhale, then hold for as long as I tell you to."

Thorne says it as such an idle aside as he stretches my asshole with three fingers now.

"Ember? Are you listening?"

"Yes," I manage to breathe out, my fingers digging into the mattress.

"Inhale," he demands again.

I'm fighting against the instinct to tense up with the desperation to keep breathing, but I do as he says, taking a deep breath and holding it, pressing the side of my face into the pillow and scrunching my eyes shut.

Submit to the feeling.

It's a pleasurable stretch. Adrenaline shoots into my veins, amplifying all sensations underneath my skin, and I wriggle my butt closer to his fingers.

He pulls them out. "Don't you dare exhale yet."

I want to whimper but can't, keeping my breath locked in my lungs as they burn and beg, the same way my pussy is.

Thorne rises up, aligning his dick with my asshole. The one eye I'm using to track him widens.

He sees. His lips tick up in a closed-mouth smile before he gets back to it, collecting more wetness from my where my pussy is simply *dripping* now and coating his shaft with it.

His tip prods against my back door with more girth than his fingers. Thorne uses his free hand to hold my hip as he guides his dick in a little bit farther and then a little bit farther still.

My vision's going dark, the stretch of him competing with my body's natural reaction to the lack of air by going through the motions anyway. My stomach pitches. My chest rises and falls in a desperate attempt to breathe. My ass muscles must also be contracting because Thorne groans as his tip goes all the way in.

"Your virgin ass is so fucking tight." His head bows forward. Gritting his teeth, he lifts his chin back up and orders, "Breathe."

My desperate inhale comes in as a wheeze, the rush of air causing a lightheadedness and the feeling of falling in my chest as though I've just taken the deep dive on a roller coaster.

It takes me a few seconds to remember where I am and what I'm doing, my eyes blinking rapidly. I attempt to lift, but a firm hand between my shoulders keeps me down.

"That's enough ass play," Thorne muses, mostly to himself. He pulls out, and I hear more than see him shuffle around. The sound of a packet ripping comes next.

A condom, I think. *Oh god, this is actually happening. I'm losing my virginity to a psycho...*

Yet you don't see me trying to escape.

I lie there with bated breath as Thorne puts on the condom and comes back behind me. He smacks his hard dick against both my ass cheeks to let me know he's returned. I arch into him both times.

He gives a tight laugh under his breath. I hope it's because he's as desperate for me as I am for him. To think he's been patient and taking his time through all of this, without any desire on his part, is almost too much to bear. My arousal is evident, as the soaked pillow under my hips will attest. His is more mysterious, with only snippets of his hard dick nearby to give me any sense of his horniness.

"I'm…" I pause, hoping for some resonance at this moment, but nothing comes.

Thorne doesn't ask if I'm ready or if I'll be all right. I didn't expect him to. A guy like this doesn't take virginity with incense and candles.

"Just—be gentle," I whisper. I doubt he hears me.

Thorne lifts my hips, the tip of his dick now exploring between my lips. He kneads my ass cheeks as he does it, coaxing me to relax. What he doesn't say, he communicates in actions. That's as gentle as he'll be.

I'm wet enough that it doesn't hurt at first. He pushes in farther, cursing under his breath as I clench around him. "Fuck, Ember, I can't—I'm not about to go slow."

"That's okay—" My reassurance is caught up in a scream into my pillow as he thrusts all the way in, burning through my walls and sending fire into my belly.

Ow, ow, ow!

I curl my hands under my chest and heave, lifting up. When I move, the feel of Thorne inside me is a strange, exotic pressure. Pain mingles with previous pleasure, confusing every synapse in my brain.

Thorne doesn't push me back onto the bed, nor does he give me time to comprehend how fast he broke my fucking hymen. "Hold your breath, little pretty."

"I can't—"

A smack rings out, my right ass cheek stinging right along with my lost virginity. "Fucking *ow!*" I cry out this time.

"The next words out of those lips of yours better be 'yes, sir,' or I'll spank you again."

His warning is clear, and as I've come to know, he always makes good on them. But at the same time as he bites it out, he massages where he slapped me, soothing the hurt. That complicates my anger. Thorne isn't meant to do anything sweet, and I knew that going into this.

His dick remains a hard rod inside me. Remembering what happened a few seconds ago, I clench around it —hard.

He fucking *moans*.

"You spiteful little plaything," he grinds out, settling his hips against my ass. My stomach does a small flip of warning, but it's too late. Once he gets the angle he wants, he starts pumping.

My head almost hits the headboard with his unforgiving thrusts until I put a hand there to prevent an embarrassing bruise.

"Hold. Your fucking. Breath."

His grunts should be terrifying, especially combined with the smack of my skin against his. All it does is turn me on. The burn at my core has turned into a building warmth, the tingles promising a greater release if I just relax into it.

Sweat breaks out on my skin, a hot flush creeping into my cheeks as that feeling builds, the foreign and exotic mixing with the natural act that all humans do.

Another *smack* hits my ass. There wasn't even a break in Thorne's thrusts as he spanked me again. "Hold it, Ember."

This time, there's no soothing massage. He's in the throes of sex as much as I am, so I do as he asks.

Thorne glides his hands up my ribs until he finds my breasts, squeezing hard.

Pain.

Bliss.

Adrenaline.

The concoction fries all brain cells, and I give myself over, allowing sex and death to collide and do what they want with me so long as I can stay in this feeling.

Thorne's so thick and big, I had to accommodate for him, and now, I can only fit him. No others will ever compare to the new shape he's created inside me—dark and dirty and completely his.

"Don't breathe until I come."

Thorne's breathless command reaches my ears, and I arch my back, my chin tilted up as I take him in, again and again, my chest tight and aching, my pussy clenching and releasing.

He releases my breasts, their sting intermingling with the struggle in my chest, and slides his fingers over my clit, rubbing and beckoning.

I moan, a little bit of air escaping, and he punishes me for my slip-up with another hard spank in the same spot he'd landed before.

It hurts. It *kills*, but I love the overstimulation. I don't know what's pain or pleasure any longer. I'm only attuned to *him*.

Saliva bubbles on my lips, my diaphragm trying to pry them open to breathe.

"Fuck. I'm coming. I'm fucking come—breathe, Ember. *Breathe*!"

Thorne pulls out. Something slaps against the floor before I feel a warm spill on my back.

Stale air spools out of me while fresh oxygen coats my lungs. I wobble on my hands, swaying sideways as I try to stay conscious. The rush is almost too much. I'm falling under...

Thorne catches me, laying me on my side. He lies down alongside me.

He catches my bleary eyes. He asks hoarsely, "Did you come?"

I shake my head. At least, I think I do.

"The first time doesn't usually come with an orgasm," he agrees. But his hand goes to the small of my back, where he collects some of his fluid. Then his voice comes out as a dark promise. "Let's change that."

My brows furrow.

He brings his slick fingers back to my pussy, coating himself all over my clit, rubbing and stimulating so suddenly, I flop onto my back on a moan, his cum sinking into my sheets.

"Spread for me, baby." His husky tone drifts close to my lips. I want to taste it.

Am I drunk? I feel drunk.

My hips have other ideas, all too sober and begging for his agile fingers. Thorne chuckles, his fingers darting in and out of me, stroking and flicking, pressing his thumb into my clit. "I'm all over you, little pretty. It's a sexy sight to see how sticky you've become. Here."

Thorne uses his other hand to scrape up some excess, then shoves the two fingers into my mouth. "Suck on it while I get you off."

I moan around his fingers, the knuckles rough on my lips. He shoves them almost to the back of my throat, but I wrap my mouth around them and stroke my tongue on the underside.

Thorne's eyes grow dark as he watches, my hooded stare catching him at his most satiated.

He doesn't stop playing with my pussy, his strokes more demanding the longer I take. Blood, semen, *me*, coats my tastebuds. My nipples turn into hard tips at the thought of how hot this must look.

"I'll even let you breathe this time," Thorne whispers into my ear, his hair tickling my temple. "Come for me, little pretty. That's an order."

I do.

And I'm not sure if I'll ever be the same again.

EMBER

I pause in the middle of the main staircase when I hear the knock.

Did I really hear that? Malcolm and I don't get visitors. It's not a thing. Especially at seven thirty in the morning when I'm the only resident at the manor. Malcolm left late last evening for either FBI or business-related reasons, and Thorne wasn't anywhere in my room when I rolled over and opened heavy-lidded eyes—

No. Don't think about that yet.

Knock-knock-knock.

The raps come in faster intervals, the lost tourist clearly in need of immediate directions.

"Uh ... Dash?" I call out.

Sadly, Dash does not materialize from the shadows, likely because he didn't hear the baritone of his employer's voice—rather, it's the unappreciative, new teenage tenant who wants something.

I billow out my lips as I adjust my messenger bag on my shoulder, stuffed with today's class assignments, and take the rest of the stairs, wincing when my vagina protests the movement.

It's sore—throbbing in a way I've never felt before, not even when I used a tampon for the first time. If I'm honest, everything feels strange down there, like I've both abused and satiated it.

I suppose that's exactly what I did.

Blinking images of Thorne's raw enthusiasm out of the way, I cross the foyer and open the heavy front door in the middle of another round of knocks.

"Oh." I stumble back in surprise.

Savannah tilts her head and smiles. "Hi, Ember. I thought you could use a ride today."

"Uh..." My ravaged brain takes its time catching up to who's standing on the front porch. "Dash usually gives me a ride. Although..." I throw a glance over my shoulder, brows furrowed. I haven't seen him at all this morning. My breakfast of oatmeal and coffee was mysteriously delivered to me on a tray outside my room, a lot like hotel service.

"He has the day off." Savannah offers her hand. "Come on. My car's waiting."

I stare at her open palm, then back at her face. She exudes friendliness, her voice light, her smile easy ... but what is it with her *eyes*? That same vacancy is back. If I squint, there's a glimmer of intelligence until she blinks, then it's gone again.

"Um..." Apparently, Thorne's turned me into a Cro Magnon, with the ability to use only one-syllable words. I throw one last glance over my shoulder. "Okay. Sure."

Avoiding her awaiting hand, I step out and shut the door, not worried about locking it. Dash is likely lurking about somewhere, and security cameras are up.

At the thought, I wince again. Thorne still lords that damn security tape over me, yet I still gave him my virginity. *How fucked up am I?*

Seriously fucked up, if I give what I allowed him to do to me any thought. And how much I liked it.

My center pulses and throbs, its former ravaging immediately forgotten as it lubricates itself for more.

I clear my throat and sway my hips, hoping to get rid of the intense want, especially in front of Savannah.

"So how was your night?"

"What? Great. Good. Boring." Inside, I'm positively *sneering* at myself. Did Thorne take my intelligence along with my virginity? I think not. "A lot of catching up with assignments. It's so easy to get behind at Winthorpe."

"That's very true," Savannah responds in a quiet voice. I realize my quadrillionth mistake.

"I'm sorry. That was insensitive of me." I reach for my dad's advice next. *When foot in mouth, try for honesty.* "I'm just wanting to make conversation with you, and it's tough because of, you know, what we did. Who we are." I laugh up at the cloudy sky. "Take your pick."

Savannah's bland expression breaks into a genuine smile as she looks over at me. "Secret societies weren't in the Winthorpe enrollment brochure, I take it?"

We lock eyes, and I share a true moment with her. My tummy wriggles with something close to kismet.

It's at that point we reach the car. Savannah breaks off contact first, heading to the other side. "Slide on in," she says to me over the hood.

The luxury car is black, of course—the preferred color of the elite's chauffeurs. This one's a Range Rover, and I get a second tug on my heart this morning. Mom always said if she ever struck it rich, she'd love to buy a pearl white Range Rover and drive over our neighbor's lawn (our neighbor, Mr. Tobias, is a cranky old man who likes to dump his garbage on our side of the fence to attract the raccoons).

The memory is so sudden and tangible that I stop opening the car door to take a breath. God, I'm even missing Mr. Tobias's curse-riddled rants to his dead ex-wife at this point.

"Ember? Are you getting in?" Savannah stares at me over the seats.

My lips tick up in apology, and I hop into the warm leather seats. *Mmm, seat warmers. I have to tell Mom about that...*

I immediately stifle that train of thought. Too much is

going on inside my head this morning. All this sentimentality will make my heart explode if I let it.

"This is Alejandro." Savannah gestures to the driver, who meets my eye in the rearview mirror and dips his head in greeting. I wave back.

As soon as we're buckled in, he smooths out of the manor's circular driveway and onto the road. I find myself staring out my window at the neighbor's house across the street—just as cranky and hell-bent as Mr. Tobias but much, much hotter.

I wonder what Thorne's doing right now. Or where he went after I fell asleep.

Thorne tucked me under his chin after giving me the orgasm of my life, stroking the underside of my jaw until I couldn't fight off sleep any longer. He's never been so tender and quiet, and I'm pretty sure I won't see that side of him again. Not if he can help it. Thorne proved that by disappearing while I was lightly comatose and not bothering with a note, text, or anything remotely considerate.

What did I expect him to write, anyway? *Thanks for your V-card. See you at school.*

He didn't come with expectations other than to warn me about risks I'm well aware of. I was the one who pushed, begged, and jumped him for sex.

And I would *absolutely* do it again.

"Penny for your thoughts?"

I tear my gaze from the window and to Savannah. The car's engine hums between us, Alejandro opting for the sounds of other motorists and nature rather than music. It's both soothing and uncomfortable at the same time. Probably because of who I'm sharing the silence with.

"There's a lot to unpack," I answer, my lips turning up slightly.

She nods. "Can I be honest with you about something? You're the only person who hasn't pushed me into talking about myself or what last year was like for me."

"Thorne and Aiko push you for information?" The question's out before I can stop it, and one my common sense answers before she does. Of course they want to know what happened. Everyone does.

"Aiko's heart is in the right place. Since I've come back, she's been my shadow, making sure I'm comfortable, constantly asking if I need anything. I found her at the end of my bed one night, watching me sleep. When I screamed, she bolted like a rabbit. You'd think she would've understood my reluctance to have someone looming over me while I was at my most vulnerable..."

I wait for a beat before responding, studying her profile. Did she just make a joke about her traumatic circumstances, or is she reliving the trauma right now? I can't tell with her. I never can. That vague mask of hers is back like there's a blurry wall between who she's talking to and what she's really thinking.

"She never gave up on you," I say. "Aiko's the only one who wanted to keep going after your trail went cold. She's a true friend."

Savannah darts a look at me. "Oh, of course. I don't mean how it sounds. Just that it's stifling."

"Is that why you offered her up?" I glance quickly at Alejandro up front, unable to say what I really want: *Is that why you offered Aiko up as our sacrifice instead of Zeke?*

I'm defensive of Aiko. I don't care if she's angry with me and doesn't want to be my friend anymore. Savannah has no idea, *none*, how far Aiko was willing to go to save her.

Savannah's lashes flutter with what I hope is guilt. "It's more complicated than that."

"Is it? I understand that what you went through is sadistic and unconscionable, but you're home now. Safe. Aiko probably just wants to ensure you stay that way. She doesn't want to lose you again."

But even as I'm saying those words, I think of the Aiko who I sat at lunch with, despondent and silent. I don't believe the Savannah she wanted was the one who came back. I finish with, "There's been a big year of change since you last saw each other. Maybe you two need to get to know your new selves. Either way, I don't think putting her in the catacombs for us to..." I glance at the back of Alejandro's head again, laying back in my seat. "Well. You know what I mean. It wouldn't have helped your relationship."

And we could've killed her.

"Why did you want Aiko?" I ask.

Savannah reaches up and starts playing with something at her neck. She pulls it out of her shirt collar, the gold glinting around her fingers.

I know, before I even see it, what the pendant is. *Forever you. You forever.*

"Because her father left my mother."

She admits it so quietly that I take a second to understand. "Wait, what?"

"When I left, I thought Mom would be okay because she had him to fall back on. She and I, we only really had each other, but then she met Kai Nakamura, and suddenly, it was all about him. At first, I was jealous, but then I started dating Thorne, and when he introduced me into the initiation of our secret school club, I quickly forgot that my mother was putting me in second place. I still loved her, though, and the whole time I was gone, I thought she was safe and loved—a lot like you're arguing Aiko is trying to do with me." Savannah levels me with a look, and I remember to close my mouth. I'm *hearing* her, but ... holy crap.

"What did it take, a month without me before Kai dropped her and chose his job over her?"

"I ... I don't think that's what happened," I say, treading carefully. "Aiko told me your mom shut down. She was so riddled with grief that she was barely a person anymore. Mr. Nakamura couldn't stay with her without losing his job and the ability to care for her. From what I understand, she left him while he was overseas, and he's been depressed ever since."

Savannah shakes her head furiously. "You have it wrong. Mom told me everything when I was recovering at the hospital. She moved in with my grandparents because Kai deserted her, and Aiko could never replace her daughter. She was alone, and I wanted Kai to feel that *same* way. To have his daughter ripped away from him while he's alone and without the support of the person he loved. To see how it felt for even a moment."

Savannah's voice takes on a cutting tone, so unlike her that I'm darting glances back and forth between her and Alejandro, wondering if this is the norm. The blur has snapped into 100 percent clarity, and I'm able to see every emotion flit across her face. Loss, hate, and vengeance.

I'm not about to ask if she really thought beating Aiko up would solve anything, since clearly she's considered it. I press into my seat, picking at the hem of my skirt, praying that we're almost at school. I aim for another tactic. "Is Thorne helping you through this ... difficult time?"

Okay, yes, so this tactic also has the benefit of providing me with needed info. Are they together? Did Thorne cheat on Savannah with me last night? Am I a *home-wrecker*?

I may be disgusted with Savannah's motives toward Aiko, but I'm not so innocent to think I don't deserve a little disgust, too.

"Thorne's playing his part very well," Savannah says cryptically.

"What does that mean?"

"It's obvious his heart isn't with mine." Her head falls back against the headrest, still twiddling with her necklace. "He's doing what Damion wants, which is to keep up the honorable image of his son sticking by the poor, damaged, traumatized girl. The Briars never shirk their duties." Her head falls to the side to look at me. "It's good for the shareholders."

"And ... how do you feel about that?" I ask it in a whisper.

"A lot's happened in a year," is all she says.

Savannah stares forward again, then suddenly points. "Alejandro, we're here."

"Yes, miss." Alejandro pulls the car to the curb.

I straighten and stare out the window, confused. "This isn't the school."

"We're taking a detour." She pushes her door open. "Come on."

"I don't think I want to." My hand hovers over the handle as I stare out, taking stock of the cemetery before me.

Savannah's found the one spot Raven's Bluff doesn't manicure and maintain. A cracked sidewalk gives way to overgrown, patchy grass. Crumbling stone columns sag under the weight of a wrought-iron gate, pitching at such an angle that it can't close all the way. It doesn't matter since there's no need to keep anyone out or in. Neglected, broken tombstones pepper the untended land until it ends abruptly on a cliffside. All that separates the ghosts from the water is a waist-high stone fence, and even that is easily scalable.

"Creepy," I mutter.

"You don't have a choice," Savannah snaps.

I whip around in my seat, assessing her true face again—hate, anger, vengeance. I ask through the side of my mouth, "Alejandro, you wouldn't mind dropping me off at school while Savannah pays her respects in the cemetery, would you?"

Savannah storms around the back of the SUV, throws open my door, and yanks me out.

"Ack—*Jesus!* Savannah, let go of me!"

My messenger bag lands beside me with a *plop.*

As soon as I'm free from the vehicle, Alejandro peels off without so much as an apologetic glance.

"Is he coming back?" I ask the back of the SUV.

"Follow me." Savannah steps into my vision. "Or do I have to drag you through the gate?"

"I'll walk."

She swivels, and I follow her into the old cemetery. It's early enough that the fog is still lifting, adding to this place's forgotten, haunting vibe. "Why are you so angry? What have I done?"

Two thoughts follow my question. *Does she know what happened between Thorne and me last night,* and *I've seen her angry—this is the toddler tantrum version of her rage. There's no way she could know.*

Savannah takes us behind a sarcophagus mausoleum with the name MERRICOURT engraved above the parapet. It's not as ignored as the other gravesites, just spots of green moss in the corners and growing over the ornamental carvings.

"You brought me to your family plot?"

"This is the only safe place for me to talk. No one comes here." Savannah spins around, crossing her arms. "What's your angle, Ember?"

I shift on my feet, uncomfortable with the sudden coastal wind barreling into my face. "What are you talking about?"

"I've missed a lot in the past year, but not once did I think there would be a girl who so smoothly took my place."

Savannah's sunny blond hair is so out of place here, whipping around her face like a solar flare while mine blends into the gray cast to the whole scene.

"Well?" Savannah prods.

"None of this was planned. I'm not positive on the details, but I'm pretty sure Damion told Malcolm that I existed over the summer, and he brought me here as his estranged daughter. I had no idea who he was"—I splay out my hands—"*what* all this was until I was forced to step into it as a long-lost Weatherby. And no, I'm not in it for the money. If I could go back home today, I would."

Savannah lowers her brows. "Why can't you?"

I gnash my teeth, chewing on how much to tell her.

Then again, what I've been through is nothing compared to what she experienced. I figure I owe her the truth. "I was stolen from Malcolm. My birth mother died having me, and the doctor who helped with the labor sold me to a couple desperate for a baby. My parents. At least, that's Malcolm's story. A paternity test proved the most important part of it. Malcolm's threatening to take my illegal adoption to the police and have my parents arrested for kidnapping if I try to go back to them."

Savannah's forehead wrinkles. She lowers her gaze to the ground, thinking. "Wow. That's not what I expected to hear."

"Believe me, I wasn't prepared for it, either."

Her chin notches up. "If you're so against this life, why did you join the Societies? Befriend my stepsister? Go after my boyfriend?"

I inwardly cringe. "I admit, it doesn't look good, but I didn't do any of that thinking I was replacing you. I just ... fell into it." I step forward, closing some space between us. "Aiko and I grew close because she told me your story and clearly needed some help. I'm good with computers and thought I could give her some closure... then I learned of the Societies, and for a while, I was convinced they were involved in your disappearance."

Savannah turns her head, staring out over the cliffs. The wind follows her gaze, blowing her hair back from her face.

"Aiko and I concocted this whole plan where we would break into Briar Manor—"

Her eyes fly back to mine.

"—to search for evidence of Damion's involvement. He's the king of the Nobles. He had to know something."

Savannah stares at me harder. "And what did you find?"

I stare back, but attempting to decipher what she's thinking is like learning hieroglyphics. I blow out a breath. "A spreadsheet. Aiko didn't tell you any of this?"

She shakes her head. "I explained to everyone all I could remember. None of it involved a spreadsheet. She must've accepted my word."

"Yeah. We were dead wrong—*I* was wrong. I thought you'd uncovered Damion's drug ring and threatened to take it to the police, so Damion silenced you." She doesn't react, but I'm compelled to continue. "Or the other half of the argument was that you were helping him acquire the ingredients. You knew all the drop times and where each ingredient was located." I press my lips together for a moment. "Why did you have that spreadsheet on your laptop? Malcolm and Damion have the same one, and since Malcolm is in the import-export business, it makes sense for him to be under Damion's control. But ... what reason would you have to know all that?"

She goes back to staring over the cliff, the strength draining from her features when she does. I wonder if she's wishing she could just shape-shift into a mermaid or a selkie and swim away from here forever.

God knows I do.

The wind picks up, and I have to strain to hear her when she starts talking again, her attention remaining out at sea. "I've run out of people to trust."

I follow her stare, folding my arms over my chest. "I know the feeling."

"You're a stranger, but I feel closer to you than any of my 'friends.' Even Aiko's different. It's a good thing, though. If she were the same sister I left, it wouldn't be so easy to push her away. To keep her out of—"

She cuts herself off.

The breeze wreaks havoc on my hair, but I don't push it away. I look at her through the tangled strands. Something in her explanation has had my instincts ping twice now. First, in the car, and right now. When it finally comes to me, my tongue sticks to the roof of my mouth. "You keep saying that you left. Not that you were taken."

Savannah lowers her chin.

I resist the urge to bite back my secret. Now that she's exposed herself, I don't have to maintain the same soft tread of respect. "I hacked into the RBPD database. The police report says that, you said you were held for ransom by three men who were out to blackmail your dad and change one of his votes in the Senate but you don't remember much else. Traumatic amnesia's a great explanation, I'll admit. It's clear from looking at you that were treated well, fed, had access to showers, and clothed. Your dad was the deciding vote in a multibillion-dollar spending plan that would hike taxes for the middle class if put into effect. These men didn't like that, according to Senator Merricourt. They had families to feed and were desperate." I spin to the sea again, unable to look at her for this part. "Yet when I was with you in the crypt, your actions weren't someone who was treated nicely. The way you hid your body, how you trembled when Luke barged in ... the abject *fear* on your face. I was on your side, then. I wanted to protect you. But then we were given Zeke."

A sound escapes Savannah's throat, a mewl of remembrance.

"And you morphed again. Into someone willing to kill. I'm not innocent in that, either, but it doesn't line up. You change personalities so often that I have no idea where you'll land anymore. And that mask of yours—the one you're giving me right now. Where you're there, but not there." I step in front of her, blocking her view of endless escape. Forcing her to meet my eyes. "What really happened to you these past fourteen months? Were you held against your will by three men in a row house, or did it have to do with the Societies? Do you know something that could bring them down?"

Savannah bites her lower lip so hard that blood trickles out. She sucks the lip in, tonguing the wound.

"Savannah, please." I rest my hands on her arms. "If they did something—if they hurt you and made you live this lie, maybe I can help. I'm a Virtue, but I'm not like them. I'm like you. You want a change—I can feel it."

Savannah's eyes slide over to mine. And hold. I hold back. "Can I trust you, Ember?"

I nod, keeping my mouth shut. I don't want to spook her.

She breaks out of my hands, retreating a few steps. Needing to see the horizon without my form blocking it. "You weren't wrong with your theories, but you also aren't entirely right. I know about Damion's drug trafficking, and I helped him perfect it."

The breeze doesn't have to turn my cheeks to ice anymore. My blood runs cold. "What?"

She swings her head back to me with a dead-eyed stare. "We were having an affair. I'm in love with him."

CHAPTER 15

EMBER

I can't be hearing her correctly.

"Savannah, I ... I don't understand. You're having an affair with Damion Briar?"

"It sounds like you're getting it." She shrugs, strands of tangled hair sticking to her blazer.

"Where have you been for the past year?" I glance around, understanding dawning. She's brought me to an abandoned cemetery at the crack of dawn and behind a standing mausoleum, blocking us from the roadway. It's probably the only property in Raven's Bluff the Nobles and Virtues don't own or have forgotten about.

She's smart. I'll give her that. But ... is she as traumatized as everyone—including me—thinks?

"You said we're the same." Savannah rests her back against the stone wall, beautiful even with gray as her backdrop. "In a lot of ways, we are. We've exposed brutal truths to each other, like the pleasure we take in other people's pain."

I grind my teeth, shifting uncomfortably, unable to admit how close she is to the real me—a person I'm only coming to know myself.

"It's for that reason I'm comfortable being honest with you, Ember." Savannah's voice takes on a strange lilt —flat and light, without much space between words. Almost like a robotic version of herself.

"Okay."

Another frantic option replaces the reason Savannah's brought me here. There are no witnesses. She could kill me, dump my body in her abandoned family mausoleum, and throw her hands up in confusion with everyone else when people start asking questions.

And who would that be? I don't have many people caring where I am at any given moment. Even if I could count Malcolm or Dash, there weren't any witnesses to my departure this morning. If it weren't for—

Thorne. Thorne will wonder where I've gone. Why I'm not at school.

Oh god, I hope he wonders.

A bark of laughter escapes my mouth. I throw my hand up to cover it as Savannah squints at me suspiciously. But, come on, it's funny. I went and gave one of the most important, coveted parts of myself to a guy who may or may not care if his ex-girlfriend legitimately murders me.

Well, fuck him. I can take care of myself.

Turning back to Savannah, I repeat without an ounce of fear in my voice, "Where were you?"

Savannah works her jaw while leveling me with a look like she's daring me to question her. "I was with him."

My arms go slack at my sides. "Damion?"

"Yes."

I stretch my eyes wide. "But where? At the manor? No, that's impossible. Thorne would've—" I stop as I try to control the thoughts tumbling over themselves in my head. "Is Thorne in on it? Did he know you were in the house? Did Julie?"

Savannah presses her palms to either side of her head, closing her eyes. "You're asking too many questions. Stop, just stop and let me finish."

"Sorry." I lift my hands in surrender. "I'll shut up."

And listen. I'm getting the sense Savannah's bottled this up for so long and is desperate to unload.

"It started when I was initiated into the Societies. Damion took control of my trials." Savannah pushes out her lips. "A lot like Thorne did with you."

If she thinks my situation with Thorne is anything close to an affair with a sadistic pedophile, Savannah really *is* as traumatized as everyone thinks.

But I keep my thoughts to myself, biting down on my lips.

"He pushed me to limits beyond what I thought I was capable of. Made me experience things that were terrifying at first, then exhilarating. I became addicted to the challenges and to him. It wasn't long before we took my new fetish to bed. Does any of that sound familiar?"

Her question dares me to argue that Thorne and I are different, that father is *not* like son ... but I can't. My fingers curl into fists at my sides, battling the sickness within myself.

"Damion told me so much about you from the moment you enrolled at Winthorpe. Before that, actually. He asked me if it was a good time to reveal you to Malcolm Weatherby. Obviously, I said yes."

My focus narrows, my horizon tunneling into a scope of only Savannah, her bright, amber eyes locking mine in place. "What ... what the *fuck*, Savannah? You're telling me that while your family and friends were killing themselves looking for you, you were with Damion practicing in puppetry? Malcolm and I aren't *toys*. We're people, and you've completely screwed up my life."

"I wouldn't say you lost much. You've gained Thorne, haven't you?"

The image of Thorne on top of me, bare-chested and gleaming, returns, sending my heart racing. I blink it back. "Where did Damion keep you? At a hotel in Greece? Did you get a new identity? How come no one could find you? How did you evade the police and private investigators for so long? Your dad is a senator, for crying out loud."

Savannah clutches her temples again, moaning

quietly. Good. That'll teach her to stop being so cocky when she continues her revelation *that she was with Damion all along.*

Ugh. Ew.

I keep going. "Did you lose your soul along with your pledge to Damion? You keep saying Mr. Nakamura was responsible for your mother's depression and isolation, but you know what—"

"Stop."

"—*you're* the problem here, Savannah. Your mom left because *you* left her. Aiko's family fell apart because *you* chose your secret older boyfriend over the new family your mom, Aiko, Mr. Nakamura created—"

"Stop. *Please.*"

"—and prevented them from experiencing any happiness. They fell apart when you disappeared. Did your little messenger pigeon Damion tell you that? How badly your family was broken, how lost and desolate your mother was, and how eventually everyone stopped looking, probably just as Damion wanted, except for Aiko, the girl you call *stifling*—"

"I got pregnant, okay? *I was pregnant!*"

I fly back on my heels. My jaw snaps closed.

"Are you happy?" Savannah shrieks, her face a mottled red as she glares at me. "Damion got me pregnant, and because I was a minor, he didn't want anyone to know. And I didn't want an abortion. We were at a stalemate because he really does care about me, despite all the hatred you're spewing. He doesn't deserve that. We decided that I'd stay in one of Briar Manor's underground rooms, unknown to the Societies and behind walls no policeman would think to break down. He decorated a room just for me, promising that when the baby was born, we could forge a birth certificate to change the birthdate so I'd be of age when I had her. It was all legitimate and planned, okay? I didn't want to leave Mom or Kai's house. I liked it on the coast, and I loved having Aiko as a sister. She understood me in a way Aurora never could. Aiko didn't care about social status or the latest trends or who I was dating. She just..." Savannah releases a garbled cry, rubbing her hands across her face too hard.

I reach up in an effort to stop her but fast realize my position here. I'm hearing about a crime Damion's committed. One of many, yes, but this ... I could get proof of this. Savannah's confession. A paternity test, a lot like the one Malcolm forced me to take to prove I was his. I could bring it to Malcolm to give to the FBI, maybe providing enough probable cause for them to get a warrant for Briar Manor...

My heart starts racing again, but not for Thorne. It's against him, now.

Shit. Thorne...

I'd betray him if I did this.

Swallowing, I drop my hand to my side, allowing Savannah to keep going, scrubbing her face until it's as red and plump as a tomato.

"He paid off a midwife to visit me," she continues, tremulous. "A Virtue, of course. For six months, everything was going fine, and then..." Savannah lowers her hands from her face, gently laying them on her belly.

My stomach drops. "Oh, no. Savannah."

"It—I'm told there's nothing I could've done. But I had to give birth to her, you see. To the stillborn. But I don't like to call her that. I named her Aria. Ari. She was— she's..." Savannah's shoulders hitch on a sob. Snot and saliva run down her face as she falls to her knees, and I can't be stoic anymore.

Landing on my knees beside her, I rub her back, letting her sob and cry out until she's hoarse.

"She's here," I think I hear Savannah say.

I lower my head so I can better listen.

"My baby's here," Savannah repeats, her chest heaving with sobs. Eventually, she straightens, taking a deep breath. I keep rubbing her back in soothing circles.

"Damion wanted her cremated, turned to ash. I couldn't argue against it. I got to hold her for a few hours, and then ... he took her away. I was able to convince the midwife to bring me the box when Damion thought she'd destroyed it. She felt sorry for me."

Savannah stumbles to a stand.

"Maybe you should take it easy..." I say but rise with her.

Savannah ignores me. "Here. Right here."

She points at a sprout of white roses remarkably in

bloom despite the cold weather. And now I understand why. She planted them there. Over her baby. Aria.

"Oh, Savannah…" I whisper.

"He told me the midwife to flush her down the toilet. So there would be no record of her … but she couldn't do it." Savannah cups a white petal, stroking it as she would the top of a baby's head. "He let me go for walks at midnight sometimes, along the beach where nobody would see me. I kept her in a safe place. Once I was well enough to return, I brought her here. Buried her here."

"I'm so sorry."

Savannah shakes her head, remaining focused on the flowers. "Damion was there for me. I was in a bad, bad way after we lost her. It took me months to recover, and even then, I had to be well enough that I could return to my family without admitting the full truth. Damion told my dad that I was sequestered for Societal reasons, and that as king, Dad wasn't to question it. He was told to go along with the ransom story once I reappeared." Savannah pauses. "Not once has Dad asked me what I did, where I really was. That's how much the Societies mean to him, Ember. To everyone. No one would dare lose their place among the elite, not even my father, who lost his child for over a year and now has to lie about it for the rest of his life." She takes a deep breath, then loosens her chest with a heavy exhale. "Damion helped me create a plausible story that no one could be suspicious of. Except for you. Somehow, I couldn't entirely convince you, could I?

You've seen too much yet stay separated from it all at the same time. How do you do it? And why?"

Frowning, I massage the back of my neck. "I felt—I feel just as adrift as you. Having no real parents, being dragged from the familiar and plopped into a *very* sadistic, foreign environment. All I have left is information, and I'm gathering as much of it as possible, so I can—"

"Stay in control of your fate," Savannah finishes. She pushes to her feet, walking closer, her stare less intense and burning. I hope her unloading cleared her vision some. "See? We're almost the same, you and I, in so many ways."

I'm unable to argue. I nod, my cheeks hot despite the cold, my vision blurred. Savannah's pulling on emotions I thought were long dead. "Why did you tell me all of this?"

"Because I needed to." Savannah tucks her hair behind her ears. "And because if you come forward with any of what I said, it won't be me facing the worst of the punishment. You're the one who dealt the final blow to Zeke. Your fingerprints are all over the deadly weapon. I have the paddle. Took it before we left the catacombs. You're screwed, Ember, if you breathe a word of what I said to anyone. Even Thorne."

"That's—" I clear my throat of my panicked heart scrabbling up my esophagus. "This is a hell of a monologue."

"I'm well aware of your relationship with him. As you've probably figured, I could give two shits about it.

I'm still with Damion. We're keeping it a secret, for now, until I graduate. It feels good to tell *someone* the truth and get it off my chest. To have someone else know Aria existed and that she's here. And it feels extra special because your lips are sewn shut. My secret baby isn't worth your jail time, now is it?"

"No." What else can I say? My mind's working over-time, parsing through exactly what the hell's going on right now.

"Good." Savannah folds me into a tight hug that I endure, stiff-backed and confused. "I'll text Alejandro. We're going to be late for school."

CHAPTER 16
THORNE

Where is she?

Ember isn't in any of her morning classes. As a Beckett, she should be beside me in almost every class, yet her seat is empty for all of them.

Slipping out of her bed and leaving Ember before dawn was a feat unto itself. Laying beside her was a comfort I had trouble admitting. Surrounded by her scent—caramelized peaches—and inches from her warmth, I figured this was the closest I ever came to being happy. *Happy.* An exotic, rare word in my vocabulary that I'm starting to associate with Ember.

Not good.

Hence, my burglar-level exit from her bedroom, then her home. She didn't stir as I collected my things, so heavily sedated by our sex. As I buttoned my shirt at the foot of the bed, I took the time to imbue her moonlit profile into my memory, the howling manor doing little to distract from the serenity of the moment. It was that second of realization that I lurched backward and half-walked and half-heaved myself out of the room.

Sleeping with her was meant to *remove* this ridiculous ache from my body. The need for Ember. The want. The *obsession*.

Little did I figure that her sweetness would cling to me. I licked my bottom lip as I snuck out the door, hoping to collect one last hit of her pussy.

My dick was soaked in her. She's drying along my shaft, sinking in, laying her right to it as permanently as a tattoo.

Son of a bitch. My obsession has turned into an addiction.

The only reason I was able to leave the softness of that bed instead of flipping her over and giving Ember her first morning fuck was the thought of seeing her again at school, flushed and nervous as she approached me cautiously—maybe even with a little limp because of the relentless pounding I gave her.

My cock twitches at the memory, straining against my slacks as I stalk the hallways for her. When the bell rings for lunch, everyone streams out of the classrooms and scurries to the various places they belong, their lunch seats designated through the hierarchy of coolness. Jax will guard our table, Aurora and her supplicants soon filling it. With Savannah back and acting as Virtue princess, Ember should be there, too.

I do an about-face toward the cafeteria, thinking about all the ways I'm going to punish Ember for putting me through this ... whatever this is. Concern? Longing?

Fuck. I need to see her so I can squash it.

She better not be skipping school because of me. If she is, I'll break into her home again and demand she never hide from me. That's not how it works when prey comes to my attention. Especially this one.

Movement catches my eye as I storm past Winthorpe's main entrance. Two girls are slinking inside, their cheeks flushed from a prolonged outing in the cold.

Wait.

I come to a severe halt, my legs practically *electric* with anger.

"Where the *fuck* were you two?"

Ember jolts, her eyes snagging on mine. Savannah slows to a stop and crosses her arms.

"Getting to know each other better," Savannah supplies, despite where my attention has *very* clearly landed. "We're sisters now that Ember's been officially proclaimed a Virtue."

My eye tics in response. That's another reason I need eyes on Ember at all times. My father has plans for her, and with how he handled his supposed best friend, Malcolm Weatherby, I don't have much faith in Malcolm's ability to defend his daughter.

But I can.

As Savannah talks, the pink in Ember's cheeks drains to her neck, leaving her face paler than usual and staining her collarbone bright red. If I didn't know any better, I'd say it was shame coloring her body. My lips curl.

A line forms between Ember's brows. She looks at Sav, then back at me, as if trying to solve a mathematical problem between us.

"You have a sister," I say to Sav. "Go see how she's doing. I'll take care of Ember."

Ember steps farther away from both Sav and me, breaking our little triangle. "I don't need any taking care of. And I'm hungry, so I'm going to lunch."

She walks between us at a fast clip, her head dipped low so she doesn't have to make eye contact with either of us.

That's odd.

I swing my arm through the space between her elbow and torso, snagging her against me.

"What the—"

My mouth brushes her ear so the movement of my lips sends tingles down her neck. "I said, you're coming with me."

She tries to push out of my hold. Obviously, she fails. As her plan B, she swings her face to mine, glaring. "You made your intentions pretty clear last night. I'm not a basketball you get to bounce around and score whenever you feel like it. If you really wanted me, you would've stayed. But you didn't, so fuck you very much and let me go."

Sav's brows shoot up. I frown. It's through slitted vision that I growl at her, "You can go now."

"Right when it's getting interesting? That's not very fair," she says.

My frown turns into a warning sneer. It's not like she's jealous. We've both been playing our parts for our parents, being the good little heirs. When I first saw her after she returned, I was sincere in my concern, but her actions soon showed me that her trauma wasn't entirely real. I'm well versed in how to be fake, and it seems Sav collected a few tips while she was gone.

Sav holds my stare but ultimately concedes, as everyone does. Nobody comes close to melting my ice. She backs up a few feet, but adds, "Remember what we talked about, Ember," before swiveling on her heel and walking off.

"Well, that was unnecessarily ominous," I muse over Ember's head, but her struggles quickly redirect my efforts.

"Let me *go*, Thorne."

"Every time you say that to me, it makes me want to fuck you harder."

She stiffens. Releases a frustrated growl. Then aims a kick.

Shit. She got way too close to my goods. I toss her over my shoulder to put her legs out of commission.

"*Hey!*" She bats against my back. "We're in the middle of school! What the hell do you think you're doing?"

I spin, taking us in the opposite direction of the cafeteria. "Taking us somewhere more private."

"I don't *want* to be anywhere with you! Put me down!" She smacks at my lower back again.

"Keep going. You know I like it rough."

She tries to arch out of my hold, but Ember's core strength isn't what it once was now that she's off the swim team. After a few attempts, she flops down. "You're such a twisted fucker sometimes, you know that?"

"Obviously."

Ember doesn't give up. She wiggles, grabbing for my hair and yanking hard.

"God—*fuck*." My neck cricks as she forces it at an angle. "Let go, little pretty. This is your first and final warning."

"Nope, nope, nope," she says through clenched teeth. Ember grips harder.

My arm tightens around the backs of her legs, holding her in place and leaving my other hand loose. The halls are deserted, most heading for the irresistible call of food and a break from school. Maybe a few teachers remain behind in the classrooms, but the doors are closed and the lockers unattended.

I smile. "Don't say I didn't warn you."

Using my free hand to go under her skirt, I push aside her underwear and sink two fingers in.

Wet. Just as I suspected.

She shrieks, bucking against my grip, but that only wriggles my fingers in farther.

"Keep struggling, and I'll stick my entire hand in, little pretty, and fist you in the middle of the Winthorpe halls."

Ember stills. She must be sore from last night. Tender. Sensitive. She buries her face in the back of my blazer and cries out as I curve my finger and press against her G-spot.

The exposure of her pussy to the air and parting her lips release that scent I've been pining for since leaving her bed. It envelops my face, tickling my nose and sending saliva cascading into my mouth. I pick up the pace, more eager than before to find a vacant classroom.

I stick another finger in. Then another. That's four fingers now. She leaks against my joints, dripping onto my school blazer and covering my palm. Ember's scent is so strong, so sensual, that my dick demands to be a part of it, poking through the top of my pants.

Ember moans, wriggling her ass, driving my hand in deeper.

"Do you want my entire hand, little pretty?" I murmur, not expecting her to hear me.

Her hands come around my front, feeling across my belt, finding my cock...

"Argh." I falter in my steps as she goes under my shirt and swirls my precum around the tip.

"Two can play at this game," an upside-down Ember

says, her voice tight. My shoulder's digging into her stomach, both hurting her and restricting her breathing.

I know she fucking loves it.

Resuming my strides while peering through the frosted glass of the classrooms we pass, I maneuver my hand so my thumb gets in her pussy, as well.

Ember lets out a groan of pain. She's only just been deflowered, and here I am, introducing her to more pain, more fetish.

I don't ask if she wants me to stop. We're too far gone for that. She grips my dick and squeezes, her nails biting into the flesh.

Cursing, stumbling, I shoulder through the door I'm 100 percent certain has no one in it. Professor Lowell loves his lunch breaks and refuses to re-enter his class until his students do, and therefore never locks his door.

The light's off, but the squared-off windows let in enough light through the cascading ivy outside that I can see where I'm going. I stop at the teacher's desk and unceremoniously pull my hand out and dump Ember on her feet.

She trips, her side butting against the desk, but gets her bearings quickly. Her palms smack against the wood. "You have a lot of nerve."

"And you have a lot of pussy juice for me." One by one, I put each finger in my mouth, sucking her off me slowly.

Ember's squinting, furious glare softens, then grows hot. But she blinks, retreating and throwing her hands up.

"No. I'm not doing this. I'm so *tired* of these games you entitled, spoiled kids play. Ever heard of *normal* daily life? Like eating breakfast, then going to school, then doing homework, then watching your favorite show or reading your favorite book, then going to bed? Is that so hard? Why aren't any of you capable of that?"

"That sounds fucking boring as shit." I press my thumb into the pad of my tongue, lowering my eyelids. "And you're not that, either, Ember. You're like me. You *like* it when I do these things to you. Hell, if we had longer to walk, you would've begged for my fist in your cunt."

She winces. "Don't say that word."

"Why? Does it disgust you?" I step closer. She takes one step back, yet her rebellious expression doesn't waver. "Would you like to slap me for saying it again?"

"Yes," she says, chin high.

"That's too bad because I love talking about your *cunt*." I take another step. She retreats again. I'm loving this dance. "I want your cunt dripping for me. I want to shove my dick in you so hard and so high, you taste my cum in your throat. I want it to stretch and fit the length of my cock—and only my cock, for the rest of your stay here at Winthorpe Academy. Your cunt is beautiful and delicious, and you gave it away last night. It's mine, and I'm going to take, and suck, and ram it until nothing in the English language exists for you but *Thorne*." I step closer still, listening to Ember's ragged breaths as she holds so tightly to resolve. Poor girl, she's going to lose.

"And when you're not around, I'm going to jerk off to it. I'll slide my hand down my cock, picturing your tight, wet *cunt* sheathing it instead. I'll feel the memory of you spasming around me, coming and screaming and rocking against me until I've had my fill." I *tsk* while she tracks me with wary eyes. "Problem is, I don't think I'll ever be satisfied. I'm constantly going to want to fuck you. My pretty, little, cunt."

Her back smacks against the wall nearest to the windows. We've been here before, and I resist an eye roll at her sweet unoriginality. "Turn around and go back to Lowell's desk. Then bend over."

"N—"

I clamp a hand on her mouth. "Are you really going to test giving me the wrong answer?" I snake my hand up so I cover her nose, too. "Because we both know I'll get my way."

Ember pushes my hand off. I let her. "Thorne, there's too much going on. I don't think this is the time to order me to have sex with you."

I cluck my tongue against the roof of my mouth. Little does she understand that I *need* to have her and be rid of this ... thing ... inside me. It'll go away once I'm finished with her. I know it. At least for a little while.

"I see. You've chosen the testy route. Very well." I spin her until I'm holding her wrists at the small of her back, then drag her over to the teacher's desk.

"Thorne—stop!" she squeals.

I don't. Not until I have her bent over the wood with her short skirt riding up her thighs. Keeping her in place with one hand, I use the other to pull down her panties, leaving them skimming her ankles.

Ember bucks wildly, scattering Lowell's stacks of papers with her head and hair as she whips them around. To stop it, I grab her ponytail and give it a hard yank, tilting her eyes almost up to the ceiling.

"Your pussy tells me otherwise, Ember. You're fucking *glistening*."

And she is. Even in the unlit room, the small beams of sunlight cascade down her folds, shining them like a beacon. Her thighs are sticky with it.

To prove it, I stroke down her slit, swirling and dipping as I push my thighs into hers and bend close to her ear, keeping her still.

"My body's betraying me," she grits out. "That doesn't mean I want this."

"Doesn't it?" I purr. I'm so confident in her submission—in her obsession with me just as I am with her—that I dare to say, "Then tell me to stop."

My thumb circles her clit. Her ass presses into my forearm, and she moans, positioning herself for more.

"Yes, a lot is going on," I admit, tasting where the corner of her jaw meets her ear. She shivers. "But I can't seem to shake you. Not yet. And I can't concentrate until I've done all I want with you and you're out of my system. There's *a lot* I'm desperate to do."

As I slide down her body, my dick positively screaming to be let loose, I bend to my knees and spread her ass cheeks, then go in for a feast.

As Ember moans and writhes, I bury my nose and mouth inside her, releasing her by her wrists and allowing her to stabilize herself on the desk. I groan into her center, devouring as much of Ember as I can, consuming her pain, pleasure, and regret over falling for me again.

Tinges of blood come with her juice. I'm swallowing remnants of last night with eager gulps, making her a part of me as much as she's burrowed into my unwelcoming soul.

Her muscles clench around my tongue as I thrust it in and out. Ember releases a closed-mouth scream, slamming her palms into the remaining paper stacks and sending them flying out on either side.

I don't waste time. Sitting back on my heels, I wipe her off my face and stand, undoing my belt and pants. At last, my dick bursts free, tight and desperate to unload.

Swiping my hand along her slit, I collect enough lube needed to coat myself, then line up to her folds.

Shit. Condom.

Growling with frustration, I release my cock and knead her butt cheeks instead. "Do you have anything on you?"

My voice is barely controlled.

"Like, a condom?" she asks, her tone supple and satiated. Her cheek is pressed against the desk as she splays out for me, the perfect time to spear her with my cock.

DAMMIT.

"Just. Answer the question," I rasp, my abs tightening along with my balls.

"No," she says. "Unlike you, I don't carry condoms around while breaking into people's rooms."

I assess the situation in front of me, licking my lips. We can't risk the pull-out method. And I'm too far gone for her mouth. I want more than her tongue. I'm here to take, and spurting my cum all over her face just isn't enough.

Then I get an idea.

My mouth curves into a slow smile.

"I regret to inform you, little pretty, that you're about to lose your virginity in a second spot."

CHAPTER 17

THORNE

She lifts her head, eyeing me from the side. "What?"

I answer in the obvious way, pushing the tip of my thumb into her ass.

Ember spears up on her hands, the stimulus so intense and unexpected that she resembles a deer in headlights. "Fuck! No, Thorne! Not that. I mean, eventually, maybe, but not right now. In fact, I should really talk to you about Savannah..."

"Do *not* say her name," I snap, pushing my thumb in to the second joint. "Or anyone else's. It's just you and I in this room, and I'm going to fuck you whether or not you're prepared for it. Do I make myself clear?"

Ember goes silent. I watch the muscles work in her cheek as she thinks it over. She also tightens against my thumb to a degree where I wish my dick was already inside her, enjoying it instead of my hand.

I'm about to pull my thumb out and slam into her, if only to relieve this unbearable ache when her lips fall open, and she says, "Yes, sir."

Well, *fuck*. She's done for, now.

My throat vibrates with approval. Slowly, I remove my thumb, then press close to her pussy with my dick, sliding it up and down, coating the shaft in her wetness, then using my hand to both pleasure her clit and swirl some of it around her ass.

She pushes into my hand, her head falling forward as she keeps her palms on the desk.

I want to see all of it. Everything. So I unclasp her skirt and send it somewhere over my shoulder. Getting the hint, Ember kicks off her panties at her ankles, leaving her in a shirt, blazer, and black loafers. It's so schoolgirl hot that I have to tip my head to the ceiling for a few seconds to maintain control.

I don't want to cause her complete pain. Only a small bit. As much as I want to, I can't just shove my dick in and hurt her. No, this has to be slow. Careful. A torturous burn that will end in a desperate, filthy release.

God, yes.

So I start with my fingers. First one, then two. Three...

Ember arches at the sudden discomfort but eventually relaxes. I spread my fingers, stretching her, and she starts up again, but I soothe her back to submission, promising her that this is crucial, that I need to massage enough space to fit into.

To keep her supple, I keep working her clit with my other hand, bringing her to orgasm not once but twice. Each time she twists and mewls with pleasure, my ache ratchets up more. If I keep this up, all I'll have to do is lay my dick on her back, and I'll spew my load all over the place.

That's it. By the third stretch, I can't wait any longer.

With a haggard exhale, I push my tip into her ass, pressing in with excruciating slowness. Ember tenses up again, but I knead her ass cheeks, coaxing her to take me all the way in.

My balls are so tight, they've become baseballs. I resist shoving myself in and pounding the life out of her, going slowly, inch by inch, until my balls touch up against her slick, dripping pussy.

"Oh, fuuuuuck," I groan to the ceiling, exposing my throat.

Ember moans with me, warring with pleasure over pain as she adjusts to my girth and length in a place she'd never thought would be violated.

But it's a good place. Grinning, I let my head fall forward. I'm about to show her just how good, and where a hidden G-spot is.

My thrusts start gently. I'm only a beast when I want

to be, after all, and after putting her through what I did the night before, she deserves some coddling.

"That's it…" I whisper hoarsely as she begins to meet my thrusts. "Exactly, baby. That's exactly right … yes, little pretty. *Yes.*"

Her ponytail calls to me, and I wrap it around my wrist, then grip it, pulling her head back. She moans in approval. I can't see her face, but I can picture her closed eyes and her delicate, plump lips, wet from her tongue as she opens them to moan my name.

I go harder. Harder still. Soon, our skin *smacks* with contact, again and again, her ass cheeks rippling with impact. I stare down, holding her hair and watching my dick slide in and out of her, my shaft simply throbbing and the veins popping out…

"Fuuuuuuuuuuuck!"

My curse will be heard all around Winthorpe as I hold her and ride the release, plunging and milking her asshole until she's so full of me that she'll be walking with clenched cheeks for the rest of the week.

Once the black stars disappear from my eyes, I realize Ember's coming, too. While I worked her ass, she was working her pussy, masturbating while I fucked her, finding her orgasm while I pushed against her G-spot and brought her along for the ride.

Panting, I pull out of her, stumbling back. My ass hits the student desk behind me, sending a wrenching, scraping sound through the room.

Ember's gasping, lifting herself off the desk and turning to face me. Her inner thighs are a mess, slick with her and sticky with me. She holds a hand to her chest and leans back against the teacher's desk.

"I..." She stops. Swallows. "I don't know what to say after that."

Breathing heavily, I stare at her. Waiting. Expecting the ache to have been released along with my load. There's no way I still want her after all that. I've had every capable hole of hers. I've taken her precious virginity in the most undignified and selfish manner. I've choked her, held her down, and ordered her to humiliate herself, all for my sick pleasure.

I keep staring at her.

Why? *Why* isn't the tumor of Ember Beckett Weatherby removed from my goddamned brain by now?

Ember stares back, blinking innocently. Unaffected by my treatment of her because she's not stupid. She's aware of what I'm doing. She would only be this way if...

...if she liked it.

A resentful cry tears from my throat. Ember's eyes widen, but she otherwise doesn't react to my outburst.

Almost like she expects it.

Like she knows me too well.

I step into my pants with fucking arrow precision, buttoning up with sharp jerks of my fingers. She watches without comment.

Once finished, my eyes snap up to hers. "Clean this

up. Lowell won't approve of all these papers covered in your pussy juice."

The classroom door flies open with a bang as I storm out.

Ember doesn't say a word.

CHAPTER 18
EMBER

Shit.

Shit, I like him.

I like him so much.

Rising up from my lean-to on Lowell's desk, I should've spun around and slapped Thorne for the way he treats me, taking without asking, expecting without working for it.

That's exactly what I was *about* to do if it weren't for the look on his face once I'd turned and saw him.

Shock. Abject pain. Hope.

Three emotions that shouldn't precede each other, yet they turned his expression into a perfect crescendo—enough to pull on my heart and send goose bumps across my arms and legs.

It's like I was seeing his soul before he jerked it back

and shoved it down, deep inside the pit of himself before I could latch onto it.

That image of him haunts me as I straighten my uniform more than it should. I'm supposed to be sick over what I've done—both with Zeke *and* Thorne—but all I can think of is the addictive mix of pleasure and pain I've been exposed to.

I'm changing.

And I don't care if it's for the better or worse. My moral compass is shrinking, but I have to believe there's enough of the old me left that I can still cling to doing the right thing and exposing Damion Briar for what he is.

I hope.

I peer into the hallway, ensuring no one's around before hobbling through it and finding the nearest bathroom. Cleaning myself up is the first priority. I'm aching and sticky in places I'd never thought possible, but the walk isn't too bad. When my thighs brush together, I'm reminded of Thorne, and the swelling turns into sweet fire. I never really pictured how I'd lose my virginity, but I can sure as hell say I didn't think it would be both holes in two days.

It's bad. It's wanton. And it's all Thorne.

Ugh, I'm already reminiscing. I hate the way my belly flips for it.

Pushing into the bathroom, I grab a wad of paper towels, soaking them in the sink, and start heading into a stall when I hear someone come in after me.

Thorne?

My vagina literally throbs at the thought. I don't know if I can take another round with him, but my body sure wants to try.

Luckily, a girl rounds the tiled corner, holding a navy messenger bag. Aiko.

I pause with my hand on the open stall door. "Hi."

Her eyes slide to the mirrors across from us as if regarding my reflection instead of the real me will prevent whatever curse I'm likely traveling with.

It's not far from the truth, actually.

"I found this in the foyer." She lifts the bag in the direction of the mirror. "I saw you drop it when, uh, when Thorne sort of..."

"Tossed me over his shoulder like a sack of potatoes?" I stroll forward, flinching only slightly when my body reminds me of the sweet damage he did. I lift the strap from her arm and put it on my shoulder. "Thank you."

I'm eager to talk to her and desperate for a piece of how we used to be, but Aiko's made it clear where she stands. I don't want to push it.

With a sad tic of a smile, I turn away. Her voice stops me when I head back to the stall.

"I saw you. I mean—I followed you guys. To the classroom." Aiko clears her throat, staring down at her feet as she shifts her weight.

I raise a brow. "Oh?"

I'm outwardly calm but internally freaking out. The

classroom doors have a square of frosted glass. We didn't turn the lights on. Thorne locked the door.

There's no way Aiko *saw* us. But ... heard us? Oh yeah, that could've 100 percent happened.

"I didn't mean to eavesdrop," she continues. "It's just, the way he manhandled you and how you yelled for him to let go—"

She has no idea it's part of the games we play...

"I thought you were in trouble and wanted to help. I tried the doorknob, but it was locked, and, um, then I heard the kind of noise that meant you weren't in trouble."

"I'm sorry you had to hear that." I run a hand through my ruined ponytail, digging my fingers into my scalp in hopes of redirecting the humiliating heat in my face.

"Dude, you were in a *classroom*." Aiko's voice rises in times with her hands in a gesture of *what the fuck?*

And just like that, my embarrassment wanes. I start laughing.

Aiko shakes her head with furrowed brows. "What's so funny, weirdo?"

"It's you!" I say between laughs. "It's really you! I'm finally seeing the Aiko I've come to know, with horrified emotion and everything."

Aiko shuts her mouth. Her hands clamp in front of her. "Oh. That's not—that wasn't my intention. I'm still mad at you."

My laughter subsides. "I ruined it by calling you out, didn't I?"

She sighs. "No. I've missed it, too. Missed *you*. I figured with Savannah back, I didn't have the bandwidth to deal with our stuff and hers all at once, so I made a choice. The right one, considering what I just witnessed."

A ball of shame lodges in my chest, but I pull my lips in and keep my face blank. "I'm aware of my choices, too. If I wanted to feel regret, I wouldn't have slept with Thorne in the first place."

Aiko gasps, forgetting her anger again. "You slept with him?" She points at the bathroom door. "At *school*?"

"No. Well, yes. Kind of."

"EMBER!"

A squeak of laughter breaks through my façade. "Come on, did we not all see it coming? I had to know! He'd been dangling his skills in front of me for months. You had to know I'd cave eventually."

Aiko sobers, regarding me quietly. "You're making a joke out of this?"

"What do you mean? I'm just being honest."

"Em, you gave him your virginity. Your first time was with a sociopath. A hot one, sure, but also one who's guaranteed to break your heart. He's not good for you. You deserve someone who cares, not a guy who'll bend you over a table and grunt his way—"

I hold up a hand. "Stop."

"We've been distant lately, but I still know you. This is going to hurt, Ember."

Heat swells, different than before. "I've changed. You have no idea what I've gone through. *None.* I'm perfectly aware of Thorne's emotional limitations, and I don't *care.*"

"You do."

"I *don't*! What is with all this, anyway?" I flap a hand in her direction. "You're done with me, remember? Don't be showing concern now."

"Ember, I still care about you. And I love you."

"No." A sharp pain forms in my chest, too close to my heart. "I'm not doing this." I move to go around her, but she spins with me.

"I'm a dummy, okay? Ember, please." She grabs me by the hand, bringing me to a sharp halt. I still can't turn around and face her.

"I shouldn't have iced you out. I can see what it's done to you, and if I'm honest, that's partly why I *haven't* been talking to you. Because I can't stand to see the hopelessness on your face like you have no one left who loves you. *I* do. And yes, I come with the baggage of a broken home and a kidnapped stepsister, and let's not get into the secret societies that run this school that I've never been chosen for ... but I always prided myself on being a good friend. And I failed you when Savannah came back. I couldn't balance the both of you."

My throat is thick. It burns, and I'm terrified that burn

will travel into my eyes, and I won't be able to stop crying. "I don't blame you."

"See? That makes me feel worse. I don't want to desert you anymore. Please, don't go down this path…"

"I'm a big girl, Aiko. You can't stop me."

"But I can help you."

I slowly lift my head, regarding her.

"I feel … useless. I'm trying so hard to help Savvy, but it's like she doesn't want it. She can't stand to be around me, and all I want to know is *why*. What did I do? Does she hate me?" Her eyes cloud over. "I've gone this far. I might as well make a full confession. I'm jealous of you. You get to spend so much time with Savvy, especially with both of you being members of the Virtues, and I'm—nothing. A speck in her spotless cloud. She pretends to include me by having me sit at your table and stuff, but come on, we all know how she's treating me."

My face softens. I stare at her for a long time, watching her fight off the overwhelming sadness that comes with not feeling good enough.

It helps me come to a conclusion. And maybe, gifts me with the ability to remove some of the poison infecting my body. I squeeze her hand. "Aiko, can we get out of here? There's something I need to tell you about Savannah."

She sniffs and wipes her eyes with the back of her sleeve. "Sure. I hate Macroeconomics, anyway."

I smile. "It's one of my favorite subjects. I'll catch you up if you need it."

Aiko snorts. "You don't have to forgive me so easily."

I blow out a breath as I finish what I need to do in the stall, and we trudge out of the bathroom, the weight on both our shoulders curving our spines. "Save that thought for after you hear what I have to say. Let's go to our favorite coffee shop in town."

AIKO SIDE-EYES my caramel macchiato with extra whip as she nurses her steaming cup of milk-only coffee. Because it's the middle of a school day, we've scored a window seat that looks out into Main Street, where some stores and boutiques have kept their Christmas lights. With the light snowfall, it's picturesque and quaint, like Scrooge is going to lumber out of his countinghouse any moment to declare the existence of Christmas spirit.

It would all be true if I didn't know what Raven's Bluff harbors under its purity.

"You already look so sad, and you haven't said a word to me," Aiko says, redirecting my focus.

"I was just star-gazing. It's beautiful out there."

Aiko stares out the window. "Very true. When Dad said we were moving here, I thought I was going to die alone in a small town with no Starbucks to save me."

I chuckle. "Me, too."

"Gosh, we've come a long way from our respective urban lives."

"Yeah." I warm my hands on my hot cup. Aiko drove us, but her Bug was acting up and only managed to cough up spurts of heat. She has enough money to replace it, but there's no substituting loyalty and love, and she admitted to me on the drive that it was her mother's car. One of the last treasures she has left of her.

"Okay, so what did you want to tell me off school property?" she asks.

I look up from the mesmerizing ribbons of whipped cream on my coffee. "I don't know where to start."

Aiko perches her elbows on the table. "Just dive in. I promise I won't yell at you and storm out ... like last time."

She's talking about our argument over the necklace. The one Savannah's wearing as we speak. The 'Forever You' pendant from *Damion*.

My coffee doesn't look so sweet anymore. I push it away.

"You say that now, but wait until I'm finished." I gulp down a lump of saliva, at first choosing to stare out at the townscape, but no. Aiko deserves my full attention when I tell her who Savannah truly is.

I start with, "I'm hoping to God you believe me..."

Aiko nods, her eyes bright, eager, and sincere. "I'm here for you. For good. I promise."

I take her for her word, regardless of whether she'll

keep it. The old Ember reaches up, pressing against the cage of my heart, ready to escape and reclaim her turf. Aiko offers friendship, safety, and love. I can't help but be drawn to it, even if I end up ruining it again.

So at the risk of everything, I tell it all to her.

CHAPTER 19
EMBER

I'm worried Aiko's about to go blind. She refuses to blink.

My coffee sits cold in front of me, the whipped cream melted into a white glob. "...which is how I ended up in Winthorpe's foyer this morning, too stunned to fight Thorne off."

Aiko's mouth has stayed in a frozen 'O' throughout my entire confession. It started with being held with Savannah in the Noble's crypt, then Zeke's battery, and finished with the graveyard with Savannah earlier today.

"Aiko? Say something." I rip shreds of a paper napkin, the pieces scattering our tabletop like snowflakes, while I wait for her to speak. Or move.

Aiko's shoulders heave as she sucks in a breath. Something comes with it because she sputters and coughs, her eyelids fluttering.

"Shit—I'm okay," she says in a tight voice, covering her mouth with her hand. "My mouth is unused to having no saliva for so long."

I crumple the napkin shreds into a ball. "That's okay. I know what I've said is ... a lot."

"Understatement." She hacks up a few more coughs, waving me away when I offer to go get water. "I'm fine, I'm fine. Just processing. That's ... oh, my *god*. Savvy? With *Damion*?"

"Shh!" I glance around wildly, clocking the handful of patrons in the coffee shop. They're all strangers to me, but who knows who Damion has in his pocket. Half of Raven's Bluff storefronts contribute to his drug trade. I haven't yet figured out if the owners are aware of it or not.

When I'm satisfied no one shows any interest in the two schoolgirls cutting class at the window, I turn back to her. "Does that mean you believe me?"

Aiko falls back in her seat. "Honestly, with the way she's been acting, if you told me Savvy unzipped her skin in front of you and an alien popped out, I'd ask you what color it was."

"I take that as a yes."

"Unfortunately." Aiko reaches up to rub the back of her neck. With her head bent at that angle, the purple shadows under her eyes are more pronounced. "I wasn't stupid, you know. I assumed she'd return different if she came back to us at all. No one endures that amount of time against their will and stays the same person. That's what I thought, anyway." Aiko returns my stare, her eyelids heavy with exhaustion. "The last thing I considered was that she disappeared *willingly*."

"This is so hard to hear. I'm sorry."

"Don't be. You're the only one who wanted to help me figure out what happened to her." Aiko's shoulders shake with silent laughs. "I completely cut you off in anger, and you *still* uncovered the truth."

"It was kind of by accident. I had a feeling Savannah was hiding something, but ... a baby? With Thorne's father? Nope, I didn't think of that, either."

Aiko's head moves in a disbelieving arc. "Is it wrong that I wish she'd told me and not you? I would've been there for her. Given her a shoulder to lean on. She didn't have to run away. She had *me*. Her mom and dad. *My* dad." Aiko lifts her head with an agonizing sheen to her eyes. "Why would she leave all that behind and go to *him*? He creeps me out on a good day."

"Probably because she was scared," I answer quietly. Savannah's miscarriage wasn't my story to tell, yet I spilled all to Aiko. If it weren't for Savannah's threat hanging over my head or the danger Malcolm's playing with by becoming a mole for the FBI, I would've held off telling Aiko and waited for Savannah to talk to her, if she ever chose to.

We're not living through normal times, though. Savannah had an affair with the leader of a secret society and a man who is willing to kill to protect his drug dynasty. I have my suspicions that Damion orchestrated the miscarriage. But just as I'm keeping the secret of Savannah offering up Aiko for the Virtues' beating, I've kept that theory from Savannah.

A small part of me still wants to protect these women from the terrible truths of the people they love the most.

"What are you going to do with this information?" Aiko asks.

I reach for my coffee, drinking down half despite it becoming cold, grainy swill. "That's my dilemma. I wanted to be honest with you—please know that. But I also need help."

"I'm listening."

I take in a deep breath and let it out slowly. "The right thing to do is to take this to Malcolm. He can leak the information to the FBI. Damion having sex with a minor is a good start toward a warrant. She says she was held by him willingly, but she was sixteen at the time. According to my research, she can't consent."

Aiko's lips flutter with a hard exhale. "If they find the room she stayed in, that will break Savvy's case wide open, whether she cooperates or not. The press will descend like vultures. Raven's Bluff will never be the same again."

I nod. "If the agents keep only the most essential personnel in the know, Damion won't see it coming and won't have time to wipe his computer or destroy incriminating evidence." My vision lowers to the table. "I'd make sure of it."

"That solves it, then." I watch Aiko's hands lift from the laminate. "It's what you should do. If you're worried about me and how my family will handle it, don't be. Savvy's deliberately lied and put a lot of people through absolute, utter hell. I'm convinced a lot of it comes from Mr. Briar's manipulations, but this affair started long before she left. I'm sure of it. Remember when I told you how she acted strange for our entire sophomore year? I blamed Thorne, but now I see the truth. It was Damion. I wish she admitted it to me, Ember." Aiko's voice breaks. "I would've—I would've convinced her to break it off. *Shown* her how messed up it is that a grown man wants to have sex with a fifteen-year-old!"

I don't try to shush her this time. Agony laces her voice and lines her face. I reach across the table and catch one flailing hand, offering a soothing squeeze. "There's not much you can do when someone is blinded by love."

"Is that what you think it was between them?" Aiko blinks back tears.

I pull my hand back, my forehead stiff while I think how best to explain this to her. "I'm not saying how she felt about him is right. It's just that when the wrong person hooks you by the heart, it's so hard to untangle yourself. They become the air you need, the blood that keeps you alive. You spend your nights alone in bed, obsessing over the fast and fervent moments you spent together. It's not something you're proud of. You don't like who you become when you're with them, but ... you hate how you feel when you're without them."

Aiko stares at me over the table, unmoving. "We're not talking about Savannah anymore, are we?"

I peer at her through the corner of my eye. "Um, that's exactly who I'm talking about."

"Are you in love with Thorne?"

I rear back as if slapped. "What? *No.*"

"Ember, we're in our safe place. You've told me literally everything terrible that's going on under my nose. Admitting you have feelings for the crooked prince of Winthorpe shouldn't be that much of a reach."

"I can't admit to something that's not true."

"Fine." Aiko folds her arms across her chest. "We'll table that since it's not a top priority. *Yet.*"

I roll my eyes.

"When will you explain to Malcolm what you've found out? I'd like time to warn my father of the incoming shitstorm if that's okay. I don't have to give him all the details. Maybe just enough to keep him out of the country for a while."

"Oh—well, that's my dilemma." I have to force the words out, considering what I've only seconds ago denied. "A raid will only work if a small, limited number of people know the truth."

"Uh-huh." Aiko tips her head, waiting for more.

Dammit, she's going to make me say it. "For the FBI to

succeed, no one at Briar Manor can know what's about to go down. That includes Thorne. I can't tell him what I know. I have to lie to him when it happens. If he ever finds out that I knew what his father had done well before the police broke down his door—that *I* was the leak who tipped off the FBI, he'll never forgive me. Ever."

To Aiko's credit, she doesn't wag her finger at me, singing *I told you so!* She makes a clucking sound with her tongue, then says, "Yeah. Thorne doesn't seem like the forgiving type."

"Tell me I have to do the right thing. Convince me to explain everything to Malcolm tonight."

"I'm sorry, Ember. I can't do that."

"Why?" My voice cracks. I clench my hands. "I'll save Raven's Bluff. Damion will be stopped. Not even the best lawyers could get around the mountain of evidence against him if this goes through. Maybe I'd even expose the Societies, given that some of them actually assisted in hiding Savannah. I told you about that midwife, right? Right. I'm sitting on too much *not* to tell the police. In fact, I think it's an actual crime if I don't speak up."

"It's not worth it. Not at the expense of your soul."

"Excuse me?"

"You've been through so much. You lost your parents and gained an absentee father. A secret society embroiled you in their fucked-up ways. A mysterious, handsome boy hooked you with his unsavory intentions—your words, remember." Aiko holds up a finger to stop my counterargument. "Ever since you enrolled at Winthorpe, I've watched more pieces of you chip away. I fucking hate to admit this, but the first time in a long while I saw your face light up was this morning when Thorne approached you. You walked into school dejected and pale, Savannah trailing behind you, inanimate as always, yet ... I sensed she was the reason you looked so shell-shocked. Now I know why. But back to Thorne—he's awakened something in you, hasn't he?"

"I..." *Yes*. His shadow's entwined with mine, the dark forms coming together whenever there's a chance.

"If you do this, you need to be sure you can handle it." Aiko leans forward and rests her hand on my forearm. "I'm not talking about Thorne's anger. You've withstood his wrath more than once. I'm more concerned with how you'll defend against betrayal. Because that's how he'll see it. There's no coming back from that, and it might just rip you wide open. He'll devour the last, tender parts of you and spit you out." Aiko adds in a softer tone, "He'll find out. Thorne's smart and horrifically good at sniffing out traitors. Somehow, he'll deduce that you're responsible for his family's downfall."

I search her eyes, my jaw involuntarily clenching.

"Savvy's not kidding around, either. You're the only one she's told, and she made sure to do it with a failsafe—you'll go down for Zeke's assault."

That sick feeling swirls, brushing against the back of my tongue. "I might deserve it."

The more distance that grows between the mania I experienced in the Nobles' tomb and now, the more I regret my actions. "Keeping my membership in the Societies or not, I shouldn't have done it."

"I agree it's not like you. Not the Ember I've come to know. But, it's in the past. You have to look forward, and you'll be no good to anyone if you're under arrest."

Sighing, I rub my eyes. I'm between a rock and a sharp-edged knife. Having Aiko to talk it through with is helpful, except I'm nowhere near a solution that could punish Damion yet protect Thorne. I'm willing to sacrifice myself, but Aiko's right. What good could I do in chains? Raven's Bluff is far from purged. If they don't find anything in Damion's home, it would all be for nothing, with no plan B.

It's then that an idea wriggles its way into my mind.

I lower my hands. "Not if we figure out another way."

"Like what?"

I lean back. "Zeke."

"The aiding and abetting jackass you practically put into a coma? What does he have to do with this?"

Saying his name out loud solidifies the thread of a plan weaving through my head. I give a confirmatory nod to a confused, information-overloaded Aiko. "Zeke will be the mole who tips off the FBI."

CHAPTER 20

THORNE

Ember has disappeared *again*.

My little pretty is being a bad little girl. Skipping classes twice in one day now after achieving a flawless attendance record so far. It must be worth it, whatever she's up to, to tarnish her record. Ember's nothing if not a stickler for perfection.

Suspicion gnaws its way through my annoyance as the afternoon drags by with still no sign of her. I've noted the people Ember's most likely to disappear with (a pathetic few), and all are accounted for, except Aiko.

Strange.

Last I checked, they were still at odds with each other. And I have many ears in the halls of Winthorpe.

Clearly, those ears require some cleaning.

"Where is she?" I snap at the first sophomore I find,

gripping him by the bicep and dragging him close to my bared teeth.

"W-Who?" he stutters.

"I'm in no mood to explain myself. Where the fuck did you or anyone else last see her?"

"I ... I don't know, Mr. Briar. Sir."

He trembles in my grip. The poor idiot's teeth even start chattering.

Proving his uselessness to me, I toss him aside. He slams into the lockers, rights himself, and scampers in the opposite direction while I continue prowling the halls.

I swear I can smell her in the air. Or maybe it's on my fingers. She's certainly on my dick.

It doesn't surprise me that I'm losing control when it comes to Ember. It's just that I simply don't care. I want her. I have to see her.

"Looking for someone, Thorne?"

The lilting voice slithers into my ear like a de-fanged snake.

I pause in my journey to last period, not bothering to turn to the voice. "Unless you have something else to add, Aurora, you can go about your soulless day."

I catch her leaning up against the lockers in my periphery. "She's with Aiko."

"No shit?" I widen my eyes comically, then pierce her with ice.

I'm six feet away from her, yet she shivers under my scope. It seems to annoy her, though, because she straightens her blazer with a scowl. "Ember's off-campus. She left a few hours ago."

"When will she be back?"

"I have no idea."

"They're friends again?" I despise asking Aurora questions and proving my cluelessness, but she's the only lead I have so far.

Aurora shrugs, then checks her nails. Pretending aloofness while standing within my target range. How cute. "All I know is Ember's doing the rounds. First Savannah, and now Aiko." She raises her eyes coquettishly. "What do you think she's planning?"

"Don't play dumb with me, Aurora." I step out of the middle of the hallway and closer to her. "I'm sensing we're on the same side with this."

Aurora stiffens at my proximity. "I don't like losing my title. I'm glad Savannah's safe and sound, obviously, but I was having fun at the top. So if I *do* know something you might want to also know, you'll help me get that spot back. Right?"

I sneer. "I don't make deals with beggars."

"Savvy's not in the right mind to take such an important position in the Virtues. Everybody knows it, but no one's doing anything because of what she's gone through. We're protecting her delicate feelings while sacrificing the defense of the Societies. Do you think Savvy's in the right headspace to guide a bunch of baronesses? Because I sure don't."

"She proved her value at the last meeting. Both Ember and Sav did."

"Yes, but how long can they keep it up? Neither of them has the fortitude to complete another challenge. I'll prove it to you—set up a challenge worse than what they did to Zeke. See if either of them complies."

An exhale hisses through my clenched lips. I can't argue with her, but I'm sure as hell not about to give her the satisfaction of agreeing with her. "What's worse than battery? Murder?"

Aurora lifts one shoulder in a shrug and goes back to checking her nails.

I laugh.

Her eyes shoot up, glaring. "What do you think is so funny?"

"Who the *fuck* would complete a challenge like that? *You*?" I laugh harder, seriously amused at the image of Aurora brandishing a knife on a freshman.

"I almost succeeded with Ember," she seethes.

The back of her head slams against a metal locker with my hand locked around her throat. Aurora doesn't have time to so much as gasp. All she can do is claw at my hand with her fake pointy nails, breaking off as soon as they try to dig into my skin. *Like declawing a cat*, I muse, my arm steady.

I don't say anything as she chokes and struggles. Just stare at her with a flat expression, communicating without a doubt that I wouldn't "almost" succeed at anything. I'd win, even at murder.

"S-s-*sorry*," she gasps.

I drop my hand. Her feet hit the ground, and she slumps against the lockers, massaging her throat.

There's nothing sexy about clamping around Aurora's neck. She doesn't have Ember's flawlessness, nor do I picture her pussy getting wet for me as I squeeze her soft points. This is merely business, and so far, I've wasted my time.

"See you around, Aurora," I say, then spin on my heel. I don't need to warn her never to mention her assault on Ember again. I already have. Next time, I won't be so gentle.

Aurora raggedly calls out, "Don't—don't you want to know what Ember was doing with Savannah this morning before school?"

I stop. Turn. Wait.

Realizing she's not going to get any more from me, Aurora reluctantly says, "I spoke to Savvy's driver."

She means paid him off. The help of other aristocratic families is relatively easy to convince to talk with the right presidents in your hand.

I raise a brow. *And?*

"He said he drove them to the old cemetery. Why would they go there, do you think? There aren't any Society treasures hidden under broken graves, right?"

If there were, I'm not about to tell her.

I turn on my heel in silence, my mind working with this new information while Aurora blubbers behind me. She was never princess material, and she has to know after what she did to Ember, she'll never come close to royalty again.

Social Studies has started by the time I duck in. The professor notices me as I wander to my desk, choosing to refrain from saying anything when I take my seat, knowing there's little point in attempting to punish a Briar.

I stare at the back of Sav's head for the remainder of the period, my hand taking notes on autopilot. All I can do is stare at my fingers, remembering what they were doing a few hours ago and who they were doing it to.

I've taken Ember in all the ways that matter, yet I'm still unsatisfied.

Aurora's given me enough that I should be calm enough to endure the rest of the school day. Ember was with Sav this morning, me after that, maybe did a little schoolwork, then fucked off with Aiko for the rest of the day. I have a relative idea of where she is and who she's with—but it's not enough.

There's a small prickle at the back of my neck. It's hot and pokes like a needle, relentless and itchy. I scratch at it, no amount of digging in relieving this feeling. It lingers and grows, traveling into my gut and pushing against my ribs.

It only occurs when I think of Ember, fading when I

focus on other things. The problem is, *she's* my focus. It's like I ... I wonder if it's...

Fuck, no.

Concern? Worry?

Those emotions were beaten out of me years ago. It's such a foreign feeling that I almost don't have a name for it anymore. It's just a nagging tug that comes every time I think of her name...

The bell shrieks at the end of the period. I scowl at the speaker above the door.

"That's it, folks! Have a great weekend," the professor says. "I expect those ten thousand words on the archeological significance of the original Raven's Bluff mansions first thing Monday morning."

A chorus of groans answers him. He grins and waves at all of us.

I would shoot him if I could.

Sav pushes to her feet, and I'm at her side before she rounds her desk.

She jumps at my sudden presence. "Thorne. Hi."

"Hello, sweetheart." My voice drips with sarcasm.

She catches it and rolls her eyes. "No need to put on an act. No one's watching."

"Everyone watches all the time." I take her hand, squeezing hard with warning as I lead her out of the classroom and to somewhere private where we can talk. "I have a few questions for you."

"I'm sure you do, but I don't have any answers to give."

As soon as we're out of the wave of escaping students, I whirl on her. "That's—"

My phone buzzes in my blazer's inner pocket. I frown.

"Are you going to answer that?" Sav crosses her arms and cocks a hip.

My, isn't she confident today? I immediately wonder why.

I pull out the phone, checking my display. My frown deepens as I lift the phone to my ear. "This better be good, Jax."

"You wanted to know where she is, didn't you?"

My back turns ramrod straight. I shift away from Sav, murmuring, "What've you got?"

"Well, not Ember, exactly, but Aiko. She just walked into Zeke's hospital room."

My brows slam down. "What? Why?"

"I'm as confused as you, man. I didn't think they hung out with each other."

"They don't."

"Then why—"

I hang up, spinning to Sav. "I'll come back to this. Right now, I have somewhere else to be."

"Sure, fine. Corner me another time," she says dryly, then sweeps her arms out in an *after you* gesture.

It's the most personality I've seen from her since she's returned.

I don't trust it. Not one fucking bit, but there's nothing I can currently do about it.

Ember is my top concern. She's up to something. *That's* what the niggling at the back of my neck has to be. She continues to plan and put herself in danger, somehow roping Aiko in to do her dirty work.

And I have to stop her before my father catches wind of it.

CHAPTER 21

EMBER

I meet Aiko in the oncology wing's visitor room of Boston General. It is a quiet, somber place that I thought would have the least prying eyes.

When the elevator doors slide open and Aiko steps out, I rise from one of the sofas. No one else is here.

"Well?" I ask her as she walks up to me. We sit together on the same muted gray couch I occupied. Purple irises bloom in a vase on the small table in front of us, complementing the lavender-painted walls. So far, none of the staff walking through the adjoining hallway have questioned my presence.

"Those nurses mean business," Aiko says, angling to face me. "I had to put on my best teacher's pet face and swear to them I was the student council president bringing Zeke homework."

I smirk. "I don't think one has anything to do with the

other."

Aiko shrugs. "She fell for it, regardless."

"Good. So you got in?"

"Yeah, and I had to leave a few of my textbooks behind. I hope I get them back."

I resist the urge to shake the information out of her. "Priorities, Aiko. What did he say?"

"Zeke had no idea who I was when I walked in. And boy, does he look rough."

That *irk* of guilt hits my belly, but I nudge it aside. "Could he talk?"

"He could. Um…" Aiko shifts against the cushion. "Do you want to know what he looks like?"

Maybe. No. Yes. "I'd like to know if he'll be okay."

"He will." Aiko rubs my arm reassuringly. "I may have perused his chart while he was busy trying to understand who the hell I was."

I wheeze out a breath. "Good."

"Zeke's banged up, for sure. His head is all bandaged, and he sports some serious bruises. He did have surgery to reattach his pinky finger, though," Aiko quickly adds as she watches my face. "Bandages around his ribs. A cast on his hand. He's otherwise comfortable. They're giving him the good stuff."

Nodding, I clear my throat. "That's a relief to hear."

"Savvy did the most damage," Aiko adds softly. "Zeke knows it. He told me to thank you for putting him out of his misery."

I vigorously shake my head. "I didn't do that. I hurt him." *And basked in the blood...*

"You stopped a beatdown that was only going to get worse. You're smart enough to know that." She pats my hand. "Anyway, I made sure to lead with the fact that he owes you. After getting you poisoned and almost killing you in the pool, and then when you saved him by preventing Savvy from maiming his face, it's the least he could do."

That was exactly my plan, to blanket the guilt over him until he couldn't breathe. If anything, I'm becoming an expert on the subject. "Did he go for it?"

Aiko's expression becomes pinched. "Not at first. Zeke's too cowardly to agree on the spot. He needed more incentive."

I smile tightly. "You went to plan B."

"Yup. I told him that the Societies were behind it all. He believed it was Thorne who wanted to sacrifice him for personal reasons. I guess because of what Zeke did to you."

"If Thorne was responsible, I would've heard about it. From his own mouth."

Thorne would never let such a barbarous move go unnoticed by me. He'd preen under my horror, swearing he was doing it to protect me. Eventually, I'd believe him. That's how it works between us.

"No kidding," Aiko agrees. "Zeke had no idea the Societies totaled his car to cover up their part in his attack.

How they even made the type of crash consistent with his injuries. I reminded him that if he thinks the kids the Societies recruit are ruthless, what does he believe the alumni are like? Forensics was covered. The police report forged. Everything you told me about the accident scene, I told him."

I nod, pressing forward, urging her to continue.

"I swear, his swollen eyeballs almost popped out of his head when Zeke realized he was expendable. Zeke may have given valuable information about you to Damion, which is what got you facedown in the pool and kicked off the team, but that info is outdated now. Used up and wasted because here you are, still alive." Aiko gestures up and down my body with her hands. "Once someone has outlived their usefulness, what does he think Damion's going to do?"

"Wow, Aiko." I regard her with newfound respect. Why the Societies disregarded her, I'll never know, but I'm so glad they didn't realize this diamond hidden under the Raven's Bluff rocks.

"Zeke was confident he'd recover, leave Massachusetts and go back to California for his show, and that no one from the Societies would touch him." Aiko shakes her head. "To think I was obsessed with him in ninth grade. I thought he was the hottest guy on the planet. Never considered how dumb he'd be."

"That's why we're told never to meet our heroes," I say.

A tiny flame flickers behind my ribs. I press a fist to it, stifling the craving for him. I can still feel Thorne inside me, hot and demanding.

Thorne isn't my hero; he's my villain, and he doesn't disappoint.

"You're telling me. Long story short, it took way more chatting than I would've liked, but Zeke agreed to anonymously call the RBPD and put in the tip about Savvy's..." Aiko goes quiet. "Affair."

The air around us becomes thick with sadness. It turns out I really did pick the right place to meet with Aiko. I couldn't risk going to Zeke myself. Someone might see. If anyone noticed Aiko, they probably wouldn't put two and two together. She and I are still fighting, according to the entire school.

Soon, Winthorpe will be inundated with so much more. At least two other people know the truth about Savannah—Zeke and Aiko. Within hours, it'll be the entire town, then the nation.

Oh, god. Nausea swirls, threatening to burst out of me. I've deliberately put thoughts of Thorne aside, despite my body constantly reminding me of him—the delicious aches and the newfound hollowness that comes when he's not pleasuring me—but Aiko and I have reached the point where I can't turn back or change my mind. *I'm doing the right thing. Please, let me make the right choice.*

I try to redirect Aiko's and my desolate thoughts. "You gave Zeke the burner phone we bought?"

She nods, her head down. "If the Societies try to follow the lead, or if they have the police in their pockets, they'll be told it was a male caller—and not from one of those speech doohickeys, either. An honest to God male with no connection to you. I made sure not to attach your name to this bomb."

"Just yours." I wrap an arm around her. "Thank you, Aiko. You did an amazing job. Savannah may not realize it at first, but you're saving her just as much as you're saving everyone else from Damion. He won't be able to touch you after this."

She rubs her nose. "I hope so. I think I'm so good at this because it doesn't seem real to me. Not yet."

He might go after me. I have no doubt he'll climb down the funnel until it's so narrow, it'll only be me at the end.

Let him. I put Aiko into this position, and I'll gladly submit to the punishment in her place.

I'm more worried about Thorne.

My eyes scrunch shut. I can't think about his repercussions right now.

I rest my chin on Aiko's shoulder. "It's done. There's nothing more we need to do."

"I did run into one small snag."

"What kind of snag?" I ask slowly, lifting my head.

"Jaxon was at the nurse's desk. His expression was pure confusion when I strolled past, but I swear I stayed confident like I belonged there. Besides, what link could he possibly make between Zeke and me? Jaxon barely knows I exist—for all he knows, I really *was* there to distribute homework."

I nod along with her words, but my brows grow tight. "Sure, but what was *he* doing there? He and Zeke aren't friends..."

"I don't know. We didn't speak, and Jaxon didn't come into the room when I was there. But when I did leave, Jaxon was still lurking in the hallway."

I bite my lower lip, thinking quickly. Jaxon's helped me before, during the challenge where I had to beat Thorne's time swimming and then scale the cliff. I'd be a fool to think that proves his loyalty to me, however. Everyone knows he's Thorne's best friend, his second-in-command, his do-or-die...

I bolt from my seat. "We have to go."

Aiko jumps up with me. "What? Why?"

"We need to get out of here before Thorne comes."

"Why would Thorne—oh." Aiko goes pale. "Jaxon's keeping watch. He's noting Zeke's visitors and sending them to Thorne."

"Yes, and it won't be long before Thorne figures out you're here for me."

And Damion. Oh fuck, Damion could have Aiko's name on his lips right now...

I keep that hellish thought from Aiko as we scurry down the emergency exit stairs and into the hospital's parking lot.

CHAPTER 22

EMBER

Aiko doesn't need much persuasion to get on the next plane to her father.

I hated to do it. I practically screamed at her during our drive back to Raven's Bluff to pack her stuff and beg her father to disclose his location so she could join him.

It wouldn't be a hard sell. Mr. Nakamura was making noises that his daughter spent way too much time home alone and that it might be better if she started traveling with him.

If anyone could protect her from the Societies, it'd be a military base.

Aiko argued to stay. I countered that if she did, she could be used as bait, and everything we worked for, *risked* ourselves for, would be for nothing.

It took over an hour to convince her that remote

learning was a thing, even on Army bases. I promised her that as soon as it was safe, I'd text her and she could return.

I swore to Aiko I'd do everything in my power to protect Savannah, too.

Waving to Aiko at the end of my driveway, I hope I can keep my promises.

Once Aiko's headlights disappear around the corner, I head into Weatherby Manor. My turn forces me to glance across the road at the copse of trees I know shroud the Briar home, and the two stone ravens who guard it.

An arc of light distracts me from my too-long stare into the darkness on the other side of the street.

Dash has opened the front door. "Come in, Miss Weatherby. Master Weatherby is waiting for you in the drawing room."

"He's here?"

"Yes." Dash responds to the stupid question without judgment, but a closer inspection reveals the deepened, disapproving grooves on either side of his thin, wrinkled lips.

Uh-oh. My instant thought is that Malcolm's been notified I skipped school.

He steps aside as I walk through the door, shutting it quietly behind me. The black, sparkling chandelier is lit at full brightness, casting the main foyer in vivid relief, from the faded wallpaper to the unpolished wood staircase to the impeccably dusted portrait of Malcolm and Julie.

I squint, unused to such exposed lighting in the manor. A further sweep of my eyes to the balcony above and hallways that I can see show that those lights are on, too. *Why is every light turned on in this house?*

Usually, when Malcolm returns from his trips, he wants me to forget he's home, floating between rooms like a ghost until dinner. He doesn't flick light switches while he wanders, not even in his office.

"Malcolm?" I call, dropping my messenger bag to my feet.

"Master Weatherby is in the drawing room," Dash repeats. He hasn't moved from his spot near the front door.

"Yes, I heard you. I was just..." *delaying the inevitable.*

Exhaustion weighs me down. I released a lot of emotional baggage today, and my body was used as Thorne's ultimate pleasure toy. I have the almost irresistible urge to go upstairs, curl up in bed, and wake up with retrograde amnesia.

I trudge through the short hallway showcasing Malcolm's nineteenth-century collection to the cracked-open door.

"Hello?" I push the cherrywood open further.

"Come in, Ember." Malcolm reclines in a leather wingback chair near a crackling fireplace. I assume the fire is for ambiance. Unlike all the other areas I've encountered in the manor, the drawing room is dark, save for the fire.

"What's going on?" I ask as I perch on the wingback across from him. The chair is made up of maroon leather stretched to its limit. My tailbone lands on it uncomfortably.

He turns his head away from the fireplace. Half his face turns into shadow. The other is cast in a soft glow, his eye glittering with tiny, reflected flames. "Why would you ask something like that?"

I lick my lips. Fold my hands on my lap. "Nothing. Never mind."

After the day I've had, I wouldn't be surprised if I'm reading too much into things. Maybe this evening is the night Malcolm likes to test for wonky light bulbs that need replacing in his house. I don't know him well enough to question it.

"The school called me today."

I nod, unsurprised.

"You never skip class, Ember. Not from your Boston school and not from Winthorpe since you've attended."

I cross my legs at the ankles, keeping silent. I swear one of the shadows behind him moves. Closer inspection proves it must be the fire dancing over the bookshelf. I chastise myself for being a wimp.

"Do you care to tell me where you were?"

"With Aiko."

"Mm." Malcolm lifts his drink from his side table. The crystal tumbler shines between us. "You're choosing to speak in half-truths, then."

"I was with her, Malcolm, I promise."

"I've noted as much, considering there aren't many cherry red Volkswagon Beetles tearing out of my driveway while the moon is out. What else?"

"Okay. I'm—overwhelmed. I thought taking a day off from the pressure of Winthorpe would be good for me."

Lame, but it's all I've got.

Malcolm's chest deflates. "That's my fault. I've put too much on your shoulders, demanding you keep to your Societal duties and maintain an impeccable academic record. I've spoken to my ... source." Malcolm shifts forward, his incredibly blue eyes landing on mine. "We've agreed I've asked too much of you. I've grown desperate. So much time has passed since I—chose—to work for them, and nothing's come of it."

As he moves, the firelight caresses more of his features. His eyes are overly bright, spearing right into me, demanding I pay attention. But to what?

"I've been thinking about that." My folded hands tighten their hold on each other. While the fire shines on Malcolm, the shadows close in on me. Warning skitters across my shoulders. "Is that why you brought me to Raven's Bluff? To help you?"

"No." Malcolm's voice grows hoarse. "I swear to you, no. I brought you into my life to get to know you. I was devastated to learn I'd lost almost eighteen years with you."

I shake my head. "That doesn't make sense. You

haven't stuck around long enough to sit down for more than a few dinners with me. I've grown closer to Dash than I have with you. If you really wanted to know your daughter, you would've *stayed*, Malcolm."

"You don't—" He pauses. Scrubs a hand over his face. Sets his tumbler down. "No, you *can't* understand. This is my fault."

"You've been beating yourself up for decades. I've felt sorry for you for most of it, but not for this. I've needed someone, Malcolm. To belong. To be part of a family. To understand where I come from. I ..." To my horror, tears threaten. "I feel like I'm swimming in dark waters, and I've lost where the shore is. I can't swim home."

"Sweetheart." Malcolm lurches forward in his seat, but something stops him short of reaching for me. "I'm so sorry for the hurt I've caused you. For what I've involved you in. You don't have to do this anymore."

I whisper, "What?"

"I can't keep living this double life. I need to regain control, and the only way I can do that is if I shed one of them."

"Malcolm, what are you saying?"

Malcolm's expression sags. "He's removed all the best parts of me already. The last I have to cling to is you, and I'll be damned if he gets it. This is what I'm trying to tell you, Ember. I'm offering Damion a trade. Me in place of you."

"Nope." I stand, and though I only reach his chin, I

feel stronger on my feet. "I refuse to let you do this. We're so close, Malcolm." I suck in a breath, reaching for bravery. "I wasn't going to tell you this, but—god, we're both putting ourselves in ridiculous situations trying to protect each other. Tonight, I—"

A voice comes out of the shadows. "Yes, do tell us what you were up to tonight, Ember."

The fire in my belly turns to ice.

I look at Malcolm in hopes that his reaction will tell me which Briar it is. His sallow expression confirms my greatest fear.

As soon as Damion melts out of the darkness, Malcolm spears forward.

The backs of my thighs hit my chair.

"He's here for you," Malcolm whispers harshly. "Go. Now."

"What—? Malcolm—?"

Damion drags Malcolm back to his chair, pressing the back of his head into the hard leather and holds a knife to his throat.

"*Run!*" Malcolm shouts.

There's sacrifice, and there's self-preservation. Refusing to leave Malcolm's side would only put both of us in danger. The two compete in my mind for a single nanosecond before I'm sprinting for the door.

"Dash!" I scream.

"He's otherwise indisposed." Damion chuckles behind me.

I throw open the drawing room door and rush through.

"Go ahead and try to run, girl," Damion calls. His laughter echoes into the hall, invading the spaces between my harsh breaths.

I try for the front door first—of course I fucking do. No amount of pushing and shoving opens it. A muffled voice comes from the outside, halting my frantic twists of the doorknobs.

"You're barricaded in. A Virtue stands at every possible exit, Cum Bucket."

"Aurora! Don't do this!" I cry, pounding against the wood.

"It's already done. Welcome to your next challenge. I doubt you'll survive this one."

Cursing Aurora, I push off the door and run for the atrium. It's all glass. I can break one of the panels with a garden chair.

My shoes skid on the floors as I lurch around the staircase and haul ass to Malcolm's sanctuary. As I sprint, I'm hoping it'll become mine, too.

I slide to a halt at the atrium's entrance. Spotlights beam onto the rosebushes, their leaves a garish green in the artificial light. Worse, the outside's halogen lights are turned on, too, illuminating a row of gold and black cloaks on all three sides of the windowed atrium.

My heart hammers. The tips of my fingers pulse. My throat closes up.

One particular asshole raises his hand and waves through the frosty glass.

"Shit," I croak and do an about-face back into the manor.

I run for the stairs, banging into one of Malcolm's life-size knights and sending the armor clattering across the ground.

Shitshitshit.

If there are Society members outside, there must be some on the inside, too. Damion can't be the only one.

My arm stings from where it smacked into the pointy end of the Medieval knight's spear. I clamp a hand around it as I pick up my steps. And—

—it hits me. Why all the lights are on.

Damion's ensured I have no place to hide.

CHAPTER 23

EMBER

The secret passageways.

Those cobwebbed, crumbled remains of a nineteenth-century underground society's creepy invention drive me to the top of the stairs, panting.

I know there's one close by. Thorne used it to get into my bedroom the other night. And if I can't find that one, I'll use what Zeke and I crawled through to get to Thorne's Halloween party.

It's easier to focus on my options rather than what Malcolm is going through downstairs.

Don't make his sacrifice be in vain.

With hardened resolve, I push off the banister and head deeper into the second-floor hallways.

A flicker of movement at the other end of the corridor snaps my chin up. With every crevice in Malcolm's mansion so glaringly illuminating, I quickly spot Savannah making her way toward me.

Her gold robe flows behind her, blond hair cascading in waves down both sides of her chest. The robe parts at the collar, her body enhanced with a tight, bloodred dress matching her lipsticked mouth.

Something glints in her hand.

"Don't make this so easy, Ember."

I don't dawdle enough to see what she has before I dive into the nearest room and slam the door, twisting the brass lock.

Spinning around, my breaths aching inside my lungs, I take stock of where I've landed.

It's a guest room, one I've never wandered into. Dust immediately coats my nostrils, and I sneeze.

The doorknob rattles behind me.

"Ember? Are you in there?" Savannah follows up her obvious question with dulled laughter.

My eyes snap back to the door. I don't know if they've scored the master key from Dash, but if I were them, that's one of the first things I'd do—other than turning on all of the fucking lights. I have to find a place to hide. Now.

I do another sweep of the room. Blue walls, white lace bedding and canopy, bay window with a reading seat—I can't be forced to hide under the bed. I absolutely *cannot*. I may not have the best odds of outwitting a secret society, but I certainly won't be their sitting duck.

An armoire catches my attention. It's huge, one of those incredibly old ones used instead of closets. It's not any better than crawling under the bed.

I lift the large rug positioned underneath the wooden bedframe, praying for a trapdoor. There's none. That would be too easy, of course.

Swallowing a cry of despair, I honestly debate jumping out of the window.

But no, I won't give them the satisfaction of handing them a dead Ember, either.

I go back to the window. Narrow my eyes.

Could I ... get to the roof that way?

I have to try.

After throwing one last look over my shoulder, I press my hands to the cold glass panels, searching for a give. My eyes dart to the ledge, noticing an iron circular lever in the corner.

"Oh ... fuck." I give it a twist. It won't budge.

"Ember? You doing okay in there?" Savannah trills.

I jump up, throwing my entire weight into unsticking this old, rusted window crank.

I'm fully committed to getting this window open, but my ears are attuned to all other options. I hear a scuffle on the other side of the door. Muffled voices. Then Savannah's squeal of glee.

"Not to worry if you're stuck. I have a key," she calls.

Shit, I was right. They scoured Dash's room—or Dash —and came up with the master key. Someone must've just passed it to her. Otherwise, she would've used it to catch me as soon as I trapped myself in here.

And that someone other than Damion and Savannah are in the house.

How many Society members got in?

No time to ponder. I shimmy the handle back and forth, gritting my teeth. I'll force it to move with my mind if I have to.

There's a *snick* of a lock drawing back. The doorknob turns under Savannah's hand.

I give one last motherfucker of a shove, resigned that I'll either break it or get it unstuck. I have no other choice.

The black handle gives under both my hands. I don't celebrate, immediately spinning it until there's a wide enough crack for me to slip through right as a flash of red enters my periphery.

I can only go by memory when I swing a leg over the ledge, the icy stone sinking through my uniform with chilling speed.

Savannah's gaze leaps around the room before landing on me. Her eyes widen at the same time mine do.

She dives forward.

I scurry all the way out of the bay window, skirting the edge and thanking the founders for their dedicated detail in the stonework.

A gargoyle's on my left, sitting on a column etched into the house. I step on his head, dig my fingers into the old stone, and climb.

Savannah's manicured hand sweeps out, clawing for my ankle. I kick at it as she blindly tries to grab on.

She could climb out after me. I keep that in mind as I scale Weatherby Manor, my fingers already stiffening with cold. Savannah's head pops out next.

She finds me, her gaze drifting up as she tracks where I'm going, and smiles. "What are you doing out here, Ember? Are you going to the roof to wait for your helicopter?" She laughs.

I ignore her, turning my face forward and finding purchase to move up and away from her.

"Sorry to say, this isn't a Bond film," she continues.

I grunt, "I don't care where I end up, as long as it's away from you."

"Why are you running?" she asks. "You could just stay and talk."

"We've done enough talking, don't you think?"

I take some hard breaths, amping myself up to take my foot off the gargoyle's head and position myself even farther away from the ground. My aim is to jump to the domed turret on top of the windows I'd just climbed out of. If I can do that, I can shuffle over to the main roof and get as far away from Savannah as possible.

I can do this. My fingers turn into claws. One of my nails breaks on the chipped stone.

"What makes you think we're here to hurt you?" Savannah's voice changes to a calm, placating tone.

"Damion and I only want to sort through Malcolm's and your plan to hurt us."

"There is no plan," I lie, then take the leap.

My right hand grips where I intended on the tower's cornice. My left slips on a clump of snow I didn't initially see. Yelping, I dangle one-handed before I swing my left arm up and grip the cornice hard. My shoe tips squeal against the windowpane as I frantically attempt to climb up.

"I trusted you, Ember. You were supposed to be my secret friend."

Savannah has the perfect opportunity to grab my ankle and send me plummeting to the frozen ground below. For reasons I've yet to figure out, she doesn't.

"Ember, don't be stupid. Come back in here."

Even if I wanted to... I stare down wryly, then back up to the roof. I'm pretty fucking stuck both ways. My hands start to shake, and despite the freezing weather, sweat prickles against my hairline.

I use my elbows to get a small side-to-side going, hoping to swing myself to the angled part of the roof. On the third swing, my right foot scrapes against the slate, then slides off. *Dammit.*

"You'll kill yourself out there, and for what?" Savannah perches her elbows on the window ledge, resting her head in her hands as she watches me. "All Damion and I want to do is ensure your silence. Not by murdering you, obviously, but your father's admitted some concerning things. You need to prove you're on our side—on the Virtues' side. Where's your loyalty, Ember? I don't think you'll find it between that gargoyle's ears."

My finger joints are screaming. I can't hold on for much longer.

"And how was I supposed to prove my loyalty? By watching Damion kill Malcolm and then giving a thumbs-up afterward?"

"Hm." Savannah pretends to think that over. "It was a possibility until Malcolm offered Damion his business in exchange for not harming you."

"What?" I stare past my struggling arm at Savannah.

Savannah sighs, her exhale coming out as a white puff of air. "Can you stop your gymnastics, please, and come back inside? Let's chat over coffee or something. It's fucking cold out here."

I push my brows in. "Sorry. No can do." And try another swing.

This time, my first foot makes it, and after a grunt and a ton of core strength, my other foot makes it, too. I push until I'm steady, then move my hands to the shingles in a quick transfer, slipping slightly but keeping myself on the angled roof.

"Ember!" Savannah cries, slamming her hands on the ledge. "Get the *fuck* back here! I'm not climbing up after you in a stupid suicide mission!"

I crawl like a bug over the multi-gabled roof, all the while searching for a place to jump or crawl through...

Yeah, I really didn't think this part through. Weatherby Manor is infested with Society members. Anywhere I go, they'll catch me. While it's true I've found the one place where they won't follow, I can't stay up here all night. I'll freeze to death in my school uniform.

My breaths are clouds of smoke. I can't feel my cheeks and my hands and feet are basically robotics I'm controlling with my mind. I have to figure out my next move and fast.

I shuffle to the other side of the house, my head constantly swiveling. Once I'm high enough, I pull myself to the top and belly flop on the uppermost roof ridge until I can swing a leg over and straddle it.

One of Weatherby Manor's gable tops looms in front of me, featuring a compass that I never realized housed an iron raven in the middle.

God, I wish that raven could help me figure out the safest direction *down* from here.

Cursing, I lock my hands on the back of my neck and look up to the starry sky, parsing through my next steps. I don't have my phone—it's in the messenger bag I left in the foyer. I've escaped Damion and Savannah for now, but Malcolm's still with them. They could be hurting him. Other members could be enduring their own challenge, with Malcolm as the target.

Each possible threat becomes worse than the last. My heart rate ratchets up, impervious to the winter air.

I'm about as useful to Malcolm as one of his stone

gargoyles up here. I have to get down, regardless of who catches me. I have to be with Malcolm. There's still time for Aiko's and my plan to succeed—the FBI could be planning a raid on Damion's house as I sit here, wafting in the wind.

"Ember!" someone whisper-shouts behind me.

My hands smack against the roof's ridge. I twist my torso to the sound of my name as much as I can.

"Come quickly."

I squint into the surrounding trees, seeing nothing until a flash of light snaps my attention to a cloaked figure between the branches.

The hood is up, but I can tell it's black. A Noble, holding up their flashlight app high enough to highlight the outfit, but not their features.

So much for thinking I won't be followed up here. Savannah's reluctance made me too confident. I start shimmying away on a hiss, basically riding a roof horse to get away from him.

"Wrong way, little pretty."

Thorne. If I thought my heartbeats were erratic before, now they're breaking through my ribs.

"Get over here before another member figures out tree climbing as a way to retrieve you."

"How do I know *you're* not retrieving me?" I whisper-shout back.

"It's pretty obvious that's exactly what I'm doing."

"Then I'll be just fine. See you."

"Ember."

"*What*? Can't you see I'm busy here?"

"If you'll stop humping the roof for one moment, you'll realize I'm here to help you."

"I'll ... I'll get down when they all get tired of waiting for me and leave."

"That'll be a while."

"S-see if I care."

"You're cold. Freezing. I have a cloak here for you. Stop being like a stubborn cat stuck on a roof and come over here."

"They're trying to hurt me, Thorne! And your dad has Malcolm by the throat!"

Thorne answers quietly. "I know."

"How can I trust you?"

I hear his deep inhale before he speaks. "If you're willing to have my cock in your ass, I'm fairly certain I own some of your trust. Now get. Over. Here. I'm running out of time before somebody notices I'm missing."

I crick my neck, trying to stare him down through the branches. "Why are you helping me?"

"You're really doing this right now."

It's not necessary to see him to know his eyes have turned to the same flat color as the slate on this roof.

"I have half a mind to climb down and leave your ass for the vultures, Ember. Eventually, some dipshit desperate enough to impress my father will figure out how to get to you." He pauses. "With force."

My lips peel back from my chattering teeth. "*Fine.*"

"Good girl."

Shivers unrelated to the cold spread across the back of my neck and curve around my nipples. Even now, his verbal approval is full of sexual promise.

I shimmy across the ridge backward, getting closer to him.

"Just FYI, you're giving me an excellent view of your ass."

"Shut *up,* Thorne."

My hands have gone from cold, to numb, to frost-bitten hot. That's not good. I press down harder, scooting back until I hit the edge, wobbling at the sudden air against my butt.

Thorne's palm presses into my back, steadying me. "Good. Turn around carefully."

I swing one leg over, buttressing myself with both hands gripping the ridge as I turn. Once I've done a full one-eighty, I swing the same leg over again.

Facing Thorne.

His eyes have the sheen of a predator under the moonlight, peering at me through his cover in the trees.

That same predator holds out a hand for his prey. "See that branch closest to your foot?"

I look down to where he's directed. "Yes."

"It's too thin to bear your weight. You're going to have to do a little jump, but I'll catch you."

I gulp. We're at least three stories from the ground. "If you miss..."

"I won't."

There aren't many other options other than to hang onto Thorne for dear life. I inwardly groan. *God, when did this happen?*

His hand hovers in the air between us. "Make a choice, little pretty."

With gritted teeth, scrunched shut eyes, and a prayer to whatever's out there, I clasp Thorne's hand and push off the ledge.

His grip is solid and firm. My feet are not.

My shoes slip off the bendy branch and hit air. I swallow back a screech as I dangle from his hand, swinging uselessly between the branches.

Thorne grunts, bowing forward to hold my weight. I look up in full pleading mode. *Don't let me die, please don't let me die...*

His features are tight, tense with effort. Thorne's curved one arm around the trunk, and on a roughened groan, he uses his other to pull me up. Muscles bulge underneath his long sleeve. Veins pop out of the top of his hand.

I cover his hand with both of mine, using my legs to scrabble up the trunk and hopefully lift some of my weight off his straining arm.

Sweat grows between our fingers as we both expend effort. My heart creates a new home in my throat, but I keep my mouth shut despite the overwhelming urge to wail and scream before I plunge to the ground.

"Hang on..." Thorne rasps.

Our eyes lock.

"Thorne. I can't——"

"You can. Don't let go."

"I'm slipping."

My palm slides from his grip.

Panic flashes in his eyes. He pushes himself farther from the trunk.

"No——Thorne, don't. You'll fall, too."

"I'd rather fall with you than watch you die."

A pained gasp escapes my throat, both at his conviction and the realization that he'd rather die with me than without.

Thorne tightens his thighs around the thick branch holding him up and lets go of the trunk.

"Thorne——"

He's operating on pure core strength, bending forward and catching my slippery wrist with his free hand. With a low, determined growl, he pulls me up, inch by inch, until I can finally help out and use my legs to join him on the branch.

Soft velvet hits my cheek as I land against his chest. The soothing scent of salt and forest hits my nose. I inhale it like I've never breathed in before.

"I've got you. You're safe." His gravelly voice brushes against the top of my ear as he throws an extra cloak over my shoulders, thick with expensive fabric and as dark as the night surrounding us. A Noble's cloak. Thorne pulls the hood over my hair.

Closing my eyes, I murmur, "That was…"

"One of the dumber things you've done."

Aaaand he's back. "It was either this or submit to whatever Savannah has planned for me." I lift off his chest. "I wasn't about to give her the pleasure."

He cocks a brow. "Pleasure's all mine, then."

Thorne's hands were wrapped around me, but slowly, he pulls them back, his thumb and fingers grazing along the bottoms of my breasts.

My belly clenches at the contact. He smiles under his hood as he feels my muscles tighten. Using those blasted thumbs, he flicks both against my pebbled nipples.

I'm cold. I'm scared. I'm insanely turned on.

I scowl. Glance below us. "How are we supposed to get down?"

"We have to wait. We're up high enough that no one will see us unless someone decides to stand at the base of this oak and look up."

"What are the chances of that?"

"Slim, I'd say. The alumni aren't here. Just the current Winthorpe members of the Society, and their efforts won't extend beyond scouring your house."

"But—Malcolm."

Thorne nods. "He's with my father. There's nothing you can do right now to stop it."

"I have to. If Damion's discovered what Malcolm's done, he'll kill him."

Thorne's features soften. He lifts a hand and brushes his fingers across my cheek. "Sweet pretty, you're assuming my father never knew in the first place."

I struggle to speak through numbed lips. "Your father knew? This whole time?"

"Of course. Why do you think Father brought you here? To reunite long-lost father and daughter?"

"Obviously, I didn't think that. Your dad always has ulterior motives. Malcolm was so careful. He only confessed to me because he had to."

"No, because he was desperate and was forced to involve you." Thorne's features grow dark as he retreats into his Noble hood. "He couldn't perform his suicide mission alone. Therefore, he asked you to do his dirty work. Tell me, have you gotten the information you needed? Is that why my father's attempting to grab you and Malcolm?"

I stare at him closer. "You don't know why they're here?"

Thorne shakes his head. "Only that Malcolm's due for punishment. With all the challenges that Malcolm and my father used to compete with each other, it came as no surprise. What is disturbing is that my father wants you involved in the punishment, too."

I press my lips together. We're straddling a tree branch, and I'm still holding his arms. If I tell Thorne, if I explain to him why Savannah and Damion want a piece of my flesh so badly … we may both topple out of this tree out of the sheer force of Thorne's rage.

Looking into his face, so determined to save me and ignorant of the truth, I don't think he has any idea of the lengths Savannah and Damion have gone to to keep their affair a secret.

"Didn't you say you'll be missed?" I aim to change the subject while we're stuck in this tree together.

"Soon. Now that they can't find you, Father will take Malcolm to the catacombs, and the members will follow."

"What kind of punishment do they have planned for him?" My fingers tighten around Thorne's biceps. It's like digging into rock. "Maybe I should've let them take me. I have to be there. Malcolm's sacrificed himself for me. I can't let him do this."

"I thought you didn't give a fuck what happened to Malcolm?"

"Circumstances change." I glare at him. "You should know that better than anyone. You helped me, didn't you? The girl you were determined to fuck and then ditch because it was so terrible? You even went back for seconds, and it still sucked. What are you doing in a tree saving my life?"

Thorne growls, "Like you, I have trouble ignoring my stupid side."

I smack him in the shoulder. "Oh, so now you think I'm stupid as well as unfuckable."

"I have never, not once, said you were a bad fuck." Thorne's voice lowers to a warning decibel. "You are the opposite. Too irresistible. The fact that you've solely experienced my dick, that you've stretched to fit only me ... I can't stop thinking of the feel of you, Ember. I want to re-experience every opening you have because those are places only I've had the pleasure of discovering." In a sudden move, he hooks my jaw, keeping my growing desire in one place. "As the first explorer, I should have you cry out my name every time you experience an orgasm from here on out."

"Even when coming to my rescue, you're a cocky asshole."

He shows his teeth. "Absolutely."

Heat builds in my center, warming all the spots that shouldn't be activated while hiding. We need to be focused on what's below us, not what is between us. With the way he's straddling the tree, Thorne's erection tents out like a branch of its own. I can't stop staring at it, even as he hangs on to my neck to keep me still.

I garble out, "Is there another section of this tree I can wait on?"

Thorne's eyes grow hooded. "Why would you want to leave when I have a great way to pass the time while we wait?"

My mouth falls open. "No way. Don't you dare. Not here."

"Why not?" He releases my neck, cupping my pussy

through my underwear instead. "You're wearing the robe. Part of maintaining a membership in the Virtues is rising to every challenge."

"This isn't a—"

"Now it fucking is." He pushes his thumb between my folds, the thin fabric of my underwear doing nothing, absolutely *nothing*, to prevent entry.

My hips push forward of my own volition.

"We can't," I say in a ragged whisper. My body's well on the way to betraying my words. "I have to … we have to … Malcolm…" My head tips back on a quiet groan when Thorne pushes my panties aside and circles my clit.

The combination of his freezing fingers and my wet warmth is magical. My hips match his circles, the wetness transforming into a chill as soon as he spreads it around.

I bite my lip. My hands move to his shoulders, nails digging into his cloak.

"Ride me," he coaxes.

I tilt enough for two of his fingers to slip in, forming a U that I would bounce up and down on if I could.

With our position, I can only rock, but it's enough. My movements turn furtive, bucking against his fingers hitting my G-spot and his thumb pressing into my clit. The pleasurable sensation bursts from my center and weakens my thighs, turning my stomach into jelly and my nipples into aching pebbles.

Thorne pulls away.

"W-What?" It takes a couple of hard breaths and slow blinks before I can say even that.

"Take me in your hand," he orders. "You're going to make me come, then you're going to take my cum and spread it all over your pussy while I watch you get yourself off."

"E-Excuse me?"

"Do that, and I'll help you down from your particularly sexy perch."

I realize my thighs are pretty much spread wide open on the thick branch, showing off my white cotton underwear. It's probably transparent by now.

I'm forced to clarify, "We are in a dire situation, and all you can think about is me jerking you off?"

Thorne shrugs. "Fear and danger are huge turn-ons for me. Or haven't you figured that out?"

"Oh, I have." *Because they're huge turn-ons for me, too.*

I work my jaw. Glance at his erection. Lick my lips.

He lifts his lips into a mischievous grin. "Or blow me."

Dammit, I want to.

It's like the fear of being caught and the very real risk of dying once I face Damion act like a conduit to the best sex of my life. While stuck in a tree.

How I got here, I'll never be able to explain, but what I want to do with my time while I'm trapped...

Thorne grips the hood at the back of my head, guiding me down. Our cloaks camouflage us enough that we could get away with this.

He unbuttons his pants as I bend, his dick spearing out, hot and throbbing despite the cold air rushing against it. The tip shines in the moonlight, his desperate need leaking out where his words fail him.

I part my lips and take him in.

Thorne's rough moan and tightened fingers on the back of my head encourage me to do deeper. I suck him all the way back until he hits the back of my throat. Saliva collects in my cheeks at the intrusion and drips down his sides. I gag but fight the reflex until I fit him all the way in.

Thorne leans back on both his hands, his torso jerking up before he forces it down like he's trying very hard not to plow into my throat.

I pop him out of my mouth, swirling my tongue along his tip and collecting the precum. When I'm confident in my stability, I reach down and cup his balls, massaging them with cold fingers in hopes he experiences the same hot and cold sensations he gave to me.

Thorne curses under his breath. His thighs start to shake.

I'm getting good at this.

I curve my spine until I'm able to lick and nibble on his balls while stroking his dick. Thorne's short, pained grunts are all the incentive I need to suck harder, first one ball, then the next. When they tighten against my tongue, I bob up and swallow his dick, his veins pulsing against my tongue.

At the first spurt, I reel back, collecting his cum

exactly as he demanded and painting it on my exposed pussy while it is still warm.

It's both soothing and sexy to lean back and use his cum as lube while he watches, his Noble cloak billowing off my shoulders and tickling my ankles. Being dirty with him in public, submitting to his orders, always at odd times and in unfathomable situations, I can't resist.

Why should I? It feels good. *Thorne* makes me feel good.

My eyes are closed. I can't see his reaction as I bring myself up to his level and dampen this branch the way he has. There's no need to. Thorne's in my head. His face is constantly on my mind, exquisitely unmatched and one I'm obsessed with. He can be naked in my imagination or in reality—both will stun me into orgasm.

I practically hew my lips shut as I reach my breaking point, my own fingers spearing in and out of myself and my thumb doing the work I wish Thorne would.

The comedown nearly tips me out of the tree. My legs are boneless, my chest filled with prickly static. Thorne has to steady me with both hands at my clavicle, his fingers kneading the back of my neck. "Good girl."

I hum in pleasure as goose bumps form under his ministrations.

"I'd bend you back and fuck you right now, but unfortunately, we have to leave."

His words bring me back to real life too hard and too

fast. "I can't believe I just did that. It's too easy to escape with you. With everything going on—"

"You deserve pleasure, Ember." His quiet voice becomes even softer. "It's me who doesn't deserve the pleasure of you."

I meet his eyes. "I choose what I want. And I want you."

Thorne lowers his brows, creating crescent shadows over his eyes. "That's your stupid side coming out agai—"

I don't give him time to humiliate me out of my decision to keep him.

I jump forward and catch his lips with mine.

THORNE

I don't kiss.

It's been a rule of mine since I can remember. The very idea of exposing a softer side of myself is unappealing and pathetic. I'll happily ram my cock into a girl's mouth. I'll eagerly put mine on a pussy. But mouth-to-mouth contact and the brushing of tongues—that muscle we use to speak, so small compared to the rest that comprise our bodies yet so crucial at exposing our vulnerabilities—yeah, no thank you. No girl needs to come close to that.

Until Ember.

I should be revolted by her wet, sticky touch. She pulled free from my dick with drool and cum collecting on her chin and didn't bother to wipe before capturing my mouth.

I should push her away, grab her by the neck and

brutalize her with insults so venomous she'll never dare to kiss me again.

I don't.

I'm taken aback by her softness. She's swollen from me, all that sucking and swallowing, but it adds an unexpected plushness as she parts my lips with her tongue and explores my most protected area. Her tongue does an inquisitive dance against mine, enough for me to unfurl and let the velvet of her take over.

Ember angles her head, and I grant the deeper access by cupping the back of her neck and pressing her closer.

Her teeth dig into my lips. I press harder, wanting the hurt, the pain, the blood to come from too much roughness.

Ember doesn't allow it. She pushes against my grip, keeping her touch soft, drawing her tongue in and butterfly kissing my lips.

"What are you doing?" I ask roughly.

"Touching you," she murmurs.

"That's not—this isn't the way it should be."

Her arms come up, wrapping around my shoulders and neck. "This is what caring about someone looks like, Thorne."

My hand falls from her back, slackened by her confidence.

Ember drifts across my senses, her smell, touch, heat, and sureness enveloping my comfort zone in a way I wasn't prepared for.

I want to push her off. I can't.

It feels too damned good.

"Ember," I demand in a pained voice. "I'm not the guy for you."

I am. I fucking am. She's mine, and she will forever taste me, suck me, fuck me, and no one else.

I quiet my inner voice by forcing it to the back of my head. "You need someone better than a guy who wants to name all your fuck holes after him."

She chuckles against my lips. Even her breath is sweet. "Not if I get to name your dick in my honor."

"You are not calling my cock Ember."

"I was thinking *little pretty*."

Laughter threatens to peel out of my throat. I staunch it with a scowl and push Ember off. "I feel sorry for you, wanting someone who treats you the way I do."

Ember looks down at the ground, assessing our height and appearing unaffected by my brush-off. I sit back, wary of the type of Ember who can withstand my venom and come out smiling.

She'd be unstoppable.

"How did you get up here in the first place?" she asks.

"I'd ask you the same thing."

"I got onto the roof by nearly killing myself. How'd you do it?"

"By never looking down."

She lifts her head, her eyes a little wider than before. "Right."

I swing my leg over. "Let's go."

Without waiting for her response, I find a lower branch and twist until I'm standing on it while pressing my hands against the trunk. "Follow me. You'll be fine. And—"

"Don't look down. Got it."

Ember adjusts her skirt and pulls my spare cloak tighter around her shoulders. After ensuring the hood covers her beacon of hair color, she scoots toward me, the branch in a death grip.

I'm not one for encouragement, but I remain where I am, unwilling to move until I'm sure she's safely off the first branch.

After a few minutes of quiet, careful maneuvering down the tree, Ember gains more confidence, descending smoothly as I lead the way down.

At each step, I scan the area for straggling members. Every window of Winthorpe manor shines a cascade of light across the lawn, giving me a broad view of the flat lawn and surrounding trees. All is quiet. I wasn't lying to Ember when I stated my father would be taking Malcolm to the catacombs as quick as possible, relying on Savannah to secure Ember. Father's flock would've followed him.

The fact that Sav has become Father's new pup is disquieting, to say the least. It's one of many mysteries I'm committed to unraveling as my time at Winthorpe ends, and I become part of the full-fledged peerage of the Nobles.

I chance a look at Ember as she climbs above me, that gorgeous ass of hers in my view again every time the wind hits just right and billows my robe around her, but I'm not thinking of spreading those cheeks right now. Maybe later. What I am thinking of has much worse consequences.

I want to use her mind, not just her body. I want her to ... help me.

Fuck, that can only end badly.

"Come on." I land on my feet and reach up to help her down the rest of the way.

Ember settles in beside me, looking up one more time before we start walking. "I can't believe we were all the way up there."

"I only wish we could stay there," I mutter, leading her around the manor and through the gates.

"Weatherby tree house. I like the sound of it."

I turn back enough to give her a sardonic smile. "Maybe I'll build you one for your birthday."

"That would presume you know when my birthday is."

"June twelfth."

Ember's shoes scrape against the asphalt as she halts. "I'm sorry, but did Thorne Briar just admit to remembering something about me?"

"I remember you," I respond without turning around. "All the time."

That shuts her up. She can't see it as I stride in front of her, but I smile again, this time at my ironic ability to quiet her with kind words rather than vicious insults.

I guess that says as much about me as it does her.

Ember follows me across the road and up the driveway to my house. We're not going in, but we need a car to get to Winthorpe.

"Father has a good headstart on us," I toss over my shoulder, "but he loves his rituals. We should get to Malcolm in time."

"In time for what?"

I ignore the tremble in her voice because that would mean I care. "Malcolm committed the worst sin in the Society. He spoke to outsiders about our existence. Worse, to law enforcement."

"Not the Societies," Ember corrects. "Just Damion. That's all he wanted to expose. Maybe if I got the chance to convince the members the Societies are safe..."

I swivel around, walking backward while I face her. It takes effort to ignore the eagerness on her beautiful, innocent face. "You're as much an outsider as he is. You're Malcolm's daughter, previously unknown, currently untrustworthy."

"I've excelled at every task the Societies' have given me."

"True. But you're new and unpredictable. You don't

have the years of rule and commitment my father has for the Society to believe you over him. So unless you have a piece of info that could trump a traitor, I suggest we come up with another plan."

Ember slows her pace. Something like pain flashes through her expression before she schools it into deliberate blankness.

My vision narrows. I stop my backward motion and stroll forward instead. "Ember? What is it?"

Her throat bobs with a slow swallow.

"If you have something to say, spit it out." My voice cuts like shards of glass, but I can't help it. There's something about her expression that's put me on edge.

She takes a breath. I'm about to throttle her when she finally starts talking.

"I may have some information which will freak you out, but I need you to stay calm. I'm the messenger, okay? Not the enemy."

I arch a brow. It's meant to cue her into continuing, though I suppose looming over her while I do it causes a threat.

Ember tilts her head until she's almost at my eye level. She doesn't shrivel under my stare.

"Promise me, Thorne."

I scoff. "Fine. But it better be good."

She swallows again. "It's worse than good. It's about your father."

"There's nothing you could say that would surprise

me about my father." I plaster on a fake smile. "Are you about to tell me about his hidden drug trade? I'm well aware of it, Ember. He's grooming me to take it over."

She purses her lips. My grin stretches wider. Nailed it. "Rather than waste our time going through the moralities of my father's business, let's fucking move our asses. *Your* father gets the priority this evening."

"It's about Damion and Savannah."

That gives me pause.

Ember flutters her lips on a sharp exhale, then bursts out, "They've been having an affair. That's where she's been all this time—hidden away by Damion while she was—while she was..."

"Don't stop there." My voice comes out deadly quiet.

"—when she was pregnant." After too many seconds without my response, she peers hard at me. "Thorne? She was pregnant with his baby."

"I got that much."

Ember takes a step back. The tight fury lacing my words is finally the thing that makes her shudder.

"I'm sorry," she whispers.

I look at her sharply. "What are you sorry for? Did you fuck my father, too?"

"God no!" She raises her hands, thinks better of surrendering, then jams them against her hips. "I understand this is hard for you to hear, but don't you dare take this out on me."

"Is this your next trick?"

Her hands fall from her sides. "Excuse me?"

"You've had some choice moments where you got the best of me. Is this your grand finale? If so, this is piss-poor compared to your previous attempts. What you're talking to me about is complete garbage."

"Thorne, it's the truth."

"It fucking is *not*."

Yet she stupidly forges on. "Savannah lost the baby. She buried its ashes in her ancestor's mausoleum. At the old cemetery where—"

"I know where the fuck it is."

"Stop swearing at me." She adds, quieter, "And stop looking at me like you want to cut my head off."

I lock my jaw. I'm so tense that my body vibrates under my cloak. I have to release it somehow.

On a thunderous growl, I grab Ember by the shoulders and swing her against the the side of house, my fingers denting her skin. It's not enough, so I press in harder, pushing my face near hers.

Her back smacks against the bricks. Ember cries out with the impact. "Thorne—"

"Spread your legs. Now."

Her eyes shine with petrified uncertainty as she looks up at me, her hood askew. Pieces of white-blond hair hit the moonlight. That's all it takes for me to do it for her.

"Stop," she murmurs rather than ordering.

"You want to talk about my father fucking Sav? How did he do it, huh? Give me the details. Did he hitch one leg up like this?" I release one of her shoulders to hook her by the thigh and force it up, much higher than normal, pulling at the muscle until a spasm of pain crosses her face.

"I don't know the details," she squeaks out. "I don't *want* to know."

But I'm not finished. "Did he rip her panties off? Was she wearing a slutty thong like you?" Grabbing the flimsy elastic, I pull, snapping it in half. The pale pink fabric flutters to our feet.

Her pussy is exposed, shining as much as her eyes.

The sight of her almost sends me reeling, the uncontrollable urge to fuck her first in her pussy, then her ass, then shove my cock in her mouth so all-encompassing, I have to remind myself why I've pushed her up against a wall in the first place.

To fuck my fury out.

I shove three fingers in her up to the knuckle.

She writhes. Bites her lip. Stares at me with internal rage. "Is this what it'll take for you to see the truth? To use me like a punching bag? Fine, Thorne. Do your worst. Like you said, all my holes are yours."

My lips curl. Her capitulation turns me on more than it should. This was meant to punish her for her lies. Not make her wet. Not for my cock to grow so hard, it aches.

"Did he take her pussy first, or do you think it was her mouth?" I'm relentless. "Or perhaps he engaged in ass play first. That's what you've enjoyed the most, isn't it?

Are you next for my father? Is that why he's so fixated on you?"

She shakes her head. "You're bordering on madness, Thorne. Stop this."

I pull my fingers out of her, and they freeze almost instantly, coming from a hot core and into the night air. Using those same sticky fingers, I unbutton my pants, pulling my cock out to enjoy the same hot and cold experience.

"If he wants you next, I'm going to make sure I plug your holes multiple times, causing you to be so used and stained by me, he'll finally understand what's mine."

Ember doesn't flinch at my movements. She meets me head-on, saying, "Is this what happens when you're truly upset about something? Did it take the idea of Savannah sleeping with somebody else—your father—to get to your true emotions like this? You still care for her, don't you?"

Ember couldn't be further from the truth. Sav and I were over a long time ago. After a moment of vengeful reflection, what Ember has confessed rings true. Sav's distance before she went missing. Those strange dinners where she shared prolonged looks with my father. Julie's white-knuckled grip on her spiked drink as she watched my father walk an inebriated Sav to the door because I was left to clean up Julie's vomit.

I don't admit any of this to Ember. I wait for the light to die in her eyes—the realization that Sav brings out the possessiveness in my soul and not her—before I line up my dick and plunge into Ember with a savagery she will never mistake for love.

Because I love her. Sav's face isn't holding my emotions hostage, entangling me in manipulative tentacles of her heart. No, it's Ember who's doing it. The thought of my father playing with her, too. Impregnating her. Locking her away for his pleasure. Making him the only person to talk, fuck, and own her.

No condom. Only hate sheathes my dick.

Ember quickly replaces the images of Sav in that situation, so clearly that all the pictures in my mind turn bloodred. She's *mine. She's mine. SHE'S MINE.*

I punctuate each syllable with forceful thrusts, banging Ember against the wall and burying myself all the way to the hilt. My balls hit the underside of her pussy at each impact. My teeth clench in rage—at my father, at our situation, at his continued attempts to destroy my soul...

"You're hurting me," Ember breathes.

I flick my eyes to hers. "Not enough."

Freeing my other hand from her shoulder, I take her by the throat.

Ember lifts her chin for easier access, keeping her eyes level with mine.

"Tell me to stop," I order.

"No."

"Tell me to *stop*."

"...no." It's getting harder for her to breathe.

"Fucking TELL ME TO STOP."

She responds by wrapping both her hands around my neck and squeezing, crushing my Adam's apple, using a strength I frankly never knew she harbored.

My balls almost explode at the erotic pressure.

"Fuck," I grit out. "Yes."

"I know," she wheezes, and with each of my thrusts, she squeezes harder. I match it until her face turns red—mine likely as well.

She waits until the moment her eyes start to roll to the back of her head before she submits to her orgasm, arching against my dick and digging her thumbs into the underside of my jaw.

I watch the euphoria wash over her expression, feel her spasms against my cock and collect the slippery gush of her on my pubes before I fall, too.

Now we're both stained with the other.

My head falls into the crook of her neck. I breathe hard, my cock still jerking with the remnants of cum.

Pressure hits at my chest, and I realize Ember's pushing me off her.

"So you believe me, then," she says in a flat voice. "About where Savannah was and who she was with."

I let her push me. "Yes."

In truth, the lengths my father is willing to go to dominate both his family and the world shouldn't surprise me.

"What are you going to do?"

I shove my still-hard dick into my briefs and button my pants. That traitorous appendage of mine always wants more of her. "The same thing we were planning to do before you let me rage-fuck you against my house. Track down my father and bring yours home."

"Are you going to confront Damion with what you know?" Ember follows suit and straightens her clothing. We both need showers. Sadly, there's no time to soap her up and bend her over for a third round. "Savannah threatened if I told anyone, she would send the police evidence of what I ... what I did to Zeke."

"Oh, she was, was she? I very much doubt that."

Ember takes a long look at me. "What are you saying?"

"Why give your weapon to somebody else? Or the RBPD, for that matter. They're small-town cops a step above mall rats. Don't let that threat stop you from your plans."

"My plans?"

"Cute, how you're playing dumb as if I haven't figured out your little investigator skills."

She frowns and folds her arms. "I don't know what you're talking about."

Amusement bubbles in my throat, but I shove it down. "If you're going to narc on my father to the FBI, you need to do a lot better than recruit Aiko and Zeke."

Her frown falters. "And what do you suggest, other

than taking out my frustration by sticking my dick in you?"

I don't swallow back the amusement this time. What a nice picture. "You need me."

That startles her. "But you—you're a Briar. Damion's heir. You would never go against him."

"Have more faith." I *tsk*. "And try to believe I've been waiting a long time for my chance to usurp my father."

Ember pushes off the wall, peering closer at me. "Say I do believe you. What are you suggesting?"

"Stealing all his cryptocurrency."

Ember's mouth falls open. Then shuts. She squints suspiciously. "Why are you telling me this?"

"For the same reasons you told me about Sav and my father, I suppose. We need each other."

"I didn't clue you in because I need you, Thorne. I just didn't feel right holding on to that information, considering that we..."

"We what?"

She seems to second-guess what she was about to say, choosing instead to mutter, "Considering that we fool around."

"Is that what you're calling it?"

Ember changes the subject. "Tell me more about the cryptocurrency."

I shrug, then motion to my car, hunched in the snow. I press the fob, and the headlights flash. "These days, you don't traffic drugs on foot. You use the internet."

"I know that much."

I toss her an impatient frown. "My father does things very traditionally. It took a long time to convince him to move the profits to crypto. Eventually, he caved. I planted the seed, and his advisors confirmed it would be advantageous to move the funds to a platform with no institution behind it. No monitoring by a higher power, like banks or the government."

Ember nods. "I figured crypto would be his preference."

"My father isn't a stupid man. No oversight means more security. He's put in place four verification methods to access or transfer the funds. The first is that he's taken the bulk of it offline and into cold storage."

I don't elaborate on the definition. With Ember's proficiency in computers, she already knows that 'cold storage' means moving all the crypto offline to a physical USB or other tower you can pocket, preventing any online hacking.

Ember thinks this over as we round the car. "Let me guess, the other methods would be something to do with multiple authorizations or a two-step verification when someone wants to transfer funds. Oh, or a transaction limit before a warning is sent to his phone."

I look at her over the car's roof, impressed. "Try all three."

"Are you one of the parties able to authorize access?"

"Hell no."

Ember slides into the passenger seat and slams the door. "Figures."

"I didn't know it, but it turns out I've been waiting for someone like you to help me break through his firewalls."

"And why would I help you?"

"Because you want to take him for all he's worth as much as I do." I turn on the car's engine but twist to face her. "That will hurt him more than any investigation by the FBI would. You and I both know they wouldn't find anything on him."

"How would taking his money stop the drugs? Couldn't he just acquire more bitcoin?"

I flip the car into reverse and back out of the driveway. "He has to pay a lot of people for their time, and to do that his bitcoin goes through a complicated laundering process. Dangerous men wait on the other end of that crypto ATM. If he doesn't have the funds to pay them what they're owed, there's no reason for them to keep doing business with him. And, they're known for retribution."

Ember goes quiet for a moment. "You'd do that to your own father?"

"You're trying to save a father you don't know, and I'm trying to stop one that I know all too well. Trust me on this. My father won't be satisfied ruining or hurting Malcolm tonight. He'll come after you. Then your adoptive parents. And if what Sav told you is true and not the result of mental trauma from being kidnapped..."

Ember gives me the side-eye.

"...then she's just made herself a liability. I don't know why he allowed her to return home after losing the baby or how she was able to obtain the ashes, but suffice it to say, Father never does anything half-assed."

"I agree. Involving the FBI isn't a bad idea, though."

I stop at the first red light, making sure to face her and drill the seriousness into her head. "If you do, you'll ruin everything I've worked toward. I've been collecting information on the location of his laundered profits for years, Ember. *Years* without raising suspicion. If you clue the FBI in, if you tee them up to raid Briar Industries and our home, I'll lose it all. Father will bury every cent he has." It's then I unleash the most powerful weapon I have against her. "It won't just be my father you'll ruin. It'll be me, too."

Her determined expression wavers, just as I thought it would when I brought her feelings for me into the mix. I'm damned for it, but I'll happily take up residence in Hell over being defeated by my father.

Ember stares straight ahead. "Fine," she whispers. "I'll help you."

"Good girl."

My low approval runs a tremor along her shoulders, as I knew it would. I've come to understand Ember all too well. I can only hope the same isn't true for her because my manipulations won't stop now that she's confessed.

Ember openly shared a powerful secret she harbored

about my family when she could've used it to destroy me. That move alone tells me how deeply invested she's become. In me.

If I were a better man, this would be the perfect moment to reveal the powerful secret that *I* know about her family—about her biological mother and the circumstances of her conception.

I won't, however. If I do, I'm admitting my feelings for her. I'm putting myself in the same position she is: vulnerable to another. Cared about and protected.

I'm no protector.

I'm a predator, and poor Ember keeps reaching out her hand.

One of these days, I'm going to bite it clean off.

CHAPTER 25

EMBER

I'm stunned into silence as we drive to Winthorpe Academy.

Thorne wants to take down Damion Briar as much as I do. In a way that isn't altogether legal, but our interests are aligned nonetheless.

Never thought I'd see the day.

"You're thinking hard." His voice comes out of the darkened interior. Our trip doesn't involve many street-lights, and few cars are on the road. In essence, it's just him and me, traveling through a ghost town coated with winter mist.

"I'm still coming to terms with your plans. Sorting it through my head."

"Are my revelations really all that surprising?"

I hesitate. "I don't know. I always thought you were sort of..."

"What?"

"Evil."

A raspy laugh follows.

"Like him," I add. "I thought you were going to be just like him."

Thorne shakes his head. It's a ripple of movement. His hair and cloak are the same color as the night. Shadows layering over shadows.

"You thought I'd step into the role of a secret society leader, use my childhood town as a drug lab, and kidnap myself a wife?" A slice of his profile shines in the moonlight as he turns. "Why are you fucking me, then?"

Because I'm obsessed with everything about you. The good and bad. Your beautiful body and sadistic head. I swallow. "You didn't give me much of a choice."

He chuckles, flexing his fingers against the wheel. "Very true. When I see something I want, I take it. I guess I'm like my father in that way."

"I always wanted my first time to be memorable," I admit. "And you've definitely given me something to remember."

A low thrum sounds out of his throat. He lifts a hand off the wheel and puts it between my thighs. I gasp at the contact of his cold press against my heated skin, but my body's already arching toward him.

"You're so goddamned innocent. Stop distracting me with it," he warns. Thorne's staring straight ahead, though with the way his fingers dance and explore, he doesn't need to see my pussy to know exactly what to do with it. He swipes his finger along my folds, bared to him now that he's ruined my underwear. I squeak, squirming for more, but he retreats and pops that finger into his mouth. "Mm. You're still sticky with me. That'll have to be enough. We've got a long night ahead."

His reminder straightens me in my seat. Thorne's ability to make danger cease to exist for me is unnatural and concerning. He's roaring along the curving roads in the black of night toward a ceremony involving Malcolm that may very well be violent. And here I am vibrating with the need for him to finger me before we intercede.

Where the *hell* has the old Ember gone? Who is this chick?

"You're right," I say after a determined throat clear. "What do you need me to do, other than grab Malcolm and pull him out of there?"

"I doubt there will be a paddle this time, so despite your newfound proficiency, you can't swing your way out."

I twist my head and give him a good glare, though it's as dark on my side as it is on his.

Thorne's teeth light up the dark. The bastard's grinning.

"This isn't supposed to be fun," I say. "Damion could be hurting Malcolm at this very second, all because I stupidly thought I could get away with manipulating Zeke. Malcolm's trying to protect me. If anything happens to him, I won't be able to forgive myself." My voice wobbles slightly. "I never thought I'd get to this point—caring about him. But I do. In a twisted way, I care about Malcolm Weatherby."

That sobers him. "You don't have to be so honest with me, you know."

"What do you mean?"

I watch his hands tighten against the steering wheel, the shaft of moonlight through the trees guiding me to his white-knuckled grip.

"This—what you're doing. Telling me the secrets to your heart, baring your soul, or however you want to put it. You will help me steal millions from my father and stop him from killing yours. I'll reward you with good fucks. We can put an end to it there."

I swing around to stare at him. Bite my lower lip. "What if I don't want to?"

His jaw locks after my question. He stares straight ahead.

"Have you ever considered there's more to us than sex?"

Thorne's answer is to swing the car sharply around a curve until I grip the holy-shit bar and bite down on a cry of surprise.

Thorne's trying to scare me into shutting up, meaning I'm right. He *does* think about it.

"If you believe I'll consider more than your pussy after using you for what I need, you're sorely mistaken."

His barb hits its mark. I put a hand over my heart, rubbing out the pain. "Stop denying what you know is true, Thorne. You like me."

"Shut up and focus, Ember. This isn't the time."

If he had it his way, there would never be a moment like this again. I sit back, allowing Thorne the seconds required for my revelation to sink into his thick skull. "What are you going to do if we succeed?"

"*When* we succeed," he corrects, his tone moving into a more neutral tone now that I've cut him some slack. "I'll be fine. I'm eighteen and won't need a guardian, but our butler, Josh, is a good man. A great one. I'd stay on with him until we graduate."

"And the money? Where will it go?"

He stares at me out of the corner of his eye. "Why, you want a cut?"

I shrug, mirroring him by staring straight ahead. "It's not out of the question."

"Well. Some of it belongs to Sav, with everything she endured. As for the rest, I'll distribute it to the members who Father has made suffer the most, like Julie." Thorne glances at me once, then twice, once he realizes he's under my quiet scrutiny. "The Nobles and Virtues who are basically eating out of trash cans. They deserve a few bills or two."

"It's not working, you know."

He sighs as we slow in front of Winthorpe's gates. "What's not working, Ember?"

"Your dismissive tone when you talk about helping people who can't help themselves. Your warm and squishy side is showing."

"The fuck it is."

"What about your mom?"

We're turning into the staff parking lot when Thorne slams on the brakes. I'm grateful for my seat belt when my forehead is prevented from splitting open on the dash.

"Conversation over," Thorne bites out, then puts the car in park.

"I take it she's not in the picture," I say once my heart slides back down to where it belongs.

Thorne shoves the driver's side door open, then whirls on me. "Yeah, a lot like yours."

My shocked suck of air is cut off when he gets out and slams his door.

"Fucking jackass," I mutter while shoving my door open. "What do you know of my mother?" I give my door a good slam, too. "Either one of them? That's right, asshole. I have two, unlike your sorry self. How is Julie as an unwilling stepmother, huh? I've always wondered."

Thorne's shadow seems to grow out of him, elongated and clawed, as he storms over to where I stand. I expect him to unleash and come under a dusting of his saliva as he tosses the most cutting insults in his repertoire to get me to shut up and stop talking about his sore spots.

I expect it, but I get the opposite.

"See this, right here? *This* is why I don't care for you.

We don't belong together. You, with your sweet face and stupid *fucking* fantasies." Thorne jabs a finger at me. "I come from a world of hate, and what you don't understand is I don't want to leave it. I could give a fuck what Julie wants or thinks—Do you know, at night, when my father comes home and fucks her, I listen to her screams?" He pauses to enjoy the horrified gasp that I give him. "Yeah, I'll give her money to pay her off from publicizing her abuse. And those Nobles and Virtues I spoke of, that's to buy their silence, too. As for the rest, I'm using it for my own investments. And I'm taking all my father's collateral with me. All the blackmail and leverage he has on the cloud against every single sorry soul who crosses the Briars. I *will* be king, Ember. Far from the Prince Charming you think I am." He rakes me with a cold stare before stepping back. "How's that for soft and warm?"

Thorne turns on his heel as I search for the right words. "I'm not drawn to that side of you."

"Don't I fucking know it. Go find a guy who'll—"

"I'm not talking about your good side."

He freezes, ducking his chin so he can take a closer look at me. "What?"

My lower lip trembles. I bite down on it, drawing on the pain to keep going. "I've been drawn to your dark side since the first moment I met you. It's why I'm in this position—with Zeke's blood on my hands, Savannah's secret in my head, and your cum inside me."

Thorne hikes his brows, clearly not expecting that last part to come from my *innocent* lips.

Bolstered, I step closer. "There's a part of me that you bring out. An emotion that I like. I'm addicted to your hands on me. I ache for you to be inside me whenever we're apart. All I can think of is your hands on my neck and the approval I seek when you order me around—I've never experienced this kind of sensation before." I rub my chest again, this time, not from pain. My heart's beating in tune with my desires. Just the thought of having Thorne again shortens my breaths. "I want you to teach me new things. I'm invested in this terrible world of yours, and I ... I don't want it to stop. If that makes me a bad person, then—"

"You are so far from rotten," he says hoarsely. "You are a rose with its thorns clipped. You're safe and beautiful and—"

"—and wild." I take one more step, leaving just a tiny space between us. "Maybe I started out with perfect petals in my old life with the Becketts, but when Malcolm brought me here, he threw me into the wild. And with you, I'm thriving."

He shakes his head. "I don't have the right to—"

"*I* have the right to." I point at myself. "I do. And I choose to stay with you."

For the first time, Thorne regards me with a wide-open stare. "Ember ... you can't."

"Too late." I grab him by the collar of his cloak and pull him in.

Thorne's lips are cold and unmoving at first. I glide my tongue along the seam, teasing them open. Delicate and light, enjoying his resistance as much as he likes mine when he goes after me. I lift on my tippy-toes and angle my head, covering his hard lines with my soft mouth, and...

A shuddering growl vibrates through his body. Thorne grabs me by the upper arms and slams me into the side of his car, covering my entire body with his form.

His dick is a hard piece of granite spearing through his pants and into my stomach. His teeth are sharp as they bite down on my lower lip and pull. Blood bursts between us. I dig my fingers into the backs of his shoulders, dragging them toward his neck. Wrapping them around his throat, pressing and squeezing until his breath shudders out, I feel his pulse against my fingertips like it's my own.

Our tongues entwine, warring with and petting the other in sharp, biting intervals. I breathe in his exhales, drawing his sweet taste all the way down my throat. Feral moans escape through my lips as I claw at him, willing to strip him naked in the freezing weather if only to feel his coldness brush up against my own.

On a restrained groan, he breaks our kiss. "As much as I'd like to paint this car with all the juice you're collecting for me, we have to move."

I nod, wiping my mouth with the back of my hand. Now that the headiness is leaving, I'm second-guessing my sinful confessions to him. As if Thorne wants some inexperienced, obsessed girl who he went too far with and is now regretting. He could have anyone he wants, a woman with more skills and maturity than one who's basically admitted to the equivalent of dabbling in the dark arts in her pink bedroom while her wholesome parents are asleep.

Thorne seems to sense the direction of my thoughts. He frowns, but his eyes soften. "Come on. Why don't we put your violent streak to work."

That brings out a small smile. One I'm not too comfortable wearing just yet.

"Stay in the black cloak and put your hood up to cover your face," he continues while fixing his. "I expect all members to be in their robes when we enter. You'll look like a Noble freshman." He hesitates, then states grimly, "I'll have to leave you to be by my father's side."

"I'll be fine."

"Don't let a single member figure out who you are. Not until I have a better picture of what's going on down there."

"I don't plan on it." I cover my head with the velvet hood. "Any ideas on how to get Malcolm out of there? Do you think he'll be kept in the same crypt I was? I can probably let him out before anyone sees."

"My gut says no. Father enjoys a spectacle. Whatever he has planned will be in front of the Societies."

I flutter my lips on a disappointed exhale. "Yeah, that'd be too easy."

Thorne pulls out his phone and fires off a quick text. "Jaxon will find you. Stay close to him while I'm not." He pockets his phone, looks to the school, then back at me. "You ready?"

I nod. Thorne holds out his hand then thinks better of it, squeezing it into a fist and letting it drop to his side.

I pretend I don't see it as I walk past him.

"Stay near the edges," he mutters as we head to the hidden door. He pulls his hood up, the luxurious, dark fabric framing his angles and obscuring the hollows of his face. My very own gorgeous Grim Reaper.

"No need," I respond, pulling the cloak tighter over my shoulders. "I'm living on the edge."

Thorne yanks at one of the double doors, revealing the opening to a cavern of black.

"The very edges of decent society," I add quietly.

Applying slight pressure to my back, Thorne pushes me all the way in.

CHAPTER 26
EMBER

We hear the chants before we see them.

"*Altum volair in tenebris, altum volair in tenebris, altum volair in tenebris...*"

We fly high in the dark.

I clench my hands to my sides, resisting the urge to hold Thorne so he can guide me through this mess.

It's *my* mess, though. I was the idiot who tried to recruit Zeke and ended up putting Aiko in danger. Now Malcolm's paying the price. I don't reiterate that to Thorne as we descend into the school's catacombs. My half-baked plan would be obvious to a brand new Societal recruit, never mind the prince of the Nobles.

I need to own my mistake and clean up the mess like a good little girl.

Good girl.

Quieting the dirty inner voice, I stroll forward,

keeping my sights on the flickering golden light at the end of the tunnel.

Thorne's form is bathed in the glow first. He turns slightly, squeezing my arm. His lips move within the shroud of his cloak. "This is where I leave you."

I place my hand on his, squeezing back until he lifts his from my shoulder.

Thorne's stare takes on an ethereal glow despite the shadows flowing across his face. The fire sconces behind me add to the gleam, flecks of white flame nestling in the pale blue. It contains such ferocity that I prepare for what he's about to say. *That he loves me, too? That whatever happens, we'll get through this fuckery together? That he craves my innocence as much as I covet his fetishes?*

I must look too eager. Thorne jerks back, the inner firelight dying as he blinks. "Jaxon will find you."

Those are his last words before Thorne steps into the stone octagon where Damion holds court.

There isn't time to dwell or mull over Thorne's body language. On a good day, he's impossible to read. I just accept that he's cracked my heart open while padlocking his.

I skitter behind one of the life-sized statues, clutching my hood tightly to my face as I peer around a bulging stone bicep to take stock of The Damion Briar Show.

And bite down on my knuckle to stifle a yelp when I see Malcolm, with his shirt stripped off and on his knees in front of Damion.

"We have in front of us a traitor," Damion calls. The chanting dies down.

A particularly tall dark cloak flows through the circle of black-robed Nobles and golden Virtues, peppered throughout with the bloodred of viscounts—Damion's henchmen. That cloak takes up residence beside Damion, pulling back his hood and sweeping a powerful gaze through his peers.

Thorne may refuse it, but he seems comfortable beside Damion, matching his father's charisma and owning the room with a single, forward stare. I'm drawn to Thorne even as my biological father is forced on his knees in front of him.

"You've joined us at last," Damion says to his son. "Did you find her?"

"No. Ember must've used one of the passageways she's become so familiar with these past few months. We'll discover where she is, though. She has to come back to school sometime."

Damion makes a grunting sound, half approving, half pissed-off. "I'm of a mind to set you down beside Malcolm for your inadequacy."

"Ember's in unfamiliar territory, and we've isolated her from any friends she tried to make. She won't last long, Father. I'll see to it."

Thorne's conviction is so convincing I almost fall for it, too, until I remind myself that it was Thorne who got me out of Weatherby Manor and stowed me away, protecting me from his father.

"You'd better," Damion says, then turns to address the Society. "The Weatherbys have betrayed us. The entire line is polluted, and I, as current king and leader of the Nobles, am moving to terminate the entire ancestry and future heirs from ever becoming a Societal member. Does the queen object?"

Dupris—or who I assume is Dupris—moves out of the circle and comes to a stop on Damion's other side. "Sadly, I cede to your decision, Damion. Incontrovertible proof exists where Ember attempted to expose the Society and Malcolm officially committed to exposing our deepest secrets to laypeople who would never understand the strength, loyalty, and sacrifice required to become a Noble or Virtue. For that reason, I stand with you."

My stomach sinks. Malcolm bows his head, his normally coiffed hair hanging in silver strings past his brows. His chest rises and falls in an erratic rhythm.

Half of me is desperate for him to fight or show one iota of passion when it comes to standing up to Damion. The other half hopes he stays quiet and doesn't give Damion more reason to hurt him. I don't know which one should win.

"Hey."

The male buzz at my ear makes me jump. Luckily, my lips were already pressurized shut while watching the tense proceedings so I didn't make a sound.

Jaxon hovers beside me, his hood disguising his features enough that I squint to ensure it's him.

He reaches up and pulls aside part of his hood to reveal his profile. I nod in confirmation, then get right to it, whispering, "How do we stop this?"

"We have to see how Mr. Briar will play this, first," he responds.

"Eliminating the entire Weatherby bloodline sounds like the plan," I whisper fiercely.

Jaxon shakes his head. "The king never does what you'd expect. We have to lay low until I get the signal from Thorne."

I scrunch my eyes at him suspiciously. Malcolm is at the Noble king and prince's feet, bared from the waist up. It's obvious that physical punishment is about to ensue along with the official termination of his Noble membership. I have no idea what that entails, but it can't be good. If I didn't know any better...

"Are you here to keep me quiet?" I ask. "Thorne doesn't have any plans to involve me, does he? He wants me out of the way, and you're here to help him do it."

Jaxon keeps quiet. The fact he doesn't act surprised or bother to defend Thorne tells me all I need to know.

Dammit, and I fell for it, with Thorne's long looks, deft fingers, and impassioned words...

I growl, "I am not standing here while Malcolm gets—"

Damion's voice rings out. "I asked you to assist me in

forcing Malcolm's presence here and invited all Winthorpe members to witness this moment so you may truly understand what can happen if you refuse to follow Societal edicts."

I turn my back on Jaxon and fly against the statue, practically splitting my nails from how hard I press into it.

Damion gestures to a red cloak who marches to the ceremonial fire bowl crackling and sparking behind Damion and Thorne. He lifts the handle to a stick that had been resting in the flames and passes it to Damion like he's holding the Olympic torch. Damion accepts it with just as much aplomb.

It's then I realize it's *not* a torch, but thick, heavy iron of some sort, the end glowing a dangerous red.

"Malcolm Weatherby, you are to be forever branded with that of a conspirator, a deceiver, and a treasonist. You will wear this mark for the rest of your pathetic life. Any attempts to cover it will be immediately known to me, and I will be forced to escalate your punishment to amputation. If, even then, you refuse to comport to your new rules as a disgraced member, it will result in your death."

"No," I whisper against the cold stone statue. I push off, readying to sprint around and reveal myself, become a distraction, *anything* to stop Malcolm from agreeing to such a one-sided deal.

I know which side should win now. Malcolm needs to fight his way out of here, and I'll help him.

A hand hooks the back of my hood and pulls. The clasp becomes a collar at my throat, and I gag as I'm dragged back.

I reel around to hiss at Jaxon for stopping me—but it's not Jaxon.

He bears the same eyes, but with a vicious strain to them, further enhanced by the bright red robe flowing across his shoulders.

"Dad—" Jaxon starts.

The viscount holds Jaxon by the back of the neck in his other hand. "My arrogant, *stupid* son. What do you think you're doing, harboring this girl? Do you want to be next down there? Huh?"

"Dad, you don't understand. Thorne—"

Thaddeus Murray shakes his son, then tosses him back against the wall. "Stay here and let me fix this. Do not utter one sound. Do *you* understand?"

Jaxon frantically glances at me before returning to his father. "You can't bring her down there."

"That's exactly what I'm going to do and what you should've done as soon as that boy enlisted you to do his dirty work. The Briars only think of themselves, Jaxon. I wish you'd come to learn that so I'm not continually forced to punish you."

"I'm on Thorne's side with this," Jaxon dares to argue. "You're the one in the wrong, Dad. Damion is nothing but toxic waste on these Societies."

Thaddeus clamps a hand on his son's mouth while

still wrangling me. I jerk against him like a cat in a bag, with unfortunately as much luck as the cat would have. Thaddeus's grip is surprisingly vise-like, considering his lean form. I even tried unclasping the cloak, but he's grabbed me by the hair, stopping any slippery moves on my part.

"Shut up, son. For once in your life, listen to your father and keep yourself out of harm's way. I'll deal with this the only way I know how." Thaddeus turns his glare to me. "Stupid girl, coming here. Stupid, stupid girl."

"You'd have done the same if it were Jaxon kneeling before Damion—"

Thaddeus doesn't allow me to finish. He drags me from behind the statue and pulls me down the stairs until I'm tripping on my own feet to stay upright. My hair has become my binding rope.

Thorne's the first to look up at the ruckus. His eyes widen for one precious moment before he returns to his apathetic and bored expression.

Damion's next, observing Thaddeus's catch with a slow, slithering smile. "My goodness, look who at last accepted her invitation."

"I found her skulking behind the northern pillar, likely in an attempt to save her father," Thaddeus says.

Pillar, not statue. He's deliberately misdirecting Damion's attention so he doesn't catch Jaxon. I'm motivated to out him, but better sense gets the best of me just in time. Jaxon is somewhat in my corner. Causing him to be punished with the Weatherbys won't do anyone any good.

"*Ember.*"

My name comes out as a plea, low and guttural, from Malcolm. His bright blue eyes flash between the dull gray of his hair. "Why? Why did you come?"

"I can't let you do this," I say as Thaddeus pushes me toward Damion.

Damion looks down his nose at me as I stumble to a stop. "She wears our color like an abomination. Take that robe off her." His eyes gleam with malice as he comes up with an idea. "As a matter of fact, strip—"

"I'll do the branding."

We all turn to Thorne's voice.

"Give me the branding iron." Thorne takes a subtle step forward. I realize he's redirecting his father's penchant for violence, and I've never been more thankful. I'm tough, but I don't know if I could handle three viscounts ripping my clothes off. "I'll happily burn it into Malcolm's skin."

After a murderous pause, Damion speaks. "I don't take well to interruption. You have a valid point, however. We must move this along."

"Yes," Dupris agrees. She makes no moves to save me or look in my direction. When I was in the hospital recovering from an overdose, I'd had the feeling she was rooting for Malcolm. But now... "We have a celebration to attend." Dupris stares over my head, regarding someone with deep affection. "After this terrible business is dealt with, we must celebrate the return of our princess in true Society fashion. By honoring the reunion of our prince and princess with an engagement ceremony."

What?

I fling my gaze over my shoulder, witnessing Savannah step out of the circle, clad in a golden robe and white dress, appearing like an angel from the surrounding fire. She smiles up at Thorne. With a painful tug, I follow the direction of her smile to find Thorne smiling placidly back.

He couldn't. Wouldn't. Not after what I told him about Savannah and Damion. We're meant to rob Damion of all his hidden funds. Escape Society rule. Dismantle this twisted world in which I'm standing in.

What does any of that have to do with a ruse of an engagement party?

I try to get Thorne's attention, but he's given me his shoulder while he takes the branding iron from a viscount who had the foresight to put it back in the ceremonial bowl and make it hot again.

Shit. Priorities.

I shove my shriveling heart to the side and regard Damion. "Don't you think that's a little hypocritical? Before you stake your power on Malcolm, maybe it's time the Societies knew where Savannah's been and who she—"

Damion sends me a scathing look. "Brand him."

Thorne doesn't hesitate.

"*No!*" I cry at the same time Thorne presses the iron to the back of Malcolm's neck.

Malcolm roars, beads of sweat bursting along his tense biceps and veins popping out of his temples and forehead. He bears the pain with pulled-back lips, saliva dripping from the corners as Thorne takes an unnecessary length of time.

"That's enough!" I scream at him. "*Enough!*"

Thorne catches me through his lashes, a lightning flash of apology racing across his features before he presses down harder.

"You're going to fucking brand the bones underneath his skin!" I shriek, then leap toward Thorne to stop this. Screw the plan.

Thaddeus catches me, wrapping strong arms around my chest and pulling me back.

"Now, his forehead," Damion orders.

I fight. I fight the way I wish Malcolm would, screaming and kicking and lashing out with my nails. I fight so hard, more viscounts have to come in to restrain me. My voice is so raw I taste blood, but nobody listens.

Thorne rounds to Malcolm's front. Damion happily grabs Malcolm by the hair and yanks until his forehead is exposed to Thorne.

I can't believe this. How can they do this to a powerful man? *How* have they gotten Malcolm to submit to every single fucking atrocity they've given to him?

"Malcolm," I cry. My cheeks feel stiff with salt. Wet. "There has to be something—stop. *Stop*, Damion. Or else I'll tell everyone how Savannah had your ba—"

Damion holds out a hand to Thorne, pausing him. Like a good soldier, Thorne listens. I sneer at him.

"I was grappling with the type of punishment you'd receive, Ember," Damion says, his hand remaining high and imperious in the air. "You've given me the perfect inspiration. Would you like to know how you arrived in this world?"

Malcolm bolts.

That's the only way I can describe it—he rears, seizes, and bucks like a horse bound at the wrists and ankles. "*No*, Damion! We struck a deal. You could have me—you could do anything you wanted to me. Brand my forehead with the X'd out crest of a raven. Take my company. Make me your mule. All of that in return for leaving Ember alone and saving her from the truth."

"Old friend." Damion *tsks*. "Since when have you known me to keep to a deal when it no longer suits my purposes?"

"*DAMION.*"

Malcolm's roar is the loudest I've ever heard it. Even the arms of my restraining viscounts go slack. I use this space in time to lurch out of their grip and fall to my knees in front of Malcolm. Thorne's forced to retreat, giving me room to shield Malcolm.

I'm close enough to see the tears escaping Malcolm's

bloodshot eyes, streaming down his cheeks. Once I'm in his horizon, he lets out a shuddering breath.

"Oh, Malcolm." I cup his cheeks, unable to stop tears from filling my vision, too.

He moves his chapped lips for one simple word. "Run."

"Now, now, no need for haste," Damion says. "I'm positive Ember would like to stick around for this story, no matter how much pain it causes you or her. Am I right, Ember?"

I drag my gaze from Malcolm to Damion, forming my eyes into glass shards. "Everything you say is a lie. You're a *liar*. Your leadership is a joke."

"Ember," Thorne warns under his breath.

I whip to look at him. "Why won't you fight him? Now is your moment. You have the information that could..."

I trail off as Savannah drifts to Thorne's side, wrapping her arm through his. Thorne allows it, his posture stoic and stiff as he stares down at me with no emotion. Nothing.

"I don't feel anything for you," he says in a flat tone. "I never have."

"The only liar here is you, Ember," Savannah says. "You've shown us exactly how much disdain you have for the Societies. Any words you utter in a desperate attempt to save your father will have zero credibility. You disgust us. Mocking our traditions, disrespecting our rulers, and besmirching *my* name after all I've been through. You should be ashamed of yourself. If it were up to me, you'd carry the same humiliating brand as your father."

Her words drag at me like an anchor pulling me to the bottom of a raging sea. All my mistakes. Every *should've* in my past. The kind of person I am. It's sandpaper against my soul, but I rally what little determination I have left. "Tell them the truth, Savannah. If it comes from you, the Virtues will take your side. Dupris will stand by you." At the mention of her name, Dupris peers closer at me. "What Damion's done is atrocious."

"You are the product of a whore, my child."

I hear Damion talk. Understand the words. However, they take a moment to assemble in my head.

Damion waits for me to look him in the eye with questioning wariness. I can't resist. To hear the truth while surrounded by deception...

Malcolm releases a keening wail. My hands spasm against the scruff on his cheeks. "I wanted to avoid this. I did everything in my power to shield you, sweetheart. I'd gladly take death over you knowing the truth."

I glance between them, my brows twisting, aching, with uncertainty. Malcolm's pain nestles in my stomach, making me sick, but Damion's information slithers into my head, growing like cancer in my brain.

"What could be so bad that you'd want to die for it?" I finally ask him. "It's okay if she was a prostitute. It's—I have a mother, remember. I'd never judge you for that, especially after knowing this world and the Societies' outdated traditions…"

"I ordered it," Damion cuts in. "Another challenge attempted and lost. Malcolm's punishment was to submit to sex. Doesn't sound too awful, does it?" Damion chuckles, and it's then I figure out a prostitute is the nicest part of the story. As a last ditch attempt, I glance at Thorne to see if he knows what Damion's referring to. He remains expressionless, but his eyes are intense on his father. Savannah catches me and grins.

Damion continues, "It was around the time he met dear Julia at college. You were so happy then, weren't you, old boy?"

Malcolm's head sags. "You stole everything. You couldn't even let me have her."

"Everything that was taken from you, you allowed. You could've kept her, had you succeeded in your Noble challenges. But, as a silver lining, your rape created Ember."

My spine fuses into a rod. My heart jolts with the sudden, sickening electricity. "Malcolm, what is he … what is he talking about?"

Malcolm stares at me with heartbreaking clarity. "I never wanted you to know, sweetheart…"

"He was tied down in this very room, child," Damion says. "A ceremony of sorts. Three women were ordered to get him hard, to have every sexual encounter possible with him. Toys. Whips. Plenty of pussy. They'd fuck him, then stroke him and fuck him again. And again. It's the trait of male dominance, isn't it, that even when his mind doesn't want it, the body will respond. Of course, I made Julia watch. She sat much where you are now while Malcolm was incessantly and strategically violated until there was simply nothing of him left. Or her, for that matter."

My lips part. No words follow. My tongue is so swollen it's blocking my throat. Horror threatens to spill acid into my throat with no space to release it.

"You'd become too independent from the Societies, old friend. Were making a life for yourself outside of our rule and edicts. I couldn't let that stand, not as the new king. Our members must understand how crucial it is to remain loyal, marry within the Society, and continue on to create true-blooded heirs for all we have to offer. You were about to ruin your path to a viscount, and for what? A common pussy? Being put in your place was the nicest thing I could do for you."

"You—" I rasp, "You disgusting *pig*, you are the worst kind of evil, and anyone who follows you or believes a single word out of your mouth is as vile as you are—"

"Did I not make clear how much I loathe interruption?" Damion spits. Up until now, his voice was flat with a bit of joyous inflection. The swing from that to wrath stiffens me further, but I stay where I am, on my knees and holding Malcolm. Malcolm, who won't look at me anymore.

"You're certainly making clear your hellion heritage." Damion takes a breath, straightens his lapels under his cloak, then continues. "I haven't even gotten to the finale. Julia is mine now because if I couldn't have her, I made clear to both she and Malcolm that she would undergo the same cleansing ritual Malcolm did."

"Say what it is," I spit. "*Rape.*"

I spend one last moment on the ground with Malcolm, though my stomach roils with the truth of where I come from, how I came to be...

After kissing Malcolm on his damp cheek, then squeezing his slumped shoulders, I rise, facing Damion on my feet.

Damion's lips part with a smile as he watches. "Now, here is the real punishment for you. I'm well aware of your feelings for my son and his multiple wasted opportunities to tame you the way I did Malcolm. As with everything, I have to do it for him."

"Father," Thorne says.

My hands clench into fists. I won't turn around. I can't give Thorne the satisfaction of seeing the utter confusion and hurt on my face. He's like his father. He sustains himself on conflict and grief. If I'm honest, I don't want to read whatever is on his. Protective? Panicked? Aloof?

"My son has known of your conception from the very beginning. He kept the truth from you."

Now, I spin to face Thorne, my voice rough with emotion. "You knew?"

"It's more complicated than that. There was never a right time." His eyes finally take on the warmth I've been fantasizing about.

Too late.

"How could you?" I whisper brokenly. "How could you do this to me?"

Damion interjects, "In Malcolm's defense, the woman was never supposed to become pregnant. A few weeks later, she came to me and told me she was with child, demanding money for an abortion. I had a better plan in mind. Housing her until I could have the child, then selling the baby to a family I could monitor until the time was right to inform Malcolm of the unwanted child and bring you into the fold. The final gavel, if you will. The fact that Malcolm covertly joined the FBI in their attempts to thwart me was an annoyance, but as you can see, properly dealt with. I suggest you take this information home with you, Ember, and chew on it. This is the legacy you're fighting for, the man you want to stop the torture of—a man who never wanted you. When he looks at you, he sees his trauma. *You* remind him of the worst moment of his life. You *are* the worst part of him."

My face spasms with agony as his words hit true.

"No." Malcolm grunts, shifting on his knees. "Not anymore, Ember. I swear to you. At first—at first, yes. I was sick over the thought of a child being out there, one who ... one who I couldn't fathom existed. But then I met you. You are wonderful, intelligent, beautiful, and nothing like your circumstances. I need you to believe me, sweetheart. You've become my soul where I thought I had none."

I take a step back. Shake my head. Tears stream freely.

I bump up against Thorne.

On an anguished wail, I recoil, glancing everywhere—at the silent members who all must be enjoying the show, a gleeful, maniacal Damion who goes to lengths of cruelty I could never have imagined, to Thorne.

Thorne.

Thorne.

"Oh, yes," Damion adds once he notices where my agony's landed. "Thorne was well aware of that as well."

"I'm so sorry," rips out of Malcolm's throat.

"Ember." Thorne raises his hand to me. "Don't take him for his word. If I've taught you anything—"

"*Taught* me," I sneer. "You fucking manipulated me!"

Dupris says, with a voice of calm, "Perhaps we should return to the proceedings while Ember processes—"

I swipe the branding iron from Thorne and mash it into Damion's face.

CHAPTER 27
EMBER

Sadly, the branding iron isn't as hot as it was, but it does the trick.

Damion stumbles back, blood bursting from his nose.

Chaos erupts. The members break their circle, some to come at me, others to make a run for it before their king gets *really* mad.

I swivel to Malcolm with the thought of untying him and somehow getting him out of here.

His ties are cut, dangling on his wrists and laying flat under his ankles.

I glance up, meeting Thorne's grim face as he pockets a Swiss Army knife. "Get him. Go. now." He points behind me.

I'm yanking under Malcolm's arms at the same time Jaxon appears on Malcolm's other side, and we bring him up to a dragging stumble. Ducking under his arm, I do a terrified sweep of who is the closest threat to us. *Savannah.*

But I find her running to Damion's side, uncaring about Malcolm or me.

Thorne blocks as many viscounts as he can by taking the branding iron I'd tossed aside and swinging for their legs and the backs of their necks. He spares Jaxon's father, who regards us with a leer and a shaking head.

"Take the king's quarters tunnels. And don't ever let me see you do something this stupid again."

Jaxon nods at his father's advice, and since I have no other recourse, I allow him to swivel us in the right direction. With Thorne and Thaddeus at our backs, we're able to slip through the melee and into a dark tunnel. The door is on a rusted, temperamental slider. Jaxon and I attempt to close it on our own, but it only gives a little.

Members stream closer to us, the more intrepid ones figuring out where we've gone. They start running.

"Harder!" Jaxon shouts.

"I'm—trying!" I grit out, clawing at the stone and bending my fingers backward at the knuckles.

A warm pressure comes up behind me, smelling like sweat, burned flesh, and blood. Malcolm provides the final push needed to jerk the door out of its rusted-over freeze and roll it shut with a *boom.*

The last thing I see is a robed wrist and hand getting

caught in the seam before the door slammed us into blackness. I hope it was Aurora's.

"It locks from in here," Jaxon says, breathing heavily. "They can't get to us."

"Good." I nod. "Where do we go from here?"

Jaxon points over my shoulder while turning on the flashlight app on his phone.

"Malcolm? Are you okay to walk?" I ask.

Malcolm rubs at the scruff on his face. "My neck burns like a motherfucker, but I'll be okay."

I nod again. Apparently, it's a nervous tic I've acquired.

"Are you all right?" he asks me.

"I wasn't hurt."

"I meant over what was said," Malcolm corrects softly.

"I'm not sure." Meanwhile, the cruel cackle in my head continues. *You were never good enough. You're the product of evil. Damion's sick creation. You're nothing to Thorne.*

Jaxon comes between us. "Look, I completely understand the need to figure your shit out, but not now, yeah? We have to get aboveground before the rest do."

I'm only too happy to comply. Jaxon leads the way, warning us of sharp right and left turns. This isn't like the passageways I'm used to with a straight point A to point B. Without Jaxon, we'd be seriously stuck.

Or, not quite.

I sneak some glances at Malcolm, both checking on him and wondering how familiar he is with these tunnels and secrets and lies. He was one of them for a long time. Jaxon still is. I can't lower my guard even though my worst nightmare has come true.

I was never wanted.

It takes some time to navigate through the darkness. Jaxon's phone is the one light we have, silhouetting the craggy walls and skittering, fuzzy forms like a scene from a horror movie. Malcolm only has his pants, and I have no idea where my phone is—maybe on the roof, in a tree, or in Thorne's car. I'm glad not to have it since that's likely a way the Briars could track me.

Thorne.

His name scrapes against the last section of vulnerability I have left. I feel naked when I think of him, no longer in a good way. Like all my parts were exposed, including the soft muscle of my heart. Still, he kept the truth from me. Always, he's wanted power over me.

Not anymore.

Jaxon murmurs something about a trapdoor within the forest surrounding Winthorpe. His flashlight bounces over a metal ladder embedded into the rockface that's seen much better days.

"Will it hold?" Malcolm asks.

"It has to." Jaxon jerks his chin at me. "Ladies first."

"Here." Malcolm cups my elbow. "I'll help."

His touch is more painful than I could've imagined, as

if he's transferring all his suffering, every image of torture, and all moments of enduring rage until it was snuffed out by Damion.

"I can do it." I pull out of his hold.

And just like that, I return the pain. He grimaces with it but steps back.

The steps are slippery with damp, mildewy-smelling substances. Touching the metal instantly freezes my fingers. Ignoring it, I climb, my shoes skidding with a noisy shriek once or twice. At the top, I raise an arm over my head and push against the flat wooden surface. It gives much easier than I predicted, and I pop my head out before thinking.

"Get down!" Jaxon whispers furiously.

"Sorry!" I say and turtle back into the hole.

I look down to see Jaxon nudging Malcolm up next. Once Malcolm hits the middle of the ladder, Jaxon goes next.

"All clear?" he asks me.

I'm way more cautious, allowing my forehead to appear over the frost-bitten ground. "I don't see anyone."

"Go ahead and climb out."

I do, my hands barely denting the dirt as I heft myself out. An owl hoots nearby, adding to the eerieness of a moonlit forest. I sidestep to allow Malcolm some room, Jaxon appearing soon after.

"Give me your phone," Malcolm says to Jaxon.

Jaxon hands it over without argument. Malcolm

punches the screen with his thumbs for a few seconds before saying to me, "Dash is on his way. I'm chartering a plane to get us out of here. He's packed what he could in the gap between our abduction and now and was idling in the car, waiting for my call."

I don't bother to ask what would've happened if Malcolm never made it through. He's lived through enough lasting madness to have a plan C. Or Z.

"You'll forgive me for not disclosing where I'm taking my daughter," Malcolm says to Jaxon. "Thank you for getting us this far. I can take it from here."

Jaxon looks askance at me. "Is this what you want?"

What he's not saying is, *are you sure you want to leave Thorne behind?*

Thorne, the guy who yanked my soul straight out of my body and devoured it like sugar. The boy who harbored terrible secrets yet didn't bother to disclose them and save me the pain of hearing it from the devil himself.

Thorne, who *is* the devil. My demon.

I find my voice. "Yes. I'll go with Malcolm."

We both have a lot of healing to do.

Malcolm sags with relief. I suppose I'm known to constantly argue with him.

"There's just one thing," he says.

Jaxon and I look at him.

"I'm taking Julie with us."

Dash doesn't frantically look us over as we stumble out of the brush and onto a private roadway. He slides out of the driver's seat and opens the passenger door with zero judgment on his face like he's picking us up from the airport.

"Thank you," I say to him as I crawl across the seats with shaking legs.

Malcolm comes in after me, wincing when his neck hits the headrest.

The interior light is on, giving me the chance to see in detail the damage Damion's inflicted.

It's raw and mottled, but the insignia is obvious. A raven in flight within a perfect circle. A giant X crosses it all out.

"The Nobles and Virtues are everywhere," Malcolm says to me. He must've caught me looking. "They see this, and they're instructed to either avoid me or hit me. Whichever they choose."

I blow out a breath. "I've never pictured you in a manbun, but there's always that moment when a daughter is horrified by her father's fashion choice. Even if it's to ensure your safety and disguise this branding."

Finally, he cracks a smile. "I'm glad you still consider me your father."

A needy emotion nearly chokes me. "I'm relieved you look at me as your daughter."

"Always." He twists to clasp my hands between his own as Dash climbs into the driver's seat, shuts his door, and the interior light flicks off. "Your existence may not have been a choice I made, but I am so happy I met you. This year has taught me the good that can come out of terrible experiences. And trust me when I tell you I had no reason to believe in the good anymore."

He lifts his hand to brush an escaping tear off my cheek.

"You are my sweetness, Ember. Anything I had left that Damion didn't find went into you. I'm sorry about your birth mother and that I don't know much about her—"

"I don't want to know her. She raped you."

"She was likely under the same kind of duress I was. You understand how Damion is."

"He gave her money to have me. Her first choice was to abort me. I doubt she'd like to meet me any more than I'm curious about her."

His eyes soften around the edges. Not in kindness. In grief. "You assume she's still alive."

My breath inexplicably hitches. Malcolm had previously told me she died in childbirth, but I assumed it was a lie, just like everything else. "Damion killed her?"

"I can't be certain, but knowing what I know, it's

easier to kill a woman and hide her body than it is to pay her off and keep her as a liability."

I gently remove my hands from his. I'm cold. There's a type of shiver inside me that isn't going away, regardless of how much Dash has cranked the heat.

"How will we get to Julie?" I ask.

Malcolm reaches through the middle console and into the passenger seat, where Dash has stored folded clothes. "She'll be waiting at the old cemetery. Dash contacted her."

I tear my gaze from the rolling foliage we speed past. "Wait, how? I've seen her. She's not—I mean, I always thought it'd be impossible to get through to her."

"You're referring to her opioid addiction." Malcolm finishes buttoning his white work shirt. "One she never asked for. Damion began dosing her soon after my—our separation. After what she was forced to watch, she was in no condition to argue."

"I would never judge her."

"She and I have met secretly for years."

My brows jump.

"You're not the one Weatherby who's thought to memorize the founders' secret tunnels," he adds wryly. "Before you, she was the sole motivation for me to live. Ending this ... putting a stop to Damion's constant torture, would've been so easy to do, but for her. It was Julie who convinced me to meet you."

I drag my teeth across my lips. So much revelation has

come my way this evening, and I'm not sure I can handle more. But Malcolm needs this. I see it in the slope of his shoulders, the lines in his face, and the newfound color in his stare. "When Damion told me about you, I knew it was for his gain. Another way to twist the knife and keep me castrated. She told me that she'd eavesdropped a time or two on his discussions with Thaddeus about you. That you were an honor student, somewhat of a studious loner, but with the intelligence and empathy of a woman not yet comfortable with herself. And ... that you were a wonderful daughter."

At the thought of Barb and Gene Beckett, agony hits dead center in my chest. "They're wonderful parents."

"I don't want you to think I kept you from them for my own selfish gains."

"Not anymore. After tonight, I have a much easier time understanding your decisions."

"But not pity. Never pity me."

I shake my head, unable to verbally tell him that I don't feel abject horror at the thought of what he went through. "As long as you don't pity me, either."

He offers a sad smile. "Deal."

"Can I see them again?" I can't stop hope from inflecting my voice.

"I'm taking us somewhere remote. A place I've planned for once the FBI had enough and Damion was neutralized." Malcolm sighs. "We can't wait for that anymore. The truth is, sweetheart, I don't know if we'll ever be safe from him. I *do* know I will never put you or Julie in that position again. I plan to keep us hidden."

Malcolm goes silent after that, watching me under cover of darkness. Dash keeps his head forward, politely invisible, but I'm getting the same sense from him as I am from Malcolm.

Are you sure you want to do this?

If I return to the Becketts, I'll be a sitting duck for Damion. If I stay at the Weatherby mansion, I'll be a sitting duck for Damion. Damion has a deep desire to torture me in the same way he broke Malcolm.

... except. "Damion never ended up breaking you, did he?"

Malcolm lifts his chin, his jaw a stark line of shadow against the stars through his window. "Not in the way he thought. I kept Julie. I got to know you. Both brought me back to life."

I spend the next minutes thinking hard. Chewing on the inside of my cheek.

We slow to a stop in front of the cemetery, ironically, the same one Savannah where she confessed her dark secret to me. I think of the baby there, laying in ashes behind Julie as she emerges from the cover of a mausoleum and delicately makes her way to us. Another one of Damion's victims.

Malcolm flies out of the car, jolting me out of my reverie. He meets Julie halfway, lifting her at the waist and burying his face in her neck.

I hear their sobs through the car. Unable to pull my attention away, I watch them murmur assurances to each other. Malcolm cups her face as if he's handling delicate glass, then lays his lips on hers. Julie wraps her hands around his neck, feels the wound, then jerks back, concern and worry crossing her expression as she fights his hold to get a better look.

He grabs her hand and leads her to our car. As they get closer, I can better hear him say, "Yes, I'll clean it as soon as I can. I know—it's a massive scar, and even though I despise it, I still have to take care of it so it doesn't get infected."

"If you die from this, I'll kill you," she adds.

My lips twitch into a smile. I knew I'd like her.

I come out of the vehicle as they approach. Julie hesitates in her steps, regarding me with a mixture of regret, curiosity, and affection. It's the most alert I've ever seen her.

"Hi," I say quietly, fidgeting with my hands.

"I can't believe it's really you." She comes closer, tilting her head up slightly. Without her heels, I have a whole head on her. "I know we've met before, but I ... it's all in a fog. Malcolm's been helping me detox, as well as Thorne."

My brows come crashing down. "I didn't think Thorne cared enough to help you."

Julie responds with a slight pull of her lips. "Thorne likes to consider himself a lot of things, but at his core, he wants to be the opposite of his father. He did what he could for me. I'll never blame that boy for his father's sins."

That makes one of us.

But, her statement does something to me. It helps solidify what I want to do.

"We should get going. There's only so much time before Damion considers I've chartered a jet and tries to intercept it."

"I won't give him the chance," I say.

Malcolm cuts his eyes to me. Julie regards me as if she knew what I was going to do all along.

"There's something I have to do," I say to Malcolm. "I hope you'll forgive me, but..."

"You're not coming with us," he surmises. Disappointment ripples across his face. Julie reaches over and wraps an arm around his waist.

"I can't. Not while Damion's still after my family. Because you're my family." I swallow. Meet his eyes. "Dad."

Malcolm's expression loses all muscle. Dash clears his throat like he's fighting back emotion.

"Jesus, there's nothing else you could've said that would bring me to my knees so damned fast," Malcolm says hoarsely. "Come here."

He wraps me in a hug, saying into my hair, "I don't want to let you go. I don't. But you've proven to me again and again how strong you are and how stubborn you can be. I will leave a phone with Dash. You call me if you change your mind. I'll find a way to get to you."

I'm trembling in his grip, wavering between seeking the comfort of this newly reunited family or my family of the past. Of forgetting the people I'm leaving behind—Aiko, Savannah, Thorne, Mom, Dad—and going with Malcolm to start a new, untainted life. Safe. Loved. Accepted.

I peel out of his hold before I second-guess everything. "Go. I'll be fine. I know how to get to the manor from here. You've endured enough. Dad. It's my turn to try."

"I love you, sweetheart." Malcolm squeezes my arms hard, then lets me go.

Julie takes him by the hand, and they slip into the car as silent as ghosts.

Dash drives them into the mist, and they disappear like ghosts, too.

CHAPTER 28
EMBER

Thorne had a ballsy plan to steal his father's cryptocurrency and bankrupt him.

After the nightmare of this evening, *my* plan is to derail them both.

I try not to feel any guilt as I cross my arms in the cold and make it to Main Street, where a restaurant owner takes pity on me and calls a cab. I use the time between my ride from Main Street to Weatherby Manor to remind myself that Thorne was the first to commit the ultimate betrayal.

He knew where I came from. He understood perfectly the poison that affected my family. He had the cure to my confusion, my loneliness, and the answer to why I was ripped out of the home I knew and thrown into one of hell. Still, he did nothing.

Thorne deserves to feel the pain that I'm living with. He should know the emptiness that happens when someone you love peels away your very essence, flaying you alive, then leaves you exposed, wounded, and alone.

"Thank you," I say to the driver as he pulls around the back of manor as I'd asked.

There are no signs of skulking cloaks. They're probably too busy serving their master or watching him bandage his nose as he rails about his latest plan to kill me.

Which means I have to act fast.

Out of an abundance of caution, I crouch low to the ground while making a break for the side door. The taxi driver must think I'm a nut, but I hear him motor off regardless, probably well used to the oddities of the elite of Raven's Bluff.

He'd be correct, though. I finally understand who I am. An elite. A Weatherby. Malcolm's daughter, born from violence and determined to break free.

Weatherby Manor's silent, darkened hallways are almost cold to the touch as soon as I walk in. Malcolm wasn't home a lot, but I always sensed his presence. The peaty smell of whiskey, his subtle cologne, and after-shave. There was always a light or two on, a soft gold to navigate through the insane amount of bric-a-brac this man collected over the years.

I don't dare light my way through the first floor and to the western wing where Malcolm's office sits, empty and sharp with the scent of leather. Just in case there's an errant cloak lying in wait for me. Dash might've cleared the home before leaving, and I'm hoping that's the case. I have no idea when he'll return, so it's up to me and my own devices on how I handle these next hours.

Traveling with the hunchback of a cat, I crawl to Malcolm's desk, opening drawers and sifting through using only the starry night from the bay window behind me to guide my search. At last, I come across his phone.

I perch on his chair, turning it on and dimming the screen as much as possible. It takes me more time than I'd like to guess his code—I'm locked out for a good ten minutes after too many tries. I'm tempted to open a fucking chat box on his computer and call someone that way when finally, my birthday takes me to the home screen. That was never the one I would've thought worked.

"Thank god," I mutter through the affectionate swell in my chest, swiping through his contacts. Malcolm's been smart, so I don't find what I'm looking for. A good thing, I guess.

Resigned, I dial 911 and hold the phone to my ear.

"911 operator, what's your emergency?"

"Hi, um, I have information regarding an investigation into Damion Briar. I believe the FBI is working with the RBPD on this, and I'd be grateful if you could pass on the message."

A pause. "I'm sorry, who is this?"

I take a deep breath. "My name is Ember Weatherby. And I have proof. There are ashes of a baby buried at the old cemetery carrying Damion's DNA."

CHAPTER 29

EMBER

Monday comes too soon.

I spent the weekend cloistered in a police interrogation room, meeting with the man who'd become Malcolm's confidant and friend throughout these past years. His name is Elijah Colt, and his rough, suspicious demeanor belied by his large, warm brown eyes eventually softened when my story remained consistent for hours. And I'm talking *hours*.

I told them everything. From the Societies to Damion's affair with Savannah to the tragedy befalling their baby. I informed them of the Societies' hideouts and the underground tunnels of Winthorpe. The catacombs housing their ritual items and their penchant for dangerous, deadly challenges to prove you were part of the elite. My examples included rape, assault with deadly weapons, and of course, drugs.

Did I feel like a snitch? Absolutely. Then all I had to do was remember Thorne's stubborn duplicity and Damion's maniacal glee at informing me that one of Malcolm's rapists was my biological mother, and the information slips out of me like silk.

Both of them were only out for themselves. Well, so am I, and I'm determined to give Malcolm the justice he deserves. *We* deserve.

You're nothing to Thorne.

He may have loved fucking you, but he's proven how much he doesn't love you.

His commitment to the Societies overshadows any claim you had on him.

Savannah's slim arm curving around his as they look down on me in the catacombs plays on a loop in my head, even overshadowing the pleasure of shoving a fire poker into Damion's face.

He chose her. Hechoseherhechoseherhechoseher.

The pleasure of Agent Colt's company comes to an end, and so does the safety of the police station when they drop me off at the manor, assuring me of a patrol car stationed outside my home until they confirm my story and arrest Damion.

I'm thankful to the stars when I wake up to flashing red and blue lights coming from across the street Sunday morning. It's early—around four—when I slide out of bed and run to my window overlooking Weatherby Manor's driveway. Plenty of police vehicles are parked on the private street with men barely visible in their black gear crawling over the Briar property like giant rainforest ants.

I don't get the pleasure of seeing Damion in cuffs because Dash slips into my room and pulls me from the window, muttering things about promising Malcolm to keep me safe and how that doesn't include allowing me to become target practice at an open window.

It's the most sarcastic I've ever heard him. I'm impressed enough to listen to Dash's warnings and spend the day doing Thorne's busywork and figuring out where Damion's crypto is stashed. Laptop on my knees, hunched over in bed, I form an idea before shutting the computer down and imagining the pleasure of stealing all Thorne's money. I *have* to succeed at this.

Ergo, Monday morning is upon me much too soon. I'm expected to attend school, according to both Dash and Agent Colt, who've apparently become my substitute parents. Dash purchased me another phone, and I spent most of my Sunday afternoon talking freely to my adoptive parents and promising I'd come home soon.

As soon as I can confirm Damion is behind bars for good.

I allow Dash to drive me to school like it's any other day, despite the nervous tugs in my belly and the sense of dread crushing my chest. I can be as confident as I like on the outside, but inside, I'm strangled by uncertainty. At seeing Thorne—if he's even at school—facing Aurora and her crew, and staying strong when

Savannah inevitably comes up to me and slaps me in the face.

I'm by no means perfect, but I'm committed to doing the right thing.

"You call me if there's trouble," Dash says in his deep, smooth voice as he slows in front of Winthorpe's front courtyard.

"I will." I push open my door, stepping out into the cold with my bag slung across my back and eyes straight ahead. The physical sensations are nothing compared to the chill I'm feeling inside and the heaviness of keeping my head on my shoulders.

I could be shanked for what I've done. This school isn't any different from prison when someone's betrayed them. *Am I willing to die on this hill?*

Thorne's heartbreaking face comes to mind. *Yes. A thousand times yes.*

With a deep breath, I take a step forward.

CHAPTER 30
THORNE

When Ember escaped the catacombs with Malcolm and Jaxon, I thought my father was going to kill me.

I would've welcomed it. One can face death down only so many times before you start to wonder if it's the best route to finding peace at last.

The man wanted to—oh, was he fucking *desperate* for it as he staggered toward me, his eyes vile with rage while he reached out a curled hand, skeletal and bloody like Death himself.

I stopped him with two simple words. "I know."

Father halts, one hand cupping his nose while blood drips off his chin and stains his cloak and suit. To further my statement, I glance sideways at Sav, then back at him.

Father's lips tremble with forcefully contained wrath. "If you ever utter a word..."

"I won't, and neither will you." After wiping the branding iron on my pants, I throw it to his feet. It clangs loudly in the catacombs, most members deserting the premises once they realized the huge liability of an injured, pissed-off king.

Savannah stares nervously between us before holding Father's elbow. "You need a hospital."

He yanks out of her grip, sending her stumbling. I catch her before she falls, and Sav clutches me, crying. "Why? *Why* is this happening to me? I love him. I love him!"

My hands spasm as they hold her, though I'm battling with the deep urge to toss her to my father and tell him to handle his own messes. But Sav and I were a unit once, and she was a happy, beautiful girl before my father poisoned her. Probably just to see if he could.

With the way he rakes her up and down with disgust, I decide I'm not far off the mark.

"You'll destroy any claim to the Noble throne, son. Are you willing to fuck over your future so permanently? If anything happens to me, I'll ensure your suffering. Take my word for it. That girl is unhinged from her trauma, unreliable and suicidal."

Sav tears her face away from my chest and screams. "I have the *ashes,* you son of a bitch!"

Father stiffens.

"You thought you destroyed her, didn't you?" Sav says to him. "I may have stupidly fallen in love with you and believed your promises to take care of me, but I loved *her*, too. My baby. I intercepted the midwife before she took my baby away. Do you know you used the same lady who helped you with Ember? You didn't, did you?" Sav releases a guttural laugh. "You're so cocksure you didn't consider she'd feel immense guilt over what she did to that baby since you never told her that Ember was actually better off where she was sold. Cara and I talked—that's the midwife's name, if you didn't know—and developed a friendship. I was so lonely. And she did me the favor of delivering Aria's ashes to me instead of disposing of her like you asked."

Sav sinks in my arms. I keep her upright, giving her strength where hers is fast seeping away.

Father's eye twitches. "You have no idea what you've done, you stupid, useless cunt. You will have your day of reckoning the same as my son. You'll—"

I smile. "Better hurry up with those threats, *Dad*, because Malcolm and Ember are well on their way to sending forensics to Aria's location."

I have the pleasure of witnessing Father's eyes widen with shock. "You goddamned worthless son. I'll have my moment with you. I know dangerous people, ones who would love to have Ember sold to them as the delicious girl she is now."

Father whirls, his cloak billowing as he sprints to his quarters and likely fumbles with a plan to get the fuck out of Dodge before the feds find him.

I can't say his threat didn't make my knees weaken for a brief second. In that same breath, I have the irresistible urge to find Ember and keep her beside me until the world is damned well ready to promise her safety.

"You said her name." Sav raises her face to mine, her cheeks shining with tears and Father's blood. "Thank you for saying Aria's name to him." Her hands tangle against my cloak as her knees give out, and she sobs. "It means she was real. My baby was real."

I WAKE UP DRUNK. Or high. Or both.

Sunday morning was a bitch of a time, what with Josh seizing me by the shoulders and yelling that the feds were here.

"I've destroyed all documents pertaining to Master Briar's side businesses," he rushes to say as I try to land bleary eyes on him. "But I can't be sure I put all the fail safes in place. His computers, his off-site accounts ... you must ensure—"

Josh doesn't finish. My bedroom door blasts open with a fucking SWAT team.

I'm fairly certain I'm butt-crack naked under my sheets. I lift my hand in a wave. "Hello."

I had enough clarity to understand that Ember succeeded in informing the proper authorities of my father's fetish for younger girls. As two goons carted me away and Josh pulled out his phone and lawyered me up, I asked if she was safe. No one answered until I started roaring it while they hooked me under the arms and dragged me down the stairs and some agent at the bottom, craggy-faced with the strangest, kind eyes, responded with a curt, "Yes."

That's all I needed to endure my ass-fuck of a day.

I was angry. I'm still angry. At my father, the circumstances, and the look of sheer surprise and hurt on Ember's face when she found out I kept the most important secret from her.

Why does she continue to think I'm a good man? Haven't I given her enough to hate me for?

Yet as soon as I'm released under the strict instructions not to leave the country and my lawyer works out the kinks in my involvement, the first phone call I make is to Jaxon. He assures me Ember's spending most of her weekend at the police station, not under arrest but under secure watch. I should end the call there.

I ask, "Do you think she'll forgive me?"

Jaxon hesitates. I don't have to see him to understand he's choosing the best way to avoid enraging me. "Do you really care if she does or not?"

"I did it to protect her. How could I tell her something like that without ruining her life? It's better she didn't know. If I had it my way..."

"Ember had every right to know."

I frown. Change tactics. "She stabbed my father in the face with a hot poker when he told her."

Jaxon chuckles. "I can't argue that the same might've happened to you. But seriously, dude, she's been through hell. Either apologize for being a complete fuck, or let her move on."

"Apologize?" I almost stutter on the word. "My life's fucked, too. Father's gone, the feds can't find him, and chances are she has no interest in helping me track down his hidden stash of money. The cops are going to take the house."

"The very act of forgiveness is realizing you must put your own selfish needs aside and make the other person more important than you."

"Thanks, *Ghandi*," I sneer, ready to hang up on him. I'm not enjoying how his logic invades my gut, making it lurch with contrition.

"I mean it. I'm trying it on my dad after he gave me and Ember time to escape."

"Wait, what? *I'm* the one who held those fuckers off—"

"I'll say it again. You're a selfish SOB. One that I care about, but still. If you want Ember to talk to you again—and I'm sensing from this conversation that you do—you need to put your own imploded life aside and focus on how you can help hers."

I scoff. "How can that work? She despises everything I stand for."

"Look, no one's perfect. So why don't you own your flaws? And apologize. And mean it. She's a good girl. You may be surprised what happens next."

Good girl. My good girl. I want her back.

It's that jealous streak of mine that gives me the most pause—I can't trust myself not to stake my claim on her the moment I get her in my sights.

And punish her for ever doubting me.

CHAPTER 31

EMBER

Aurora corners me in the bathroom.

"You fucking *bitch*," she says as she shoves me into a standing sink. "I hope you get gang-banged like your father for what you've done. You've ruined everything, including your own future, you dumb skank—"

She doesn't expect the knee to her vagina. I kind of didn't, either, but I'm pleased when she doubles over, clutching her center and stumbling back. I take my chance and slip past her, resisting a final kick to her forehead.

She'll suffer enough once the FBI is finished with their investigation and she's left with a normal, cloak-less life where she actually has to work to stay on top. For a girl like her, that's some swift punishment.

Savannah isn't anywhere in Winthorpe that I can see, likely sequestered with her parents until her abduction is all sorted out. I'm grateful, since the guilt of spreading her personal information weighs the most on me. She's scary and a little psychotic, but she's a victim in all this, too.

I'm stared at, whispered about, and considered *persona non grata* for the entire stressful day. News spreads as the minutes tick by, and more officers enter Winthorpe's grounds. Dupris spends most of the day in her office, lawyering up and refusing to talk to the police.

By last period, I finally relax, content with the realization that Thorne didn't come to school at all today, probably dealing with his father's arrest and interrogation instead. I've completely ruined his plans to defeat his father and truly wasn't looking forward to running into him.

For many reasons.

I shut my locker after stuffing the day's books in, relieved to have survived my first day at Winthorpe as a traitor. I don't expect to be enrolled here after next week.

Phone in hand, I turn—

"We need to talk."

—and come nose-to-nose with Thorne's chest.

It takes a disproportionate amount of effort to control my facial muscles and keep them from frowning, collapsing, my eyes leaking tears. In all these days, I didn't factor in how much it would *hurt* to look at him.

"I don't have anything to say to you," I say while

staring at his tie. A perfect Windsor knot. His whole life as he knew it collapsed, and he was able to execute flawless tailoring this morning. The bastard.

"You have a whole hell of a lot to explain to me, Ember." His voice thrums with pent-up anger, rippling the shrinking air around us in a way I've never heard before. My very soul shivers at the impending danger.

"Either we do it in front of the entire school where I choke the life out of you," he continues, "or you let me drag you to the rec center by your fucking hair, and I strangle you there. Your decision."

I hiss through my teeth. He gets what he wants when my eyes snap up to his, furious and hot. "You can't touch me."

He responds by sliding two of his fingers into his mouth, tonguing them. My head falls back in shock, pinging against the lockers while every student lucky enough to witness this falls into a frozen, awe-inspired hush.

Knuckle by knuckle, he pulls them out. I'm so thrown by the oddness of his maneuver that I don't think to keep my jaw tight and angry. He uses that opportunity to shove those same fingers in my mouth, slipping through my teeth and hitting the back of my throat.

My body seizes, my hands coming up to defend the onslaught, but he catches them like a fly, flattening them against my chest as he digs his fingers in until I gag.

"You betrayed me," he murmurs in the kind of tone

where he's handing in a late assignment rather than pinning me up against a locker by finger-stabbing my throat. "You're lucky I don't kill you where I stand."

I can't respond with words. I glare around his hand, drool dripping from my pried open jaw as his fingers stroke the back of my tongue. Any slight movement and I'll bite down on him so hard, he'll lose digits. He knows it, keeping his fingers steady in their assault.

"You're coming with me," he growls. Thorne pulls his fingers out, and I double over, coughing and spitting out the rest of the cold saliva that had built up in my mouth.

He yanks me by the braid, pulling me into a deserted classroom. Nobody comes to my aid. They just watch, slack-jawed, as Thorne treats me like his childhood, molting teddy bear and tosses me aside.

The classroom's dark. Thorne doesn't bother to flick on lights. Rather, he pulls down the shade on the door so no one can sneak in a last glance.

"You sick bastard!" It doesn't come out as harsh as I want. I'm still coughing up the taste of him—salt, fury, humiliation. "It's done. Nothing you can do will stop Damion Briar from spending the rest of his life in prison."

Thorne prowls closer. Muscle memory is a funny thing—it reacts even when you don't want it to, and mine recoils in fear, bouncing against the front desks, the force of it scraping its legs across the floor.

He watches but doesn't say a word.

"You really want to hurt me?" My voice rises with that same fear, and I hate myself for it.

"Where's your courage, little pretty?" Thorne cocks his head. "Did you use it all up with your new agent friend and your bodyguard butler keeping you cushy and safe in your manor?"

Thorne's tone flows across the room, deathly quiet.

"I did what I had to do." I straighten. "And I'd do it again. You weren't going to help Savannah. Throwing money at her wouldn't have changed what your father did to her. He deserves to be physically punished for that, not just stolen from. And Malcolm—" my voice cracks under Thorne's inscrutable stare. "My *father*, what he went through. You knew. *You knew!*"

Thorne blinks at my sudden scream.

I continue, "The first time you snuck into my room, the moment you touched me, the second I slept with you for the first time, you used it all for your gain. I meant nothing to you."

"You forgot the time when I first saw you."

I jolt at the sudden, soothing cadence of his tone.

He takes advantage of my few seconds of silence. "I was furious at the sight of you. With your white hair and too-dark eyes, so clean and *innocent.* Completely ignorant to the way you were brought into this world, living a life of safety with people who bought you on a street corner. I couldn't fathom it. I still can't—how someone so pure could come out of circumstances so evil. Yet there you were, untouched. Untainted." He pauses. "And so unlike me. I'm born from the same darkness, and I'm so goddamned *furious*—"

"And you never stop," I whisper. "You're so angry. At school, in your home, to your friends, in bed with me. So, so unhappy. I refuse to be your victim as some sort of twisted penance for a past I have no control over. Find someone else to bully, Thorne, because I'm done."

"I'm sorry."

The words come out strained. Like they taste terrible and foreign to him. Like he's never uttered that statement in his entire life.

Stay strong. He doesn't give a shit about you.

"If you're truly sorry, then let your father's imprisonment be an entry into a new world for you," I say. "This is your chance to have the life you despise me for living."

"I'm—" His face scrunches up, frustrated. "I don't know how."

"Try starting by resisting the urge to publicly humiliate a girl by gagging her against the lockers."

That was a mistake. His attention lowers to my mouth. A familiar warmth spreads low in my belly, too much like a cat unfurling into a long, satisfying stretch.

Furious with myself, I storm past him before this can go any farther, but that damned muscle memory of mine betrays me again, when I let him fuck me on a teacher's desk.

Shockingly, Thorne lets me run past him and slam open the classroom door.

He doesn't pursue me during my mad sprint to Dash's car.

CHAPTER 32
EMBER

I'm left alone for an entire two weeks. Fourteen days of quiet study sessions, unobstructed bathroom breaks, and effortless note-taking in class.

Even Aiko is suspicious of it as she places her elbows on either side of her lunch tray, guarding her food like an inmate. "Why does everyone like you all of a sudden?"

"I wouldn't say 'like,'" I respond after chewing on my sandwich thoughtfully. "Winthorpe's definitely tolerating me, though."

Aiko returned five days ago after it was confirmed Damion wasn't in the vicinity. I was disappointed to hear of his elusiveness but not surprised. He's a man with resources and a cunning decision-maker. He was probably long gone before I blew the whistle on him.

Regardless of his capture, I don't regret my actions. Aurora's been taken out of school and sent somewhere international, away from the strain of media that's clogging Winthorpe gates. Belle and Delaney don't know what to do with themselves now that their leader is gone, so they've resorted to being nice to people. The school's headed by the deputy headmaster ever since Dupris was tagged as a person of interest over the "Scandal of Scathing Societies" the press is having a field day on. Not by the police but by the shareholders. A cult leader daylighting as a high school principal isn't good for business.

With all this attention, Damion wouldn't dare show his face.

And Thorne...

I take on Aiko's same positioning across from her, sulking. I suspect he's behind everyone leaving me alone. Calling off the dogs to prove he cares.

Aiko notices the direction of my frown. "When are you planning to talk to him?"

"Not anytime soon," I mumble.

Thorne sits at his usual table, emptier than it's ever been, with more and more parents pulling their kids from Winthorpe. Jaxon remains steadfast, splayed beside Thorne and gesturing with one hand as he talks to the glowering gargoyle beside him.

I've told Aiko everything, including Thorne's decision not to preempt his father by telling me the truth. It was particularly painful to tell her what came next—*I don't feel anything for you. I never have.* Aiko's as loyal as ever, juggling her time between me and visiting Savannah when she can. Savannah, who's voluntarily committed herself to getting the therapy she needs.

"I think you should," Aiko says.

I look at her in surprise. "I'm sorry, did the military implant a device in you that makes you fond of Thorne Briar?"

She laughs, placing her fork down. "Not at all, but he's clearly trying. And without his father and the surviving Society members going underground ... doesn't he remind you of a lost puppy? All alone in the world with no idea what to do with himself?"

I return to Thorne. "Yeah, if that puppy is a rabid terrier who yips and bites any kind hand that tries to help."

"Even rabid animals can be cured."

I look at her. "No, they can't."

"Fine, whatever! Just talk to him so I don't have to watch you mooning over the sociopathic prince who nearly got you killed."

"Which is it?" I splay my hands. "Do you support me being with him or not?"

"The more important question is, do you want to be supported in that decision?"

I push back from the table. "Ugh. Stop getting tips from Savannah."

She cracks a smile, then shoves another meatball in her mouth.

Heat prickles along one side of my face. I turn to notice Thorne watching me under his lashes, pretending not to be bothered by my presence by flattening his burger with his fist. Jaxon dips his head into my vision, tipping his chin in greeting before saying something to Thorne. Somehow, Thorne manages to glower harder. But the way he raises his eyes to me...

I want to ask him how he's doing. Who he's living with now that his father's gone and his home's seized. How he's handling the lack of a Society keeping him afloat through this crisis.

Thorne narrows his eyes at me, then stands.

Crap. I'm ready to bolt.

"Don't go," he says as he strides up to my table. "Not until I ask you one question."

I sigh, conscious of all eyes turning to us. "What is it, Thorne?"

"Are you satisfied? You've ignored me for weeks. Refused to look in my direction for all that time and blocked my calls. Congratulations, you've made me feel as rotten as I made you. We're even. Now forgive me."

"Are you kidding me?" If I were standing, I would've smacked him between the pecs. "You're not even *close* to how it felt to be told you were worthless."

His brows furrow, actually confused. "I never said that."

"My bad. To quote you correctly, you said you never felt anything for me. Ever. You made me *love* you and then destroyed me with one sentence. That's all it took for you to crush me to pieces in front of your sadistic, cruel following of Nobles and Virtues."

Thorne takes a full step back. "Wait. You love me?"

"Are you *kidding*?" I don't care if I'm screeching it this time. I push to my feet. "You humiliate and degrade me, yet I keep coming back to you. You make me feel things I can't fathom. You hold my heart and squeeze it so damn hard, then breathe it back to life. I can't understand myself around you. I love myself around you. Whenever you look at me, I see who I truly am—twisted and beautiful and flawed. How can you not see that? Every time you touched me, how could you fail to notice how I fell apart, always for you?"

Thorne's lips part. Not to snarl as I expected. He takes his time building up to a cutting response that will surely decimate me in front of the remaining Winthorpe population.

He can't hurt me anymore, I promise myself. *Whatever he has to say, it won't—*

Thorne wrenches me against him, catching my gasp with his mouth and drinking me in for all he's worth. With his lips sealed against mine, he lifts me and wraps my thighs around his torso until I'm above him and controlling the kiss.

I could break it off. Shove him back, slap him across the face, and shout at him to put me down and never take me by force again.

His lips soften, plush, flavorful pillows I've missed the taste of. A tongue I've longed to dance with and a body I've fantasized marking with my nails. I'd take Damion's whip marks on Thorne's back and turn them into mine. I'd give him all of myself if it would take away the past he cannot stand and show him the promise of a future he should look forward to.

I taste salt—but not the salt of Thorne. It's me, my tears collecting in our mouths. Thorne curls his tongue as if to catch some before pulling away.

"If you're telling me," he says, his voice taking on an irresistible husky tone, "all I had to do to get your forgiveness was to tell you I loved you, then I'm a sorry shit for not saying it sooner."

I press a hand to his cheek as he looks up at me, locking me against him. "Only if you mean it. No manipulation. No premeditated games."

Thorne's forehead smooths. "I am a terrible person who's done terrible things. I possess urges I can't control and a need for dominance I'll never shake, but if you'll have me, Ember, my little pretty, I'm yours."

I press my other palm to his opposite cheek, sealing him in. Placing the key to my heart in his hands. "I shouldn't believe you," I say, watching with awe as that spark, that vulnerable light of hope, dies in his eyes. It's time to bring it back. "But I do. You love me."

"I love you," he rasps.

He cups the back of my neck and pulls me in for another kiss.

The cafeteria erupts in applause. I break the kiss to scan our audience in surprise, but really, should I be shocked at the support of their corrupt prince? Thorne is loveable even at his worst. I should know.

Aiko shrinks in her seat, too close to our passion and wishing for a graceful exit.

Thorne smooths a thumb across my over-heated cheek, redirecting my attention. "Let me make this easier for you and carry you out of here so I can fuck you senseless."

I gape at him. Aiko absolutely writhes in horror.

"Thorne, people can *hear* you," I say.

"Let them. I'd slam you on this table right here and now if it means you're mine."

Aiko bolts from her seat. "Okay, I'm out."

"Too late," Thorne tells her and swings me around. "We're the ones who get the dramatic exit."

CHAPTER 33

THORNE

There are a shocking number of places to fuck in an academy. I go through the Rolodex of my mind as I carry Ember out of the cafeteria, that delicious heat of hers rubbing against my chest with impending promise.

It doesn't take me long to choose the pool at the rec center—closed during the afternoon before practice and also the precious starting point of Ember's and my fucked-up love story.

I don't put her down for the entirety of our travels, but I don't think she minds. She's busy nipping at my ear and sucking on my neck, adept at making me pay for all those days I was forced to endure without her.

Really, I had no clue how much she meant to me until she refused to be with me. The sadist in her can be a cruel mistress, but today, I'm happy to bring it out of her.

We burst through the double doors, the smell of chlorine growing stronger the closer we get to the pool. I'm forced to set Ember down long enough to enter the code to unlock the doors, fumbling twice when she swoops in on my dick and tickles my balls.

"You'll pay for that," I warn before pulling her onto the pool deck after me.

The lights are off, a deep indigo darkness cloaking our forms as we race to the bleachers. I stumble on my pants as I unbutton them, and they slide down my hips, kicking them off and discarding my briefs when I turn to her.

Ember stalls at the sight of my hard dick, the pool's reflection playing off her body and accentuating the dark pits of her eyes. Yet they shine like a sea sprite's, a Siren's, a water goddess intent on capturing a male for her pleasure.

"I've changed my mind," she says.

I cock my head, waiting. I can't speak when there's a strange sensation closing up my throat. Like I'm experiencing ... nervousness.

"I'll forgive you on one condition."

"Oh?" I respond testily. Good. I'd much rather cling to impatience than desperation.

"You let *me* dominate you."

"Come again?" I arch a brow, thinking I couldn't possibly have heard what I think I did.

"I want you to lie on the floor, naked, dick up, and I

want to do all the dirty things to you that you've done to me, and I want you to take it like a good boy."

Both my brows reach my hairline. My cock twitches dangerously. "No one gets that privilege. Not even you."

Her eyes lower to my cock. She licks her lips, and I groan. "Let me fucking have you, Ember."

"Not until I have you wide open and unprotected." She slides out of her blazer, tossing it against the bleachers. "Then I'll know you're serious about me."

"My walls are down, little pretty."

"Not enough." She grabs me by the collar and jerks me toward her. One side of my lips curves. Fuck, I liked that.

"Take your shirt off, Thorne."

Entertaining her, I do, standing before her naked and exposed.

She tongues her top row of teeth. I have to tilt my head back to stop myself from ravishing her.

"Lie down," she orders.

I'm not sure how long I'll commit to this farce, but I must admit... "You're turning me on, little pretty."

She smiles, her preternatural eyes glittering like we're underwater, back in the caves, allowing the tide to cover our chins...

Dammit. I lie down before her.

Ember forces me to watch her strip—painfully slow. I find myself salivating over the big reveal of her tits, then her pussy. Her underwear falls to her ankles, and she steps out of them, my eyes following every single flash of skin.

"Christ," I murmur. I might as well be tied to the tiles with the way I'm splayed out for her, desperate for Ember's touch. "End this torture."

"Not yet." Ember bends down and straddles me, her pussy—soaking wet—brushing against my torso and, sadly, way too far away from my dick. I arch to get it closer. She responds by clamping a hand on my throat and smacking the back of my head against the ceramic floor. "Nuh-uh," she purrs. "Bad boy."

I tilt my chin back, allowing her better access and relishing the painful dig of her fingers under the soft muscles of my jaw.

Ember bends until her fuckable face takes up my entire vision. "I'm going to fuck you now, and you're going to let me choke you until I'm good and ready to get off. Understood?"

"Yes," I groan. With the rush of ecstasy siphoning through my veins, I doubt I'll last long, anyway.

"Wrong answer." She digs harder into my throat. "Yes, miss."

I smile. *Touche.* "Yes, Miss Ember."

She mulls that one over. "Fine. I'll accept that."

"Great. Now accept my dick."

Her eyes spark before they narrow, enjoying my witty repartee. But Miss Ember's in charge, and she quickly hardens her expression into a woman determined to cum on Winthorpe's pool floor.

She raises her hourglass hips, then lowers, her aim fantastic and true. Her heat engulfs my dick, her hot, wet muscles clenching and releasing, calling for me to buck, twist, and drill as deep as I can until she's screaming on top of me.

I can't, though. Ember isn't starting the ride yet. She leans forward, pressing the heels of her hands into my larynx, causing me to cough and gag at the pressure. Her adorable brows crinkle with uncertainty, and I know this is the time I can take control because she really doesn't want to hurt me.

But goddamn, I like where this is going.

"You're fine," I croak out. "Harder. And start fucking me."

She bites down on her lower lip. I groan and am forced to think of trees. And rocks. And anything else boring and asexual before I explode from her ridiculously innocent appearance alone.

Ember brings me back to the present by rocking her hips, small at first, then longer and deeper once she realizes how good it feels.

She arches, her tits pointing directly ahead and the column of her neck calling to me like a Church bell. Ember is so into her own pleasure that she doesn't consider how well she's encircling my throat, tighter with each bounce she takes on my cock, deadlier by the second.

My face gets hot. My eyes feel swollen. Saliva has long dried up. The draw into the black comes closer, my balls tightening with each crucial second I remain alive.

Heart pounding, deafening my ears. Ember turns into a dark silhouette above me, her nails cutting into my skin, mixing blood with her power.

Her cunt soaks my pubic hair—wet, then cold, then hot again. I'm on fire. I'm ice. I'm dying for her.

Ember coaxes the explosion out of me like it's hers to control—and I just can't allow that. She needs to feel what I feel. Turn the lack of air into hot, pulsing joy.

I rear up when she least expects it. Ember's eyes were almost in the back of her head with her rocking ecstasy. So immersed was she, she didn't consider I'd take over at the last minute and make her *mine*.

One of my hands slams into the ground behind me. The other encircles her neck. I don't start with delicate pressure because I'm too close. I want her as light-headed and dizzy as I am before we go out-of-body and our souls fuck above us.

Her eyelids flutter at my contact. Those eerie dark-chocolate irises land on mine. Fearful at first, then...

She chokes. Sputters.

Veins pop out of my forearm. Warring with each other's breaths, seeing who's brave enough, fucked-up enough, to take it all the way.

Both of us.

Her pussy tightens like a vise. A squeak comes from

her perfect mouth—an orgasm I'm in charge of. The friction between us turns rabid, fire cascading down our limbs.

My mouth forms on a curse—the curse that belongs to her.

We come together, bodiless, soulless, just two pure pleasure centers exploding together in a supernova of sensation.

If I believed in heaven, this is what it would be like.

We come down from our high gradually. Ember's hand slackens on my throat, then mine on hers. I keep my cock in her as I wrap her up in my arms, pulling her against my chest and smelling her hair. My musk mixes with her flowery scent, a smell I'm wildly addicted to and would cover myself with it if I could.

I love you, I mouth into her hair.

Ember says she's as fucked up as me, but she'll never get to my level. I won't allow it. However, if she accepts my dark nature and craves my deadly passion, I will never stop her. I'm too obsessed with Ember to ever let her leave.

"I love you, too," she murmurs against my chest. Her lips tickle my skin.

"I hope you know what you've gotten into."

She tilts her chin up at me. "I'm well aware, thank you. You've made it very clear who you are. That's part of what I love about you."

"That's true. I warned you the moment I saw you."

"And I started falling for you the second you laid eyes on me."

My hold tightens. I tuck her head back under my chin, watching the water ripple under the blue light, enjoying the feel of Ember twitching and nestling into my cock, getting comfortable.

"My father's still out there," I confess.

"I know. Agent Colt keeps me updated. They're keeping me safe."

"Like I'd trust those unlicensed proctologists with my woman." It comes out sharp and cutting.

Ember shifts in my hold, attempting to stretch out and face me. I don't allow it. "Get comfortable where you are, little pretty, because I'm not letting you out of my sight until my father's either dead or bound."

"Thorne, let me go so I can talk to you. I'm trying to tell you—"

"Nope. Shush, before I force my dick even deeper and claim you shoulders deep."

"That shouldn't turn me on..." she mumbles. "But it does."

I smile. Twitch my dick a little so she knows I'm serious.

"Fine. I'll say it to your nipple," she grouses. "I think I've found a way to get past most of your father's firewalls and access his cryptocurrency platforms."

I stop playing with her pussy. "You're serious."

"Very. If you'd let me move enough to look you in the eye, you wouldn't have to ask that question."

Instead of replying right away, I think about her meaning, our future, and the next moves we must make in order to make this work.

"Thorne? I can hear you thinking."

"Mmm."

"Talk to me instead of murdering the pool with your glare."

"If we manage to do this, we have to go into hiding. My father will be irrationally pissed. First Malcolm escapes him, then Julie…"

"And now you?"

I shake my head. She feels it since I've locked her in place. "He doesn't give a shit about me. I was a tool in his arsenal of power, and the last time we spoke, I proved I was no longer any use to him."

"Because you saved me."

"Yes."

"I'm sorry. I never meant to ruin your life."

"You never will." I'm clutching her so tight that I'm surprised she has space to breathe. "We'll succeed. With our combined efforts, there's no way we won't."

"It will bring your father out of hiding. I'm sure he's using the crypto to finance wherever he is. And without it…"

"He'll be forced to the surface. My father's never been

without money. He'll become so desperate, even the feebs could discover him."

"Hey, I like Agent Colt. He's a good ally."

My grip turns dangerous. "How good?"

Ember tries to laugh, but my possession has become tenfold. "Uggh. Thorne—you're the only one for me. Agent Colt is a fatherly friend. He's helped me. That's all."

"From this point on, I'm the one who will keep you safe. Understood?"

"Same goes, buster."

A sound hits the top of my throat. One I've never made before. An amused snort? How the fuck has this girl affected me so much?

"If I'm smart enough to follow your father's blockchain footsteps, I'm smart enough to elude detection just as much as you," she retorts.

"Fair enough."

After a few moments of hearing the comforting slap of water against tile, Ember says, "Well? Are we going to do this?"

I stroke a thumb across her cheek. Stare pointedly at the black lines at the bottom of the pool. Then grin. "Let's fucking bankrupt my father."

EPILOGUE - EMBER

6 MONTHS LATER

Undisclosed Location

"Well?" Thorne asks me as I follow the well-worn path toward him, framed with seashells and dried seaweed. "How'd it go?"

"Mom and Dad are still pissed and concerned, but I think they've finally accepted I can't return for a while." I sit down beside Thorne in the warm sand, tipping my head back to enjoy the salted ocean breeze. My long hair tickles my bare chest, and I wriggle slightly at the sensation. "All they want is for me to be safe, and as long as I keep in touch with them as much as I can, I think they'll be okay."

Thorne catches a piece of my hair, twirling it. "You're doing the safest thing, distancing yourself from them. This isn't permanent."

I nod, though sadness threatens to overwhelm me. It's been difficult these past months, being apart from my adoptive parents—this time willingly—while also dealing with the realities of my birth. Malcolm's rape. My birth mother's callousness. My black market sale. Without some expensive therapy, it's been a lot to deal with, but Thorne's become a wonderful sounding board, having his own demons to exorcise, too.

We're a wonderful, fucked-up pair. One of the first moves he made before we departed was to delete our sex tape while I watched, his oath that when he hurts me in the future, it'll be with my willing awareness, hot on his lips.

I move behind Thorne so he can splay between my legs and lay his head against my chest. He allows a full view of his scars now, though it took a lot of coaxing ... and *yes, sir's* on my part until he finally caved and let me coat those scars with fresh scratches—like I could help X them out.

We look out into the impossibly turquoise ocean, flattened with low tide and my view framed with curving palm trees, their fronds fluttering in the gentle wind.

Sighing, I lay my chin on top of his head and close my eyes.

He leans into me, wrapping his arms around my tanned thighs. Somehow, he's retained his paleness while my skin has darkened into a golden glow with all the time we spend at the beach.

I'm not surprised at Thorne's resistance to the sun, though. Born in fire, demons can't burn.

"I hate to ruin this moment, but there's been a sighting," Thorne says.

"Oh?"

"Mexico City, a man matching the description of my father was seen attempting to purchase opioids without a prescription."

"That's ... ironic."

"It gets better. The witness states he was unwashed, covered in overgrown facial hair and smelling like used cat litter, of all things."

"We knew this would happen." I massage his shoulders, activating the scent of coconut moisturizer from my hands. "That it might take a while for him to surface despite our siphoning of his funds and him making the Most Wanted list."

Cryptocurrency is a funny, dangerous way to keep your life savings if that's the route you choose. Unlike banks and even off-shore banks, where large withdrawals are scrutinized, with the right hacker, you can acquire millions of crypto within two seconds. Once we broke through Damion's firewalls, hacked his encrypted passwords, and traced the blockchain his transactions left behind, that was all it took—one, two—and we owned Damion's millions.

His drug organization fell first, his accomplices disbanding and crying ignorance the moment their stores were raided, and they weren't even paid for their efforts. The spreadsheet I provided Agent Colt helped with that. The rugged agent wasn't all too happy to learn of my exodus from Raven's Bluff—to an undisclosed location, no less—but I've been appeasing him with breadcrumbs involving Damion's fentanyl trade and information about the Societies.

I'm not optimistic enough to believe the Societies will be destroyed. There are many chapters, Raven's Bluff but one. Likely, the members stripped any evidence of themselves from Winthorpe and the surrounding cliffs and made their home elsewhere, continuing with their recruitment and testing those initiates with deadly challenges, all to live a life of watchful, tenuous privilege, until someone like Damion decides you don't deserve it anymore.

Naturally, Thorne and I are no longer members. He makes noises about finding existing chapters and confirming his theory that not all Noble members are psychotic sadists, but come on—the truth is inside him. *He* is that psychotic sadist.

There's no rush to stop Thorne. We've made ourselves

comfortable in our balmy retreat, waiting out the moment of Damion's capture with ocean breezes billowing through open windows and hot, sweaty nights under mosquito nets and his body.

"Did you call Malcolm, too, while you had access to a burner phone?" Thorne asks.

"I gave a message to Dash that we're still safe. And happy. He reiterated the same about Malcolm and Julie."

"Good."

"Mm-hmm." I go back to closing my eyes and breathing in his hair, somehow resisting anything tropical and continuing to smell like chlorine, rocky cliffs, and salt.

Thorne's chest vibrates under my hand. I'd call it a purr—though it would be one belonging to a tiger or a jaguar, not a domesticated kitten. He twists around, palming the sand as he leans his face toward me and nips at my mouth. "I'm tired of talking shop. I want to do something else."

"Like what?" I know exactly what I'm doing. Annoying him to the point that his cock spears down like an arrow toward the ground, hard and ready for a fight.

"Lie back," he orders.

"Yes, sir," I croon, taking my time getting to my elbows, then laying back on my shoulders in the sand. Part of the joy of a private beach is the ability to be nude all the time. Thorne and I have taken plenty of advantage, wearing clothes only when we need to go into the neighboring village for supplies.

I'm sticky with salt and sunscreen and gritty with sand. None of this dissuades Thorne as he crawls down my body and licks me from ass to pussy. I melt in his hands, his tongue hotter than the sun beaming down on us.

His tongue scrapes along my folds, lapping up my wetness and savoring the taste as he moans into me. When Thorne thrusts his tongue in and out like his dick, I meet him each time, clutching the back of his head and drowning him inside me.

It's a trick I've been very quick to learn—Thorne loves suffocation. Why not bury his nose and mouth in my pussy and have him pleasure me while he gets off? It's a wonderful discovery and one I use at every chance. Even at the brink of passing out, Thorne is viciously effective at making sure I orgasm first.

I lift enough to catch his eye above my stomach, his lids heavy with desire and his pupils shot despite the brightness of the day. He circles my clit, then bites, shooting pain and pleasure up my chest and into my throat. I cry out at the release, burying my fingers in his hair. Since we've left Raven's Bluff, Thorne's decided on more scruff than clean shaves, and the feel of his roughness against such sensitive places only adds to the rush.

"Mm. My favorite snack," he says as he lifts his head,

running a finger across the dampness of his lower lip, then sucking on it.

"Let me return the favor." I lift to my elbows, but he stops me from going any farther. "No. Rest. This is your time to be pampered and sexually pleasured in any way you want. All except for our breath play." He darts a forlorn stare to my neck.

I laugh at such a sad puppy dog look on such a breath-takingly handsome face. "All in due time, my love."

"That's for fucking sure," he agrees, then runs his hand down the growing curve of my belly.

THANK you for reading Thorne and Ember's trilogy!

Can't get enough of the Nobles & Virtues? Start at the beginning with Briarcliff Academy. Begin your dark adventure back into the catacombs by meeting Chase and Callie in **Rival.**

Keep an eye out for Tempest, Ketley's next dark gothic series with a snarky, irresistible asshole at Titan Falls University. **Tempest is available now.**

A Note from Ketley

ON FACEBOOK, TO TALK MORE THORNE AND EMBER! DID YOU LOVE THEM? HATE THEM? WANT THORNE FOR YOURSELF? LET ME KNOW! I'D LOVE TO MEET YOU!

xoxo, Ket.

ALSO BY KETLEY ALLISON

all in kindle unlimited

If you want more bullies and secret societies, read:

Rival

Virtue

Fiend

Reign

Tempest

If you like your bad boys and bullies as standalones (no series, one book, a happy ending), read:

I'm Not Faking You

I'm Not Craving You

If you like mafia men, read

Underground Prince

Jaded Princess

If you like a grump turned into a softie, read:

I'm Not Dating You

I'm Not Loving You

If you like your playboys with big hearts and bigger secrets, read:

I'm Not Trusting You

I'm Not Daring You

I'm Not Playing You

If you like crime with your romance, read:

To Have and to Hold

From This Day Forward